THE PALACE OF LOST MEMORIES

AFTER THE RIFT, BOOK 1

C.J. ARCHER

C.J. ARCHER

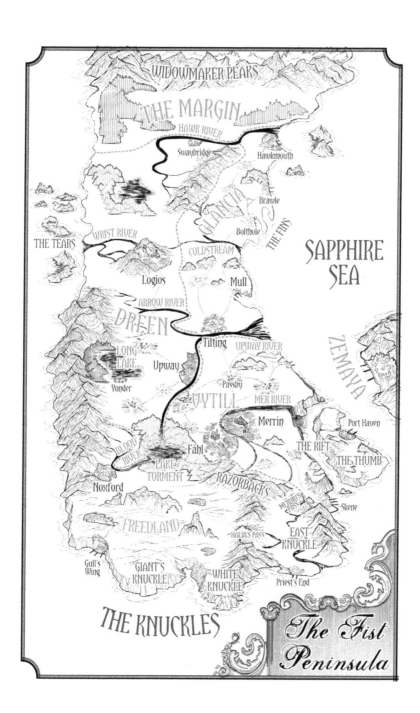

AUTHOR'S NOTE

To view the map of the Fist Peninsula within your device, go back one page or choose from the Table of Contents. To zoom in, download or print the map, go to C.J's website.

CHAPTER 1

*W*hispers of sorcery began when the palace's foundations appeared overnight. One frost-bitten day, the broad plain five miles from Mull contained nothing but grass and muddy puddles; the next, solid walls took shape as if they'd sprouted from the ground like daffodils at the first hint of spring. Looking at the completed building now, surrounded by mature formal gardens, I could see why those whispers had grown louder. Despite the distance between the palace and the clearing on Lookout Hill, where I stood, I could tell it was enormous. It must be four times as long as the street on which I lived, and it was certainly higher than the temple in the center of Mull. According to my father, it was even bigger than the main temple in Tilting, Glancia's capital city, where the last king had ruled from a crumbling old castle. That structure had taken three years to build. The palace had taken less than three months.

Three months in which not a single builder had been seen coming or going. No locals had been tasked with the labor, and according to the travelers and traders who now filled Mull's taverns to bursting, they hadn't come from elsewhere in Glancia or any of the neighboring kingdoms, either. It was as if they'd been conjured from the air and returned there after the palace's completion.

Magic.

Even I, a practical woman who believed in what she could see, hear and touch, couldn't explain the sudden appearance of the palace. It wasn't simply the speed of its erection but also the secrecy that shrouded it. Only a handful of delivery carts from the village and nearby farms had been to the palace to supply its kitchens, and guards hadn't allowed them beyond the gate. Palace servants unloaded the goods and retreated inside. They did not engage in conversation, they did not make eye contact, and they certainly didn't come to the village on their days off.

Except for that one time a maid wandered into Mull early one morning, asking passersby if they knew her. When no one could offer answers, she fell to her knees and sobbed until four palace guards collected her. She went with them meekly enough, but her haunted eyes stayed with me. Not just hers but theirs, too.

With a last look at the dazzling building, glinting in the late spring sunshine like a jewel, I picked up my battered old pack, as well as the new one given to me by the patient I'd called on, and turned to go.

The thundering of hooves along the forest path warned me to remain in the clearing. By the sound of it, more than one rider was heading my way and they were traveling fast. To move onto the path would be folly, so I waited until the reckless youths passed. No doubt it was Lord Deerhorn's sons, come to see the palace for themselves. Lookout Hill afforded the best view, after all. Either that or they'd decided to hunt here. They were supposed to keep to their own estate, but they were arrogant enough to shoot their arrows on common land whenever they pleased.

I'd learned a long time ago to stay away from the Deerhorn lordlings, but I didn't want them to think I was an animal worth hunting. I made myself visible in the middle of the clearing, facing the area of dense forest where the path briefly emerged before disappearing again on the other side. They couldn't mistake me for a fox or rabbit. Then again, they were as thick as the tree foliage in this part of the forest and fond of loosing their arrows.

The dull *thud thud* of the hooves came closer then the first rider burst into the clearing. His head jerked toward me and I caught a glimpse of a short dark beard but little else, thanks to the hooded cloak he wore. He disappeared into the forest again, his horse's stride not even slowing.

A few moments later, the forest spat out another rider, this one wearing black leather with gold trim at the shoulder of his doublet, and long black boots. He sat tall in the saddle, looking comfortable despite his horse's ferocious pace. I got a good look at his face as he slowed to study me in return. Short dark hair framed hard planes and a cleanly shaven jaw. It was his eyes that commanded attention, however. They were the blue of the shallows in Half Moon Cove on a sunny day. Those eyes made a quick assessment of me before focusing forward again.

"Question her!" he barked before urging his horse into the forest ahead.

He'd hardly disappeared when another rider emerged. He wore a crimson doublet with gold braiding. Crimson and gold— palace uniforms.

I clutched my bag to my chest.

The rider stopped and swore. He looked at me, swore again, and stared into the forest after the other riders. He swore a third time as his horse circled. Clearly good manners weren't a requirement for palace servants. Good looks, however, must be. This rider was dark like the one who preceded him, but with brown eyes and a bow mouth that turned down severely as he scowled at me.

"You there," he hailed me.

Branches and brush rustled and a fourth rider emerged into the clearing. This one also wore a palace uniform but he was younger than his companion. My theory about handsome servants was dashed by the newcomer. Though he was also dark, he had a nose like a horse and a spotty forehead and chin. His narrow chest rose and fell with his heavy breathing. He couldn't be more than eighteen.

"Who're you?" he asked me, as bold as could be.

I bristled but forced my spine to relax. I would usually treat such rudeness with silent disdain, but these were the king's men and must be obeyed. Besides, if I was nice, I might find out something about the palace and King Leon.

"Joselyn Cully," I said, still holding my pack in front of me. The new, empty one, remained slung over my shoulder. "Everyone calls me Josie. Are you from the palace?" I indicated the view behind me.

The lad sat higher in the saddle. "Huh. It looks tiny from up here, Max. Come take a look."

The man addressed as Max did not move. "Did you see him?" he demanded of me.

"Who?" I said.

"The rider in the hood."

"A little. The other man followed him." I pointed to the gap in the trees where the path led.

"The captain," the young man told me. "Captain Hammer."

Hammer? I managed to contain my snort of derision before it escaped.

"What did he look like?" Max asked. "The man in the hood?"

I shrugged. "I didn't see much. He had a short, dark brown beard."

"What shade of brown?" asked the younger man, leaning forward on the pommel. "Chestnut? Mud? Dung?"

Was he making fun of me? He didn't laugh. Not even a hint of a smile touched his lips. "Medium brown," I said.

"Anything else?" Max pressed, glancing toward the path again. Unlike the younger man, he seemed restless and eager to follow the two riders. The younger man still looked like he hadn't quite caught his breath.

"No," I said. "It was very—"

Thwack.

Max grunted and lost his balance, half falling, half staggering off his horse. An arrow protruded from his arm. *Merdu, be merciful.*

"Get down!" Max shouted as he fell to his knees. "Find cover!"

I dashed behind a row of shrubs on the opposite side of the clearing from where the arrow had been shot. I was safe but the men were not.

I swallowed hard and dared to peek through a gap in the bushes. The two men were still alone with their horses in the clearing. Max lay flat on the ground. Blood seeped through his clothes, darkening the crimson fabric. He must have pulled the arrow out, the fool. The younger man knelt beside him, his body over Max's, protecting him and making a target of himself in the process.

"Get off me, you little prick," Max snapped, easily shoving off the skinnier lad. "Do you want to get shot in the arse?"

The youth glanced behind him in the direction of the forest then angled himself behind a horse for protection. "Max," he hissed. "Take cover."

"He'd have shot again by now if he was still here." Max sat up and inspected his arm.

He was probably right and it was safe to emerge from my hiding spot. "Let me see," I said, crouching beside him. I reached for him but he leaned away. "I'm a... I have some medical skill."

"You can't," the lad blurted out.

"Because I'm a woman." It wasn't a question, but he answered as if it were.

"No. That is, I can see you're a woman." His gaze dipped to my breasts and his face turned as red as his clothes. "But you can't be a doctor. You're too pretty. Pretty women aren't smart and doctors have to be smart."

"Shut up, Quentin," Max growled. He got to his feet, only to sway a little. He was shorter than me with a wide set of shoulders and a barrel chest. If he toppled onto me, I would not be able to hold him up.

"Please, let me look at the wound," I said, eyeing him carefully. "I assure you I know what I'm doing. I've been studying at my father's knee ever since I could read. He taught me everything he knows, and he's a brilliant doctor. The best in Glancia, perhaps the entire Fist Peninsula. Even so, I've taken my learning upon myself this last year or so. My patients have seen the benefit, too." Of course all my patients were childbearing women, although I was perfectly capable of treating ailments and injuries too. Unfortunately, the lawmakers disagreed. "I'm perfectly capable," I finished.

Max put up his hand. "Be quiet. You're as annoying as he is."

Quentin beamed as if he'd been paid a compliment. I kept my mouth shut. I did tend to chatter too much when I was nervous.

The pounding of horses' hooves had us all turning toward the path again, but it was only the second rider returning, the one who'd given these men orders to question me. Captain Hammer. "I lost him," he bit off with a shake of his head. He glanced at me and looked as if he were about to speak when Quentin got in first.

"If you'd been riding Lightning, you'd have caught him."

"He doubled back," Max told the captain.

Hammer glanced sharply at the injured man and his gaze dropped to the arrow lying on the leaf litter at the edge of the clearing. "How bad is it?"

"I can't tell," I said before Max answered. "He won't let me inspect it. I'm Joselyn Cully, from Mull. It's my professional opinion that the wound needs to be bound before he loses too much blood. It may also require suturing." I held up my bag. "I have the necessary equipment right here." I was always prepared with surgical thread, a fine needle and small doses of Mother's Milk for painful births. "It's some distance to the village, and I'm your best option."

It was perhaps a little reckless, considering they were the king's men, but I was prepared to take the risk. This man needed immediate medical attention, and surely I'd only incur a fine and slap on the wrist. Perhaps not even that, if the captain chose to overlook the fact I wasn't qualified. I was, after all, doing his man a service.

I went to open my bag but the captain jumped down from his horse and snatched it from me. He was much taller than me, with a powerful frame. His shoulders were as broad as Max's, but due to his height, he didn't look blocky.

He checked inside the bag.

"It contains medical equipment," I said hotly, "not weapons."

The captain handed the bag back after a thorough inspection. "Let her see the wound, Sergeant."

"I'm fine," Max growled. "I don't need a healer."

I focused on the forest behind him and gasped. All the men spun to look, but only Max swayed and fell to one knee. He swore then sighed and sat.

Quentin snickered. "I like her."

Max glared at him, but even I could see there was no animosity in it. He tried to remove his doublet but Quentin had to help him. By the time he'd removed his shirt, Max was sweating and breathing heavily. Quentin and I both helped while the captain kept watch on the surrounding forest. He seemed oblivious to his sergeant's pain.

I tied Max's shirt around his upper arm to stem the blood flow. His veins soon bulged nicely.

"His fingers are going purple," Quentin said. "Is that good?"

"For now." I rummaged through my bag, tossing aside forceps, vials and a suction pump until I found the bottle of Mother's Milk. "Swallow a mouthful of this," I said to Max.

"You trying to get him drunk?" Quentin asked.

"It's a soothing medicine. It numbs pain and will keep him calm while I stitch him up."

"Just like ale, eh?"

"Better than ale. He won't need as much to feel the effects, although too much has the same symptoms felt the morning after a night spent drinking."

Max shook his head. "I don't need it."

"It'll hurt," I warned.

"I can cope with a little pain."

"I'll leave the bottle here. Grab it if you change your mind." I set the bottle down beside him and pushed aside the equipment in my bag again until I found the jar. It would be wonderful to move all of my things into the new bag the leather seller's wife had given me as payment after the safe delivery of her baby. It had internal compartments, pockets and straps to organize all my tools and medicines.

I removed the lid on the small jar and extracted the needle and thread stored within. "Ready?" I asked, threading the needle.

"Ready," Quentin said, crouching beside me, watching closely.

"Get on with it," Max snapped.

I stuck the needle into his flesh.

"Fuck!" he blurted out.

"Mind your tongue in front of Miss Cully," the captain said without turning around. He stood rigid, his shoulders tense.

"Doctor, not Mistress," Quentin told him. "Doctor Cully. How deep does the needle have to go in?"

Max paled. "Quentin!" he gasped. "Bring that ugly face of yours closer."

Quentin leaned in. "Why?"

"So I can shut your mouth for you."

The captain whipped around and intercepted Max's fist before it made contact with Quentin's face. "Maybe you should take the Mother's Milk," he said.

"You going soft, Hammer?" One side of Max's mouth hooked into a wry smile.

I pushed the needle in again. Max grunted and squeezed his eyes shut.

The captain snatched up the bottle of Mother's Milk. "Drink!"

Max accepted the bottle.

"Two mouthfuls," I reminded him. "You're a solid man but three will have you throwing it up."

I waited for the medicine to take effect before continuing with the suturing. The captain returned to watching the forest, his arms crossed over his chest, but his stance was a little more relaxed. I'd thought he was tense from alertness, but now I suspected it was partly due to concern for his sergeant.

"So your friends call you Josie, eh?" Quentin asked me. "Can I call you Josie?"

"If you like."

"You can call me Quentin. He's Sergeant Max and that's Captain Hammer."

"Are those first names or last?" I asked.

The captain half turned and glared at Quentin over his shoulder. The sergeant glared too. Quentin swallowed. "Is he ready now?" he asked. "He looks ready. You ready, Max?"

The sergeant sighed and closed his eyes. He finally relaxed. "The Mother's Milk isn't working. I can still hear him."

I laughed softly. "It only numbs the pain."

"Listening to him *is* painful."

I went to work, finishing what I'd begun. The task wasn't difficult, particularly with Max now calm and pain free. I'd stitched far more delicate areas than a big man's arm. It gave me time to think about the strangeness of the situation I'd found myself in. Aside from the mad servant and the guards who'd collected her from the village, these were the first people from the palace I'd ever seen. No one in Mull had been presented with such a good opportunity to learn more.

"Are you palace guards?" I asked as I stitched.

To my surprise, Quentin didn't respond. He looked to Hammer.

"Yes," the captain said without turning around.

"Who was that man you were chasing? Does he work at the palace too?"

"That's not something I can divulge."

"Have you worked at the palace long?"

The captain shifted his stance. "The entire time."

"So you saw it being built? Where did the builders come from?"

"Here and there."

"Can you be more specific?"

"No."

This wasn't going well. "Where are you originally from?"

He didn't answer.

"Why can't you tell me?" I pressed. "It's a simple question."

"You'd think so," Quentin muttered.

"You and Sergeant Max are short with dark hair," I said to Quentin. "So you must be originally from Freedland."

Quentin turned huge eyes to me. "You've been there?" he whispered. "You've been to Freedland?"

"No. My father has, and he told me stories of all the kingdoms and the republic. He traveled all over The Fist before marrying my mother and settling here in Mull. But everyone knows the sand people of Freedland are short with dark hair. You don't need to go there to know."

"Right," Quentin said. "Of course."

"Captain Hammer is different," I said, glancing at his broad back. "He's tall, like those of us native to Glancia, but he's dark like you. Glancia folk are naturally fair."

"And pretty." Quentin blushed. "Real pretty."

I smiled. "I suspect the captain doesn't like to be called pretty."

Hammer shifted his stance again. "The captain doesn't like people talking about him behind his back." He glanced over his shoulder and those eyes, so blue against his tanned skin, drilled into me. "Are you done, Doctor?"

It was a little embarrassing to be called the title I hadn't earned officially through the college—and never would. Women weren't allowed to study doctoring. Midwifery and how to make medicines, yes, but not surgery or other medical disciplines. The college system was archaic; not only for entry into the college of surgery, but into all the colleges. The rules ought to be changed, but I couldn't foresee women being allowed in any time soon. None of that was a secret. It was common knowledge. Why did these men not know it?

I finished stitching and tied the end of the thread. I asked Quentin to cut off the excess and he looked more than pleased to contribute. After removing the shirt from around Max's arm, I told the sergeant he could sit up.

He answered me with a soft snore.

"How will we get him back to the palace?" Quentin asked.

Captain Hammer tapped Max's cheek. "Wake up."

Max cracked open an eye. "The doctor's not finished." He closed his eye again.

"She is." The captain pulled Max into a sitting position. "Come on. We must go." He scanned the forest again. Did he think the archer was still there, watching?

I handed the doublet to Max. He slung it around his injured side but needed help with the other. The captain and I managed to arrange it equally on both shoulders before assisting him to stand.

Max groaned but slumped against Hammer. The captain looped his arm around Max and guided him to the horse.

Quentin gathered the horse's reins. "You can do it, Max. Upsy daisy."

The sergeant pushed off from Hammer. "I'm not a child," he growled.

He tried to mount alone but couldn't. The captain wordlessly stepped in and helped. He managed to get Max on the horse easily, even though the broad-set man must be heavy. From what I'd witnessed, Max was a barrel of solid muscle.

"Where's your horse?" Quentin asked me as he mounted.

"I don't have a horse," I said. "I walked."

"It's a long way back to Mull," the captain said. He remained standing, his hand resting lightly on his horse's neck. "What were you doing up here?"

"Passing through."

"It's a hill. No one climbs a hill if they're just passing through."

"She was looking at the view," Quentin said. "There's a nice one of the palace from over there." He pointed to the edge of the clearing where the hill dropped away too steeply for trees to grow.

The captain walked to the edge and studied the palace in the distance. He stayed there for some time, his back to us. Only the ends of his hair fluttered in the light breeze, but otherwise he didn't move. The silence stretched.

Quentin cleared his throat. "Captain? Max is falling asleep again."

The captain turned away from the view and my breath caught in my throat. He had the same haunted look in his eyes as the mad maidservant and the guards who'd collected her that day.

"Are you all right?" I asked in a rush of breath.

He halted and blinked rapidly at me. "We'll take you back to the village."

"It's all right," I said. "I can walk. I had a patient to visit at the base of the hill and decided to come up and have a look at the palace. It's such a pleasant day and the sun is shining. The palace is so pretty in the sunshine with all those glass windows sparkling like gems. Is it made of gold? It looks like gold from up here, but perhaps its something else. I imagine gold is too expensive to use as a building material." I bit my tongue to stop my rambling.

"We'll take you home," the captain said again. "You can't stay here alone."

"Why not?"

He hesitated before saying, "You saw the man we were chasing?"

"Only a little. Just his beard really."

"He might think you saw more. That's why he doubled back."

My heart skipped a beat. "You think he was shooting at *me*?"

"It's possible."

"Then why not try again after missing?"

"Perhaps he couldn't get a clear second shot before I returned."

"She hid in the bushes," Quentin told his captain.

I swallowed hard. Someone had tried to…to kill *me*?

The captain touched my elbow. "Doctor? Are you all right?"

"I… Yes. I'm fine."

"It's doubtful he'll come back for you. If you didn't recognize him then he doesn't know you either, or where to find you. If he's clever, he'll be far away by now. Even so, I'd prefer it if you allowed us to escort you home."

Quentin shifted back on the saddle and patted the front. "Climb on."

"She'll ride with me," Hammer said.

Quentin sighed. "Don't you have enough?"

"You're a terrible rider. If Doctor Cully wants to get home safely, she rides with me."

"I fell off *once*."

"Once *today*," Max piped up from where he sat slumped in his saddle.

"A ride back to the village is the least we can do," the captain said to me. "I'll send payment for your service. I have no coin on me. We left in a hurry."

I gathered up both my packs and helped myself onto the saddle, sitting aside rather than astride as I'd seen Lady Deerhorn do. The captain mounted behind me in one fluid movement. I felt small and delicate next to him. He smelled of horse and leather, and his hard thigh bumped against mine. Like Max, I suspected he was all muscle too.

We headed slowly through the forest, back down the hill. Little light reached through the canopy, making it feel like twilight, despite being just after noon. The air felt damper too, denser, as if rain wasn't far away. If I hadn't been out in the bright sunshine moments before, I would have thought the weather entirely different.

The captain remained alert and silent as we rode. His reassurance that the hooded archer wasn't a local and would be far away by now offered little comfort. I held my packs close to my chest and watched the forest too. I'd wager the archer was a burglar or poacher who thought to try his luck on palace grounds.

Or perhaps he was an escaped servant who needed to be retrieved.

CHAPTER 2

*W*e emerged from the forest at the base of Lookout Hill and rode into the village. The familiar salty scent of the sea hit me along with an undertone of gutted fish thanks to the northerly breeze. We passed the leather seller's hut, where his wife convalesced with their third born, and the clutch of other buildings built of the same warm yellow stone.

"You said your father traveled." The captain had been quiet for so long that his voice startled me. It wasn't so much the sound of it, but the way it rumbled through my body. He sat very close. "Where has he traveled to?"

"Everywhere on The Fist Peninsula," I said. "Freedland, Dreen, Vytill of course, and even into The Margin and across the sea to Zemaya. Not beyond Widowmaker Peaks, though."

"How long was he gone?"

"Years. He studied in Logios, and after graduation, he took his new education and traveled. He says he learned more in Zemaya than he ever learned in college, particularly about medicines and poisons."

"What do you know about the other nations on The Fist Peninsula?" the captain asked.

What a strange question. I turned more fully to see him properly. At such close proximity, he filled my view. "You don't have Zemayan coloring, yet you can't be from the Margin, either."

Those blue eyes lowered to mine. "Why not?"

"Because you're too sophisticated. Margin folk are simple tribespeople. You're clearly not a barbarian."

Quentin nodded sagely, proving he was listening. He did not look around, however, preferring to concentrate on the road ahead. His white-knuckled grip on the reins and stiff back were at odds with the other two, who both sat comfortably in their saddles. Max had straightened a little and seemed more alert. The fresh sea air had woken him up, and the effects of the Mother's Milk were wearing off.

"Tell me more about the Margin," the captain said.

"It's mostly plains and then the foothills of the Peaks." I shrugged. "Nomadic tribes live there. They fight amongst themselves and don't venture into Glancia. There's not much more to tell."

"What about Dreen? The college city of Logios is in Dreen, is it not? What else is it known for? What are the people like?"

We passed the Bramm sisters walking back from the main street, their baskets full. They stepped out of our path then stopped altogether and gawped at us. "Josie?" asked one.

"Good afternoon, " I said.

"What are you doing with those…?"

"Palace guards?" I filled in for her. "I'll explain later."

They glanced at each other then rushed off, their strides long and purposeful. The entire village would know I'd ridden with palace guards by nightfall.

"Dreen is large in area but smaller than Vytill and Glancia in population," I said, answering the captain. "Most of it is sparsely populated farmland. There are two cities—Upway, the capital, and Logios, the college city."

"And Vytill? What are the folk there like?"

I huffed out a laugh. "The most intelligent, beautiful, and wealthy. Just ask them. Did I mention they're arrogant too? According to the king of Vytill, it's the most important nation on The Fist. Not anymore, though. Not since the Rift. Have you heard of the Rift?"

"I have."

That was something, at least. I was beginning to think he was completely ignorant about everything to do with the peninsula.

"Tell me about Glancia," he said. "You've lived in this kingdom your entire life?"

I nodded. "In Mull. That probably makes me quite dull to you."

"Why?"

I waved at Yolanda and her three children, each carrying a package. None waved back. They were too busy staring. "You must be from somewhere very far away," I said to Hammer. "Otherwise you wouldn't be asking me all these questions about the Fist nations. So where *are* you from?"

"The palace," was all he said. "Glancia is a pleasant country with nice scenery. Is it mostly made up of fishing villages?"

It would seem he wasn't prepared to give too much of himself away to a stranger. I wondered if he was following king's orders or whether it was a personal choice. "It is, except for the capital, Tilting. It's on the River Upway, near the borders of Dreen and Vytill. Apparently being close to our wealthier neighbors makes it more strategic and affords better communication, although I don't think the kings of either Dreen or Vytill cared overmuch about communicating with Glancia until now. We were nothing to them, just a poor dog they had to throw a bone to every now and again to stop us starving over winter. Before the Rift, that is. Everything changed after that. Why did King Leon decide to build his palace near Mull and not Tilting? The capital was good enough for the old king."

"The old king kept to the old ways. The new king wanted to do something new and different."

"The palace certainly is different," I said. "For one thing, it's not a crumbling old relic of a castle."

He smirked. "No, it's not."

I directed the captain to move off Mull's main road with its shops and bustling market that now opened every day instead of twice a week. I knew far too many shopkeepers, and I was already growing tired of the stares and gasps. Soon the sheltered harbor with its two jutting piers were in view. The smell of the sea was strongest here, and the noise was incessant. Dockworkers shouted at one another, sometimes in anger but mostly barking orders. Crane ropes groaned and the machinery whirred as barrels and crates were lifted from boats onto the piers. Carts, drays and passenger vehicles came and went, jostling for space on the concourse. Everywhere foundations for new warehouses and shipping company offices sprang up. The customs building was already two-thirds built, with another level to go on soon. It looked very grand already, commanding the best view over Tovey Harbor.

Large ships anchored in deeper waters at the harbor's mouth while their smaller rowboats navigated Tovey's shallows, waiting for their turn to unload and reload at the piers. Timbers creaked and oars bumped as crews maneuvered through the crowded harbor and vied for the best positions.

The sooner the harbor was dredged and bigger docks built, the better. Perhaps. Mull was bursting at the seams with the influx of trade since the Rift, and I didn't particularly like the way my sleepy village was being swamped. I hated to think what it would be like if it grew to the size of Tilting.

"Mull is changing quickly." When he didn't respond, I added, "Because of the Rift."

"I see," he said blandly.

"I'm sorry, I'm boring you. You must already know this."

He hesitated then said, "I would like to hear about Mull from the perspective of someone who lives here."

"Very well." I indicated the busy harbor. "The Rift cut off The Thumb from the rest of the continent." I waited for a reaction. He gave none so I thought it best to begin at the beginning. "A series of earthquakes, one after the other, tore the headland known as The Thumb from the mainland. Seawater flooded the gap, now known as the Rift. The quake event is also called the Rift, for want of a better word. The Thumb was—and still is, administratively if not physically—part of Vytill. Before the Rift, Port Haven on The Thumb was the eastern most port on The Fist Peninsula, making it a trading hub. It's also on the River Mer so it was doubly strategic. Port Haven is the reason Vytill became the richest and most important kingdom on The Fist. Now that's all changing."

"Because the Rift severed The Thumb."

"Nice pun."

Once again he did not react. Not much of a sense of humor then.

"With The Thumb cut off from the peninsula, Vytill no longer has the easternmost port on The Fist. Glancia does." I stretched out my hand to encompass the activity. "My sleepy fishing village has woken up. The population has already trebled, and market prices have risen quickly. On the one hand, it's good for everyone's business, but on the other…" I sighed. "I liked it the way it was."

I directed the captain into a street to take us away from the harbor. It was quieter but we still passed people I knew. Considering I knew everyone in the village, except for those who'd settled since the Rift, it wasn't surprising.

"Is that why King Leon built his palace nearby?" I asked. "To be closer to Mull and the trading activity?"

"I don't know what's behind his thinking."

"It did seem strange to us that he'd move away from Tilting and its administrative offices. The ministers can't be too happy to travel here."

"They haven't come yet. They arrive next week for the first time."

"Will they stay at the palace? Every spare room in Mull is already taken."

"There are rooms prepared for them at the palace."

"Many, many rooms," Quentin piped up.

Captain Hammer asked me a few more questions about Glancia, mostly about its history and the various lords. I could answer many but not all. Aside from Lord Deerhorn, who lived north east of Mull on an estate that overlooked the village and harbor, the other powerful families of Glancia were a mystery to me. There wouldn't have been enough time to answer questions about them, anyway. We turned into the narrow street where I lived, and I told the captain to stop outside my cottage just as old Bessie Tailor emerged. She squinted at me.

"Who's that?" she asked.

"It's just me, Bessie," I said. "Josie. Are you here for your eyes? Could Father help?"

"Josie? Are you on a horse? Who're you with?" She squinted harder.

"Josie?" my father said, peering over Bessie's head. "What in Merdu's name...?" He took in Quentin and Max's crimson and gold uniforms, and my position on the horse in front of the captain. "Get down, Josie! Come away from them!"

"It's all right," I said. "They're palace guards. They—"

"I know what they are."

I hadn't seen him look this furious since I came home late one night after celebrating a friend's betrothal at The Anchor tavern. He'd had good cause then, but his anger didn't make sense this time. I was twenty-four, for Goddess's sake, and hardly a naive girl anymore. The captain and his men may be strangers, but it was broad daylight. Father was overreacting, as usual.

The captain dismounted and assisted me to the ground, his hands on my waist. Our gazes connected but I couldn't read his. Or perhaps I might have if I hadn't been transfixed by his eyes. Their color really was quite beautiful.

"My name is Captain Hammer, sir," he said to my father. "These are my men. You're Doctor Cully?"

My father lifted his chin in a nod. "What are you doing with my daughter?"

"Doctor Cully—Doctor Joselyn Cully, that is—assisted my sergeant after he was shot by an arrow on Lookout Hill."

I groaned silently. I'd have a devil of a time convincing Father there was no cause to worry now. It was difficult to know which was worse—the fact I hadn't come straight home after seeing to the leather seller's wife, the fact that I rode on a horse with a strange man, that he was from the palace, or that his sergeant had been shot by an arrow and called me doctor. I could see my father grappling with the overwhelming number of possibilities too. Thankfully, it rendered him speechless. For now.

It did not have the same effect on Bessie. "*Doctor* Joselyn?" She chuckled. "Very amusing."

Captain Hammer turned a frosty glare to me.

I sidled off to join the sergeant. He sat well on his horse and looked much better. "I sutured the wound," I told my father. "We were on top of Lookout Hill and he was losing blood. There was no time to bring him down here, and since I had everything I needed..." I stopped as my father's face darkened.

"Get inside, Josie," he said coolly.

"In a moment."

He arched a brow but did not scold me.

"Those stitches will need to be removed in ten days," I said to Max. "I can come to the palace—"

"No," both my father and the captain said.

"Max will come to you," the captain clarified.

"To *me*," Father added. "My daughter would make an excellent doctor, but an unqualified girl cannot attend to a servant of the palace. Or to anyone," he added.

"But he's *my* patient," I said. "What's the worst that could happen? They're the king's men."

"Thank you for bringing my daughter home safely," Father said to the captain. "Good day to you, sir. Josie, inside."

I slipped past Bessie and Father, dumped my bags on the floor, found what I wanted in my father's surgery and returned just as the captain remounted. I handed him the roll of bandage but addressed the sergeant. "Cover the wound with a thick layer of bandage so that it doesn't rub on your clothes. If it pains you, ask the kitchen staff to grind up some hollyroot. They probably grow it in the kitchen gardens. It's not as strong as Mother's Milk but it's good for mild aches and pains. You look like a man who only needs mild pain relief."

He puffed out his chest and gave me a nod. "Thank you Doc—er, miss."

"Josie will do."

"And I want to apologize for my language earlier. I was...not myself."

They rode off amid stares from our neighbors. I waved at Meg across the street, and she signaled me to join her. I glanced at my father. His deeply furrowed brow gave me my answer.

"Later," I called out to Meg.

"Josie," Father snapped as Bessie made her way carefully along the street. He shut the door behind me. "What do you think you were doing accepting a ride from those men?"

The childish part of me wanted to storm up to my attic bedchamber, but I was too old for petulance. I bypassed the front room that Father used as his surgery and workroom and entered the kitchen instead. I took my time filling the pot with water and mildwood leaves and nestled it amid the burning embers. I saw no reason to make it easy for Father. He was over reacting, as usual, and I was heartily sick of it. He'd been very close to creating a scene out there, and in front of the neighbors and palace guards too.

"The sergeant needed help," I told him. "So I helped."

"I understand that," he said, strained patience tightening his voice. "You're a healer and wanted to assist an injured man. You can't help your kind nature."

"And we were too far away from here."

"I don't disagree with your decision to suture his wound. If the captain gave you permission, you won't get into trouble, even if the sheriff hears of it. You were simply in the wrong place at the wrong time."

"Or at the right place at the right time."

"Don't mock me, Josie. This is serious. Those men could have been dangerous."

"They weren't."

"You don't know that."

I threw up my hands. "I helped one of them! Why would they hurt me?"

"Any number of reasons, none of which you're foolish enough to dismiss so easily. You're a young, attractive woman on your own in the forest on top of Lookout Hill. They're young, virile men. Do I need to spell it out to you? You're not a child anymore, Josie."

"Precisely," I spat. "I am not a child. I'm capable of assessing whether three men are a threat to me. I am well aware of what can happen to a woman alone, but you should *not* assume every man is after *that*."

"I don't," he said, sounding put out. "But they're strangers," he added, gentler. "You can't trust strangers, particularly after the prison escape."

"The prison escape! Oh Merdu. Not only did that happen a long time ago and those escapees are probably rounded up by now, but the prison was miles away! Miles and miles!"

"I've heard that they have *not* been rounded up, and nor is it a stretch to assume they would be in Mull by now. We have so many strangers in the village these days that they could easily blend in, find employment or attempt to leave The Fist on one of the trading vessels."

"These men wore palace uniforms. If I can't trust palace guards, who can I trust?"

He removed two cups from the shelf and placed them on the table. "Their authority does not make them trustworthy." He sat heavily, all the bluster knocked out of him. He looked every bit his age of sixty-five, with the deep lines across his forehead and the last remnants of his hair clinging to his head like a summer cloud.

I kissed his cheek to show him I wasn't too mad. I knew his anger was born from worry. It had been just the two of us for so long that he was afraid I'd either leave him voluntarily through marriage, or reluctantly if something awful befell me. "You think the king employs bad men?" I asked.

"Not on purpose. Besides, it's not just that. There's something odd about the palace and its servants."

I sighed. "Don't say magic. Those men are real." So real that I could still feel the captain's thigh against mine, his hands on my waist. "Magic doesn't exist outside of children's stories."

He said nothing and I poured the brewed mildwood into the cups. "Have you eaten today, Father?"

"Not yet. Do we have any eggs for breakfast?"

I smiled. "It's well past breakfast time, but I'll cook you some eggs if you like. Tell me about Bessie's eyes."

"You first. Tell me how the birth went."

* * *

TAMWORTH TAO, the Zemayan born spice merchant, sported a knowing little smile; he had gossip to impart. Meg noticed it too and dragged me by my arm through the crowded marketplace to his stall. We'd been heading there eventually anyway, preferring to leave it to the end of our marketing, but she couldn't wait and it became our first stop.

"Josie, Meg, my two favorite Mullians." Tam flicked his long black braid off his shoulder with a jerk of his head. The bells attached to the strip of white leather threaded through the hair tinkled musically before falling silent at his back. "You are a wonderful sight for my world-weary eyes." Tamworth's face-full of wrinkles deepened with his grin, but there were no signs of weariness in his eyes or elsewhere. The spice merchant was of indeterminate age. Despite the wrinkles, he sported no gray in his black hair and his slender shoulders and arms were all wiry muscle. He could be forty, seventy, or anywhere in between.

I inhaled deeply, drawing the chaotic blend of sweetness and tartness, tanginess and sharp heat into my lungs. According to Father, Zemaya smelled like the spices sold in Tam's stall, but rarely all together like this.

"What news from your travels, Tam?" Meg asked, not bothering to hide her enthusiasm. She was the same age as me, but sometimes she seemed much younger, when her eagerness got the better of her or if she became overly shy about the birthmark discoloring one side of her face.

"I will tell you," Tam said, still smiling, "but first Josie must tell me about the palace guards she rode with last week."

"There's nothing to tell," I said.

"There must be. No one else has been as close to them as you, Josie, so you must forgive our curiosity."

Meg regarded me with mischievous blue eyes. "Go on, Josie. Tell Tam how you rode with the *very* handsome captain of the guards."

Tam leaned forward, rising off his stool. He bumped his head on the string of reek roots hanging from the bar. His eyes widened, their whites so bright within the dark skin. "What did he look like? What was he wearing?"

I described Hammer's looks and clothing and those of his men. Tam listened intently, and I realized his curious little smile that enticed us over to the stall wasn't as a result of *his* gossip but because he saw the opportunity to gather tidbits about the palace from *me*.

"How did he seem to you?" Tam asked.

"Seem?"

"Aye. Did he seem…solid?"

Oh yes, Captain Hammer was certainly solid in the thighs and chest. Being close to him on the horse had given me the perfect opportunity to feel just how solid. I said none of that to Tam, although I'd already described Hammer in detail to Meg, at her insistence. "Solid enough."

"Was there anything unusual about him?" Tam asked.

"Such as?"

He shrugged. "Such as fading in and out. Or shimmering, perhaps. I don't know. Anything?"

"Oh," Meg murmured. "Are you referring to…" She lowered her voice. "To magic?"

Tam winked.

I sighed. "He was real and solid and alive. They all were. His sergeant even bled red blood. Come now, Tam, I expect a well traveled man like you wouldn't believe in superstition and magic."

"Perhaps that's why I *do* believe. Did the men tell you anything about the palace? Anything at all about its origins—or King Leon?"

"Nothing. Now, may we conduct our business? I'd like a bulb of fire breath, some reek root and one scoop each of amani, tumini and borrodi spices please."

As he packaged up my purchases, he finally imparted his own gossip to us. I was right he didn't have much to tell. He'd just come from Port Haven on The Thumb where houses lay empty and shops had closed.

"The downriver section of the Mer has been cut off from its source and dried up," he said. "It's now just rocks, sand and stagnant pools. The surrounding farms are struggling to irrigate their crops. The harbor is no longer bringing in any trade, and the king of Vytill isn't doing anything to help The Thumb folk. I heard the ministers have advised him to no longer consider it part of Vytill but rather an island nation that must administer itself. The population has been given a choice to resettle on the mainland or stay."

"They'll starve if they stay," I said with a shake of my head.

"They may starve on the mainland," Tam went on. "There's little work elsewhere in Vytill, particularly for those experienced only as dock workers."

"What about their mines?" The Fist Peninsula mined most of the stone, iron and other materials the various nations needed, but all those mines were concentrated in Freedland and in the south of

Vytill and Dreen. There were none in Glancia or The Margin to the north.

"Dock workers aren't miners," Tam said.

"They can find work here," Meg said in all her good-hearted innocence. "There's plenty to do now that Tovey Harbor has become so important."

"Mull isn't ready for such a rapid increase in population," I told her. "We're not coping as it is."

"There's a rumor that Glancia may close its borders to migrants. They must already pay a fee to cross," Tam went on. "You're right, Josie, and Mull can't cope with rapid expansion. Glancia can't cope. The villages are small and disparate, and quite primitive."

Meg bristled. "We are *not* primitive."

"Glancia is nothing but a handful of fishing villages." Tam handed me my purchases and I paid him. "Few people are educated, the roads are poor, and the ministers are too busy fighting amongst themselves to make the quick decisions that are necessary at a time like this. It didn't matter if they sat on their fat arses and twiddled their thumbs before, but it matters now. Perhaps the new king will whip them into action."

"Let's hope so," Meg said, thoughtfully. "I wish we knew more about him and his intentions."

All of Glancia wished that.

We thanked Tam and finished the rest of our marketing. Despite having told my story about the palace guards numerous times in the last week, I found I had to re-tell it again and again at each stall. Ultimately, my listeners were disappointed. I had so little to pass on, and I refused to embellish the tale as Meg suggested.

We did learn one more interesting piece of news. A farmer from outside Mull told of a procession of ministers arriving at the palace. The cavalcade of carriages, carts and wagons had stretched for a full mile along the road to Tilting, where the ministers and previous king had lived. It seemed the new palace was finally allowing in outsiders. It was a positive sign that King Leon might whip the ministers into action, as Tam had put it.

Meg and I parted in the street between our houses, and I found my father in the larder, reading labels on jars with his eyes screwed up so tightly it was a wonder he could see at all.

"Why is the Mother's Milk now stored in these pottery jars?" he asked. "We used to keep them in glass ones."

"Because the glass ones are too expensive," I said. "I told you that at the time. Why do you need Mother's Milk? What's happened? You're not scheduled for any surgeries today." Mother's Milk was used to relieve only the strongest pain because of its expense and the difficulty in sourcing ingredients. We made it ourselves to our own formula, but the ingredients came from my foraging expeditions and traders like Tamworth Tao, and they didn't always have what we needed. We only used it for surgeries, births where the mother had torn, and deep wounds. I probably shouldn't have used it on Sergeant Max, but the decision had been made and it was too late for regrets.

"Have you got the forceps?" Father asked.

"Someone's giving birth?" There weren't many pregnant women close to term that I knew of, and I thought I knew them all.

Father shooed me out of the larder. "Fetch the forceps. In fact, just give me your pack."

"Who's having a baby?"

"A woman."

I stepped in front of him and crossed my arms. "Why are you avoiding the question?"

He looked away.

"Father!"

He sighed. "A woman in The Row. Her waters broke overnight but the baby is stuck. Her sister came here and begged me to come. The expectant mother is fading."

"I'll go."

"You most certainly will not! Not to The Row."

"When I explain I'm the midwife—"

"They won't believe you. The fact is, Josie, you are a woman, and the only women in The Row are…you know."

"Whores," I finished for him since he seemed to have trouble with the word.

The Row had begun as a single street in the north of Mull, but over the years, it became synonymous with the entire area where the prostitutes eked out a living—if it could be called living. The buildings were little more than lean-tos, built from whatever materials had drifted onto the beaches. There were no proper gutters so the slops accumulated on the streets until the stench became too much and the residents themselves organized a cleanup. I'd never been into The Row, but I'd smelled it in summer and heard of the cramped conditions where the makeshift buildings couldn't keep the rain out let alone the wintry cold.

As much as I hated admitting it, Father was right. The women of The Row might trust me and accept me as a midwife, but the men would think of me as something they could purchase for a few minutes. It was too dangerous.

"Take Meg's brother with you," I said.

He shook his head. "Having a guard is as good as putting a target on my forehead. It'll make me look well off and in need of protection. I'll be safer alone."

He pushed past me and picked up my pack, the new one given to me by the leather seller. He placed the jar of Mother's Milk inside.

"You can't take the pack," I told him. "For the same reasons that having a guard will be a danger, so will carrying a bag."

"I have to take it."

I took it off him and removed the tools he'd need. "Place these in your pockets. I'll siphon enough Mother's Milk into a smaller jar."

He followed me into his surgery where I found an empty vial. "I had an unscheduled patient come this morning," he said. "Well, sort of unscheduled. Sergeant Max came to have his stitches out."

I turned suddenly, spilling a drop of the Mother's Milk. "Was he alone?"

"Yes. Why?"

"Just curious." I turned back to my task. "How is his wound?"

"Healing nicely. Your stitching was very fine. I couldn't have done better myself. Your mother would be pleased."

I laughed at that. We often joked how Mother would have liked me to be a normal girl with an interest in needlepoint, not surgery and medicine. She'd died when I was six but I'd already shown more enthusiasm for my father's books than embroidery at that age. The fact that we did laugh about it meant she hadn't really minded at all. According to Father, if she were still alive she would have been active in petitioning the authorities to change the laws so female students could study at the Logios colleges. Apparently I got my independent streak from her.

"What else did Max say?" I asked, careful not to sound too interested. "Did he mention Quentin? Or the captain?"

"Not specifically. He said everyone at the palace is busy with the arrival of the ministers and also preparing for more visitors."

"More?"

"Here's some gossip for you that no one else in Mull will have, I'd wager."

That got my full attention. I placed the stopper in the vial and regarded him. He was grinning. "Tell me!"

He chuckled. "You never did have much patience. He said the new visitors are the lords and ladies of Glancia, along with their daughters. Eligible ones, that is. The king wants a wife."

I quickly calculated numbers in my head. "Will they all stay in the palace?" There must be two hundred at least.

"They can't be put up at The Anchor, can they?" He laughed. "They're arriving in two weeks. Now, is that vial ready? I must hurry."

"I'll tell your afternoon patients to come back later."

"I wish you didn't have to," he said, pocketing the vial. "But it's for the best." He tossed me a smile and left.

A half hour later, I was inspecting Perri Ferrier's infected toe after he refused to leave. According to Perri, his pain was so intense that he required immediate attention. I cleaned up the toe, applied a salve, and bandaged it. When he left, he paid me the fee and an extra amount to buy "something pretty." I took that to mean he was satisfied with my service yet felt I ought to be more feminine. I'd never win with the Perri Ferriers of the world.

Father returned at dusk unharmed but disheartened. The baby had died; the mother, too. "The conditions in that place are appalling," he said, nursing his ale at the kitchen table. "It's a miracle anyone lives to adulthood. Someone should do something about it."

* * *

TWO WEEKS LATER, Mull was abuzz with the news that several of the country's best families had passed by the village on their way to the palace. I'd caught a glimpse of one of the processions and was surprised by how many vehicles one family of four needed. Apparently they required a carriage to transport themselves plus another six wagons for luggage and servants.

Lady Deerhorn pranced around Mull for days too, boasting how she and the other Deerhorns were staying at the palace, despite living so close. She insisted on seeing every bolt of silk and satin that arrived from Zemaya first, and bought several different colors, as well as beads, ribbons, lace, feathers and even gemstones.

Mull felt different since the arrival of the first families of Glancia at the palace. Anticipation and excitement hung in the air and gossip was rife, although how anyone could possibly know that Lady Laxley padded her bodice was a mystery. Some villagers ventured to the palace gates and were pleasantly surprised to find they were not ordered to go away. They were allowed to gaze upon the spectacle, but could not enter. Some of the visiting servants came into the village on their afternoons off and told tales of the dazzling palace and its inhabitants, but none had seen the king in person, and no matter how many I asked, none had met Captain Hammer, although they'd heard of him. His guards were omnipresent, apparently, yet he was confined to the king's side most of the time and out of view of the lower staff.

Another two weeks after the arrival of the nobles, in the final days of spring, the captain himself arrived at our house, alone.

"Josie," he said, greeting me as I opened the door on his urgent knock.

"Captain! What a surprise. Is Sergeant Max all right? Is it his arm?"

"He's fine." He glanced over my head. "Is your father home?"

"He's with a patient. He won't be long. Is someone at the palace injured? Ill?"

He nodded and once again glanced over my head toward

28

Father's surgery, where low voices could be heard through the closed door. "I need Doctor Cully urgently."

"Perhaps I can help. What are the symptoms?"

A flicker passed through his eyes but I couldn't determine what it meant. "You said your father is an expert on poisons. Are you?"

"Poison! I, er, have some knowledge, but there isn't much call for poison expertise in Mull. Has someone ingested something noxious?"

"I believe so."

"Is it the king?"

"A lady." He eyed the closed door again. "He needs to come with me now. She's very ill."

He strode off but I rushed past him and knocked on the door. "Father! Father, we have an urgent situation," I called out. "It's the palace."

The door jerked open and Father stood there. He took one look at Hammer and slipped past me. "Josie, see to Peter while I gather what I need."

I glanced at Peter, a regular patient with a bad back. He usually only needed to replenish his ointment supply. I tucked a bottle into his hand.

"You have to go," I said to Peter. "This emergency requires us both." I caught a glimpse of the captain, standing just beyond the doorway, his brows raised at me.

He turned away when my father called out some questions about the patient's symptoms from the depths of the larder where we stored more medicines than food.

"What about a massage?" Peter asked me.

"Not today," I said. "The ointment is free."

I saw him out then assisted my father. Based on Hammer's answers, he'd gathered what he hoped would be the right ingredients to ease the pain.

"Cancel the rest of my appointments for the day, Josie," he said as he strode for the front door. He never looked more in command, more energetic, than when he was racing off to a medical emergency.

I grabbed the sign hanging from the nail on the outside of the door and flipped it over. GONE FISHING it read. Everyone in the village knew my father didn't fish, and that it was his way of telling them we were both out.

"Done," I said. When he gave me a stern look, I added, "I'm coming with you. What if you don't have the right medicine? You'll need an assistant to fetch ingredients for you. This job is far too important for just one."

"You get more and more like your mother every day."

"Thank you. Oh, look, it seems we're going to the palace in style."

A carriage blocked the street. The coachman and footman both wore crimson and gold livery. Another footman held a horse's reins which he handed to the captain. He opened the carriage door and I climbed in, followed by my father. We were away the moment the door closed.

I smoothed my hand over the crimson velvet covered seat and matching door with gold embroidered LL, the king's initials, repeated in a regular pattern. I blew out a breath and watched the streets of Mull whisk past, the people I'd known all my life staring with open mouths. And suddenly the reason for their shock hit me too.

I was going to the palace of King Leon, a man whose origins were as mysterious as those of the captain of his guards and the palace itself.

CHAPTER 3

$\mathcal{I}$ caught my first glimpse of the palace as we drove along the tree-lined avenue that led to the main gate. The symmetrical building was built from the same warm pale stone as much of Mull, but that was where the resemblance ended. The palace was three levels high with one wing stretching south and the other north. The entire length of gray slate roof was capped with gold, and gilded balustrades edged the roofline in an opulent statement. It was so bright in the sun that I couldn't stare at it for more than a moment. There was more to see, anyway. Much more.

The trees lining both sides of the avenue suddenly gave way to buildings fronted by columns and arches. Servants dressed in royal crimson and gold lead horses in and out of the right building, while a carriage drawn by two black horses rolled through an arched entrance of the building to our left. These grand structures must be the coach house and stables.

"The horses live better than we do," I murmured.

Father didn't answer. He was too busy peering through the front window. The overwhelming sight of the palace up close was almost too much to take in. I didn't know where to look first. The gold-capped roof? The pink marble columns? Or the vast forecourt beyond the gate with its towering central fountain? Quentin was right. The palace did look tiny from Lookout Hill. Up close, it was enormous. The entire village of Mull could fit in it, with space to spare.

The captain rode ahead, and the guards manning the gate opened it for him. The gate itself was painted gold and topped by a golden statue of a warrior riding a chariot, brandishing a sword with a shield strapped to his arm. The House of Lockhart's coat of arms, featuring a key and a prancing deer, were picked out in gold relief on the shield, while the king's initials of LL made an impressive centerpiece on the gate.

My father gazed up at the statue and snorted. "He didn't win the kingdom through battle. I'd wager he's never lifted a sword in his life."

"Don't say that out loud around here," I warned. "Besides, we don't know if he has fought or not. We know nothing about him."

"Precisely."

We passed through the gate at a slower speed and into the expansive paved forecourt. Two identical long pavilions, fronted by high colonnades, faced each other across the area. They were not attached to the palace, but they seemed to guide visitors ever closer to it. Steps from the forecourt led to a smaller one paved in red, white and black marble. Water sprinkled from the fountain in the court's center. Beyond, the palace's main entrance was set back behind more pale pink marble colonnades.

It was not the only door, however. Others were dotted along the central part of the palace, between the statues set into the façade and the high windows of sparklingly clean glass. The upper levels sported more doors opening onto balconies.

I was so stunned by the palace that I almost missed the lady dressed in lustrous sage green silk climbing into a sedan chair carried by two burly men. An attendant closed the door and off she went across the larger forecourt toward the palace. It was quite some distance from the gate to the palace door, but surely she could walk?

Instead of heading toward the palace, we drove past one of the pavilions. It was bigger than the new customs house would be and just as grand. We did not stop there, however, but continued to a square building south of the pavilion, hidden from the forecourts. Smoke billowed from the chimney pots high above us and cooking smells blended into a miasmic stew in the air. Servants bustled in and out of the building, some dressed in palace uniforms, others in the colors associated with their house, and again others in maids' uniforms, kitchen garb or gardening clothing. I even recognized two Deerhorn servants.

We'd hardly stopped when a palace footman opened the carriage door. "This way," Captain Hammer said as his horse was led away by a groom.

Ogling servants stepped aside to allow him to pass. Father and I trailed behind, despite walking quickly to keep up. The servants watched the captain in eerie silence then turned those curious gazes upon us. One of the Deerhorn servants whispered to the other, nodding at Father and me. They knew who we were, and if the rest of the servants didn't, they soon would.

The captain led us along the breezeway separating the square servants' building and the pavilion. We entered the palace through a service door and wove our way down dimly lit corridors before ascending a flight of stairs. We emerged into another corridor through a door that, when closed, blended into the wall so well that one had to know it was there to find it. This must be part of the palace seen by the lords and ladies. Where the walls in the servants' stairwell and corridors had been unadorned stone, these were plastered and painted in a vivid shade of green. Vases on pedestals filled with white lilies flanked each of the doors along the corridor. I counted five doors, separated by long expanses of paneled walls. We finally stopped at the sixth, manned by two guards holding long pikes.

They stepped aside and Captain Hammer held the door open for us. The room beyond wasn't a bedroom, as I expected, but a sitting room with elegant furniture arranged around a black marble fireplace and gold leaf gilding the cornices. A portrait of a man dressed in furs hung above the mantel, one hand resting on his hip, the other holding a scepter. His dark eyes seemed to follow me as we hurried across the thick carpet to a door on the far side that led to the bedroom.

Hammer nodded at Sergeant Max, who stood by the wall, trying and failing to look inconspicuous between a spindly-legged chest of drawers and a dressing table topped with small bottles, a jar of cream, and hair combs.

I smiled at him. He gave me a nod then flicked his gaze toward the four post bed where my father now stood, inspecting the patient. He was more professional than me. Where I'd been distracted by the awe-inspiring palace, and the men I'd met some weeks ago, Father had immediately focused on the deathly pale woman throwing up into the porcelain bowl held by a maid. Another man and woman had moved aside to allow my father closer to the bed. Both were in middle age and looked on anxiously. They wore long richly brocaded gowns and slippers, and the man held one of the woman's hands between both of his. These must be the patient's parents.

Father placed the palm of his hand to the girl's forehead then checked the pulse at her wrist. I dipped my fingers into the basin of water on the bedside table. I touched the back of the patient's neck and she sighed from the coolness.

It wasn't a hot day but the room felt stifling, thanks to being higher up in the palace. Sweat dampened the woman's blonde hair and her nightdress clung to her curves.

"Open the windows," I said. The captain nodded at Sergeant Max to follow my orders. "Do you have a fan?" I asked the maid.

The patient had finished throwing up but the maid still held the bowl ready. I took it from her and she disappeared into the sitting room. She returned a moment later with a large fan. Under my direction, she stood on the other side of the bed and flapped it at her mistress.

"How long ago did the vomiting start?" my father asked the patient.

"Last night," the woman whispered through cracked, colorless lips. "I went to bed after midnight and woke up with terrible cramps." Her hand fluttered weakly at her stomach. "I thought it would pass."

"Did you raise the alarm?" I asked the maid.

She nodded quickly. "My lady was like this when I brought in her breakfast. I fetched Lady Claypool straight away."

Claypool. I knew that name. The Claypools were a noble family with an estate near Coldstream. Lord Claypool had come to Mull once, years ago, to inspect a fishing vessel. I'd not met him but had heard about him from those who had. Looking at him now, anxious about his ill daughter, he did not seem like the same man that Meg had called both masculine and graceful in the same awed breath.

"She has been like this all morning," Lady Claypool said.

Going by the contents of the bowl, the patient had long since thrown up her last meal and now discharged only liquid. Someone had emptied the bowl.

Father asked the patient questions as he peered into her eyes, down her throat, and at her fingers. I didn't know what he was looking for, but I would certainly ask later and make notes. I hated having gaps in my knowledge.

I did know one thing he would need, and while he was tied up investigating the patient's symptoms, I could be of use elsewhere. "Have you disposed of the other contents?" I asked the maid and indicated the bowl.

She chewed on the inside of her lip. "I emptied it into the bathtub."

"And where is the bathtub now?"

"The bathroom."

The palace had a bathroom! What a luxury.

I followed her through another door near the back of the bedchamber into a large room painted yellow with a pink marble tiled floor. An unlit furnace squatted in the middle of the room beside a bathtub raised on a dais. The tub was large enough for me to stretch my legs out if I sat in it. Not that I would want to sit in it with the remnants of the patient's stomach pooled at one end. There didn't seem very much, however, and I realized the rest had disappeared through a hole in the bottom of the tub.

"Is that a drain?" I asked, looking closer. "Where does it go?"

"I don't know." The maid held up a plug then peered into the bath. She pulled a face. "I didn't know it hadn't all gone down. I didn't look. I just wanted to get back to Lady Miranda. Will she be all right?" She blinked back tears. "She's been so good to me. She's such a lovely lady, so beautiful and kind. It's no wonder the king has fallen in love with her already. I wouldn't be surprised if they wed before the summer is out. If she... If she doesn't..."

35

Her lower lip wobbled but she managed to keep control of her tears.

I squeezed her shoulder. "You're a good maid to her. She's very lucky to have you. Don't worry. My father is the best doctor in Glancia, and he's an expert on poisons."

"Poison! You think she's been poisoned? Oh, dear Hailia, no."

"I—er...that is, we're not sure. She probably just ate something that didn't agree with her." Damn. The captain hadn't told her he suspected poison, and I'd just blabbed as if it were common knowledge. I hoped the Claypools didn't know.

The maid gasped. "Do you think someone fed her the poison deliberately?"

"No! Of course not. She most likely ate the wrong kind of salad leaf."

"But she didn't eat anything that the rest of them didn't. And she had no late night snack before bed, just the food at dinner that the others also ate. Even the king ate the same as my lady." She gasped again. "Do you think it was meant for him?"

Merdu, she had a macabre imagination. I had to reel it in before she accused someone of murder. "Do all the bedchambers in the palace have their own bathroom?"

She blinked rapidly at my sudden change of topic. "Not all. Most of the nobles have to share. We servants have a communal bathroom. Only the king's apartments and these ones are grand enough to have their own. Lady Miranda and her parents only moved down here two days ago from the attic rooms allotted to them when we first arrived." She drew in a breath and her chest swelled. "*These* apartments are supposed to be for dukes and duchesses, not for the lower nobles like Lord Claypool. He's only a baron, so the family shouldn't be here at all. But King Leon insisted on them moving out of the attic once he took a shine to Lady Miranda, even though Lord and Lady Claypool insisted they were comfortable where they were." She leaned closer and lowered her voice. "The higher up families are so jealous. You ought to hear what they say about my lady. Vile things." She shook her head. "Seems jealousy isn't just for the likes of you and me, miss."

I asked her for a towel and used it to pluck up partially-digested remains of Lady Miranda's last meal. Back in the bedchamber, I stuffed the towel into one of our empty jars.

It was then that I noticed a newcomer in the room. Another guard wearing a uniform with identical gold braiding on his shoulder and chest to Max's. He was of medium build with brown hair and the sharp cheekbones of a Vytill native. He stood by the door, his hands at his back, and stared straight ahead.

I turned to my father as he spoke, but not before I noticed Hammer watching me.

"Note the color of the fingernails, Josie," Father said, indicating the dark half moons on Lady Miranda's fingernails. "And tell me what you see in her eyes."

"The whites are milky," I said. "And the pupils are dilated. Her breathing is erratic too. Does your stomach still hurt?" I asked her.

My father nodded his approval of my question, but I guessed he'd already asked it while I was in the bathroom. He began to pack away his things.

Lady Miranda nodded and winced. She was putting on a brave face, but I could see by the way her jaw tensed that she was in pain. I touched her arm and gave her a reassuring smile.

"Don't worry," I said. "You're in the best hands now."

"Do you know what ails her?" Lady Claypool asked.

"Direweed mixed with traitor's ease," Father said. "Two poisons blended—"

"Poison!" Lord Claypool cried.

"Dear Hailia," Lady Claypool whispered, clasping her daughter's hand. Tears slipped down her cheeks. Lady Miranda lifted a hand to wipe them away but it fell to her side. She was too weak.

"Is there an antidote?" Captain Hammer asked.

My father nodded. "I'll make one up."

"Will it take long?"

"An hour once I get back to my surgery." An hour for an antidote was too long. He was holding something back, but I couldn't fathom what.

"Then go!" Lady Claypool said through her tears. "Go now, Doctor, please. Hurry back."

"Captain..." Lord Claypool began, casting a look toward Hammer.

The captain nodded. "He'll have an escort the whole way and our fastest horses."

"Continue to give her liquids," Father told the maid. "We need to flush it out of her system as much as we can before I give her the antidote." He had hardly finished speaking before he was out the door.

I hurried after him, the captain and the Vytill sergeant on my heels. Max remained behind. We caught up to my father.

"Does she have an hour, Doctor?" the captain asked.

"She has two," Father said without breaking his long strides. "If she's strong and healthy."

"She seemed to be, before this."

"Are you a god-fearing man, Captain?"

The sergeant grunted a harsh laugh.

"Pray to the goddess Hailia that she lives. Come. We must hurry."

* * *

CAPTAIN HAMMER'S silent presence was a distraction. He stood inside the front door, his arms crossed, legs slightly apart, and watched us through the open door of Father's workroom as we tested and re-tested the contents of Lady Miranda's stomach. Without a sample of the poisoned food or liquid, we had only the evidence of her discharge to go by. It should be enough.

Father clicked his tongue. "Too much riverwart." He used the tongs to remove the small dish from the grill over the low fire and threw both dish and liquid into the pail near his feet. It was a terrible waste but we couldn't risk reusing a dish the poison had touched. "Damnation." He pressed a hand to his lower back and stretched. "Another, Josie."

I handed him a clean dish and scooped a coin-sized chunk of Lady Miranda's regurgitated meal onto it with a spoon. We had precious little left. "Should I halve the quantity of riverwart this time?"

"Try one third. Going by the speed at which it burned, I grossly overestimated the amount."

I handed him the bowl of ground riverwart but he shook his head. "You do it. My hands are shaking."

I'd noticed them trembling a while ago but hadn't pointed it out. He could be sensitive about his age on occasion, but I knew he'd ask me to take over if the trembling interfered with his ability to work. He might be somewhat vain about his age, but never to the detriment of a patient's wellbeing.

I added the requisite quantities of the six other ingredients that we'd identified for the antidote based on Father's old notes from a book I'd never seen him refer to before. We only had the riverwart to go. The painstaking process of testing and re-testing to find the right quantities of each ingredient had meant we'd taken longer than the hour. Father told me upon our arrival at the cottage that he'd only said that to give the patient hope. If she had hope, she might find the strength to fight and we needed her to fight. We'd be cutting it very fine to get back to her on time. It all depended on how much riverwart needed to be added to the other ingredients to neutralize the poison left in Lady Miranda's vomit.

I heard the front door open but did not turn around as I measured out the powder.

"Aren't they ready yet?" came the voice of the other sergeant, the one named Brant. "The hour has long passed."

"Go back outside," the captain growled.

My father left the workroom to speak to them. "It's a complicated process," I heard him hiss. "It's not a combination of poisons I've come across before and the ratios used are unknown. Traitor's ease is rare. Very rare. I've only seen it once in its raw form—years ago, in Zemaya. If you want us to work faster, you'll shut up so we can think."

I smiled. Father might seem like a meek professorial type of man, but two things stirred his passionate nature—the wellbeing of his patients, and when someone disparaged me.

"Shouldn't you be in there making the antidote?" Sergeant Brant said to him.

"My daughter is more than capable."

"Is she qualified?"

"She has a lot of experience."

"I'm sure the king would like to hear how the unqualified

daughter of the local healer was left to create the antidote to save one of the most important ladies in the realm. We should have used the finance minister's doctor, as he offered."

"The king will receive a full report," was all the captain said. "Return to your post outside, Sergeant."

I heard the front door close. I added a lump of peat to the fire contained within the heatproof box set up on the desk and tipped the riverwart into the dish. Father rejoined me and watched as I mixed the powder with the other ingredients until it was fully dissolved then set the dish on the grill over the fire.

The liquid quickly heated to simmering point but seemed to take forever to boil. The other experiments hadn't taken this long. I looked to Father.

His lips twitched into a smile. "I think this is it."

The liquid in the dish bubbled and turned a yellowish-green color.

"Take it off the heat," Father said, handing me the tongs. "Quickly now. We don't want it to burn away."

I set the bowl down carefully on the tray. "That's the right color?"

He handed me a ceramic jar. "It is. Commit it to memory, Josie. I hope you'll never need to make this antidote again, but one never knows, particularly now that the palace has sprung up nearby."

"What has that got to do with poisons?"

"It's the favorite method of murder at courts all over The Fist and beyond. Has been for centuries." He pressed the jar into my hand with a grim smile. "There's no time to wait for it to cool. Pour it in now. Don't spill any."

The dish had cooled enough for me to touch it with my bare hands. With a steadying breath, I poured the medicine into the jar. Father fixed the cork stopper in place.

"Remind me to update my notes later," he said, tucking the jar into the pocket of his loose doublet.

Without a word of instruction, Hammer opened the door and followed us out.

"About time," Sergeant Brant muttered under his breath.

I hadn't thought it possible to go any faster, but we drove at such a speed on the return to the palace that we did not slow for bumps or dips. Father and I got tossed around inside the cabin but it didn't seem to bother him in the least.

He didn't wait for the footman to open the door upon our arrival at the palace. He strode on ahead, joined by the captain. I picked up my skirts and ran after them, the sergeant behind me. The hairs on the back of my neck prickled and I turned quickly on the service stairs, catching him watching me.

"I hope I didn't offend you earlier," he said. "It's not personal. It's just that the king's mistress should have the best doctor."

"And you believe the finance minister's doctor is the best?" I asked.

"So I hear."

"You hear wrong. My father is the best, and if he lived in Tilting, he'd have the sort of reputation that would satisfy you. But he prefers to be in Mull, where the people are in dire need of excellent medical attention. That's just the sort of person he is."

"I can see why Max and Quentin like you," he muttered.

I forged ahead and met the glare of Captain Hammer, holding the door open for me. His eyes had a way of making me feel as though he was rummaging around inside me, searching for my secrets. I pushed past him and followed my father along the corridor to Lady Miranda's sitting room.

A man dressed in black with gold braid at the shoulder, like Captain Hammer's uniform, stood just inside the door. He nodded gravely at Hammer, who nodded back.

Another man paced across the carpet near the hearth. He stopped abruptly and fixed dark eyes on my father. He was short and slender with black hair that fell to his white lace collar in gentle waves. He couldn't have been more than mid-twenties, and his face looked vaguely familiar but I couldn't place it. He wore a doublet of deep blue with silver leaves and vines embroidered over the sleeves and down the front. The white lace cuffs of his shirt fell to his knuckles. He tipped his head back and peered down his nose at us; quite a feat considering he was shorter.

"Are you the doctor?" he demanded.

"This is Doctor Cully and his daughter Joselyn Cully, sire," Captain Hammer announced.

Sire? So this was Glancia's new king? I hurriedly performed a curtsy that almost ended in my humiliation, since I hadn't a clue how to curtsy properly. Thankfully the king was too busy ushering my father through to the bedroom to notice.

"Hurry then!" he said. "There is not a moment to delay."

I caught a glimpse of the painting hanging above the mantel as I passed and realized why the king looked familiar. It was his portrait hanging there, although he seemed more imposing in the picture as he looked down on the painter with disdain. The real monarch was far less regal. Indeed, he looked quite ordinary.

I nodded at Sergeant Max, still standing where we'd left him, and joined Father at the bed. Lord and Lady Claypool had stood upon our entry and peppered Father with questions about the antidote.

He put up his hand for silence as he bent over Lady Miranda, who lay almost unmoving in the bed. She looked little better than a corpse. Sweat dripped from her brow onto the pillow, and her face was as white as the sheets on which she lay. Her breathing labored in shallow rasps and her eyelids fluttered. She was barely conscious, but at least she was alive.

Father removed the jar from his pocket and asked the maid to assist Lady Miranda to sit up. She struggled, and Max came to her aid. The maid settled behind her mistress to support her, and I tipped her head back and opened her mouth. Father poured a little of the liquid down her throat. She instinctively swallowed and he poured more. He continued the process slowly until the entire contents of the jar were gone.

The maid laid Lady Miranda down again, and everyone, including the king but not the guards, crowded close to the bed. The room fell silent. Father and I exchanged glances and small smiles. Lady Miranda's breathing was returning to normal. It was an excellent sign.

"She'll sleep now," Father whispered, backing away from the bed. "May I respectfully suggest that she be left in peace for the rest of the day? Only her maid is to be allowed to check on her from time to time, but not wake her."

"And me," Lady Claypool murmured without taking her eyes off her daughter.

"Yes, of course. It's imperative that Lady Miranda sleeps as long as she needs. Her body must rest to allow the antidote to work as efficiently as possible. I expect her to sleep through the night to the morning. It's vitally important she isn't disturbed. Is that clear?"

Everyone nodded. The maid looked terrified, particularly when Father signaled for her to follow him into the sitting room.

"She may grow restless in a few hours," he said quietly. "This is normal and expected. Make sure Lady Claypool is aware when it happens and does not try to wake her daughter. I don't expect Lady Miranda to purge any more. If her color hasn't returned by dawn, send for me. If she doesn't wake by midday the day after, send for me. I'll return after then to check on her anyway."

"You will stay until she is well, Doctor," the king commanded. He signaled to his man standing by the door to the corridor, and the servant approached.

"I regret that I cannot," my father said.

Merdu. Was he mad? He was certainly behaving irrationally. He might not be all that respectful when he had to tend to one of the Deerhorns, but they were only lords. This was the king, and kings' wishes were not refused.

King Leon bristled. "Lady Miranda is very dear to me. If she dies—"

"She won't if she's left alone to rest."

The king's nostrils flared at the interruption. He slapped one hand against the palm of the other behind his back. "Nevertheless, the village is too far away. If you're needed urgently, it will take too long for you to be fetched."

"I have an afternoon schedule full of patients who need me, sire." Father bowed. "I am sorry, but the people of Mull are important too."

The king puffed out his chest and lifted his chin. His manservant winced, as if he expected an explosion of temper from his master.

"I'll stay," I said quickly.

"Josie," my father scolded.

"I know the danger signs," I added. "I can answer any questions His Majesty or Lady Miranda's family may have, and I'll know how to keep her comfortable."

The king glanced at me, away, and back again. Those deep,

dark eyes scanned me from head to toe with cool assessment. "You're a woman."

"Yes," I said, biting back the sarcasm that came naturally to my lips.

"My daughter would be a doctor if the college allowed it," Father said proudly. "She would graduate top of her class."

"But they don't allow it."

A small frown creased the captain's forehead as he followed the exchange.

"Please, Your Majesty," I said. "I know it's unusual, but I also know my father will not give up his Mull patients, and I am more than capable of tending to Lady Miranda as she recovers. Besides, there'll be little to do except observe her." The more I thought about it, the more I wanted to stay. Not for Lady Miranda, who seemed to be out of danger, but because the palace and its inhabitants fascinated me. It was an opportunity to learn more.

"I prefer you to come home with me, Josie," Father said. "I need your help. My eyes are bad now and my hands…" He held up his hands. They trembled too much for it to be a natural shake.

I gave him a glare that told him I knew it. He looked a little sheepish for lying, at least.

"She stays." The king turned to his manservant, a slender fellow of about thirty with the flat face and straight hair of the Dreen. "Send someone to go with Doctor Cully and bring back the things Miss Cully will need overnight."

"Yes, sire." He turned to go.

"And Theodore?"

"Yes, sire?"

"Make sure the court knows that no noise is to reach Lady Miranda's rooms. There will be no revelries tonight, no musicales, and no games. If they complain, tell them to use the time to reflect."

"Yes, sire." Theodore hurried out of the room.

Captain Hammer directed Sergeant Brant to escort my father home. Sergeant Brant looked as if he'd question the order, but a glare from Hammer silenced him.

My father didn't immediately follow him out. "May I have a word in private with my daughter?"

"Of course," the king said, stepping toward the captain. "Hammer, you *must* find out who did this before he strikes again."

My father grabbed my elbow before I could stumble through a curtsy and steered me away from them. "Josie, I forbid you to leave these rooms."

"Why?"

"Because..." He indicated the sitting room, the window, the door, but I had no idea why. "Because this place is strange. Its very existence is strange. The sooner you leave here, the happier I'll be."

"Father," I chided. "This place may be odd, but it's not sinister. And it's certainly real, not a magic palace."

One white eyebrow crept up his forehead. "It seems there is a poisoner within these walls. Is that sinister enough for you?"

"I won't eat anything intended for the Lady Miranda."

"Don't be glib." He looked toward Captain Hammer who stood with Sergeant Brant, the king having left. "I don't like you being exposed to these people, Josie. There's something about them..."

"Something odd, yes, we've established that." I kissed his cheek. "Go. They're waiting."

Father gave me a flat smile and joined the captain and sergeant. "Where can direweed and traitor's ease be purchased in Mull?" I heard the captain ask as they exited the sitting room.

"Direweed is sold by two traders that I know of," Father said. "Traitor's ease is another matter. I've never seen it in Mull's market."

I re-entered the sickroom. Lord and Lady Claypool seemed to take my presence as a signal for them to leave. They excused themselves and hurried from the room. I sat with the maid, Hilda, but almost fell asleep in the chair. The return of Lady Claypool roused me some time later. She looked much fresher and extraordinarily elegant in a dove-gray gown trimmed with pink lace, her golden hair fixed into an elaborate arrangement that must have required at least two maids to do in the time she'd been absent.

I signaled to Max to join me in the sitting room and shut the door behind him. "You won't be needed," I said. "She'll sleep for a while."

"I don't require rest, and the captain ordered me to remain here." He checked the corridor outside then rejoined me. After a moment, he sighed and sat on a chair. He rubbed his knee. "Will she really be all right?"

"There is always some lingering concern until the patient is fully recovered, but she should be fine. My father wouldn't have left if he thought otherwise."

"The captain said Doctor Cully is an expert in poisons."

"He is, from his travels."

"Would he know who supplied the poisoner?"

"No. He can guess, as I can, and he will pass those guesses onto your captain."

He blew out a breath. "Of course. My apologies, Josie, I didn't express myself very well."

"It's all right. I can see that you're troubled. Do you know Lady Miranda well?"

He shifted forward in the chair and rubbed his hand over his jaw. "Not at all. I've seen her from afar, walking with the king, playing cards with the other ladies, laughing." A ghostly smile touched his lips before setting into a serious line again. "She laughs a lot. It's obvious she enjoys the king's company and he hers."

"You think they'll marry?"

"Not if the ministers have their way."

"Why don't they want him to marry her?"

"Because her family isn't important enough. They want him to make a strategic marriage, not a love match."

"Will he bow to their wishes?"

He lifted one shoulder. "Who know what the king thinks? He keeps his own counsel."

"He doesn't confide in his ministers? Or his trusted servants?"

He hesitated and shifted his feet before finally answering. "He trusts Theodore, Hammer and Balthazar with his life, but not with his secrets. He prefers to meditate on problems of state in his own rooms, alone."

"Who is Theodore? I noticed he wears a similar black uniform to the captain's."

"That's because he's the highest servant in the palace, along with Hammer and the Master of the Palace, Balthazar. Theodore is the king's chief valet. He organizes all personal matters for the king, from his wardrobe to his food, who gets to see him and when. Hammer takes care of the king's personal security, and Balt-hazar oversees the staff who don't fall under Hammer's or Theodore's jurisdiction, as well as the day to day running of the household. Between the three of them, they have utmost authority."

"The king must have known them a long time to entrust them with such important roles."

"It would seem so." He stood and turned toward the bedroom but stopped. "Quentin will want to know you're here. He's been driving everyone in the garrison mad with talk of you these last few weeks."

"He's sweet."

"He's a fool but a harmless one. I'll tell him you're here when I'm relieved of duty. He'll want to take over but I doubt the captain will let him. He's too..." He waved a hand, as if that explained Quentin's inadequacy.

"Tell Quentin I'll visit later. Where's the garrison?"

Max hesitated before answering, "Ground floor, almost at the end of the northern wing."

I followed him into the bedchamber and checked on the patient. She slept peacefully so I decided to go for a short walk along the corridor. I was surprised to see more guards on duty. Two had been stationed at each end. I asked one of them who occupied the other rooms and he said that aside from Lord and Lady Claypool's apartments, only the duke and duchess of Glad-stow had permission to use that corridor to access their rooms. Captain Hammer had instructed the guards not to allow anyone else in until Lady Miranda was better.

I sat with the patient and checked her pulse on the hour simply to keep her mother and maid happy. I could tell by looking at Lady Miranda that she was better. She wasn't quite so pale anymore and she slept peacefully.

The maid left to have her supper and brought some bread and cheese back for me. She whispered something in Lady Claypool's ear then her ladyship rose and left. I ate in the sitting room. By the time I'd finished, Lady Claypool returned. She smiled warmly at me and entered her daughter's bedchamber.

After another hour, I could no longer stand the boredom. I

signaled that I was going out then slipped into the corridor. Someone had lit the torches in the wall sconces and the flames danced merrily in the drafts.

I found the hidden door that opened up to the service stairs by running my palm along the wall. Thankfully the torches had been lit in the service corridors too. I headed downstairs then in the direction that I hoped was north, although I couldn't be certain. The windowless passages used by the servants played havoc with my usually good sense of direction. I asked a passing footman dressed in palace livery which way to go but I didn't like the way he licked his lips as he looked at me, so hurried on. Thankfully he didn't follow. I came across two maids moments later, talking quietly.

"Can you point me in the direction of the guards' garrison?" I asked them.

"Who do you work for?" asked the larger one.

"No one. I came to tend to Lady Miranda Claypool."

"You're that woman doctor!" the thin one cried. "Is she all right? Will she die?"

"She'll be fine."

"Good. I liked her."

The big woman grunted. "I know a few what will be disappointed with that news. Some around here want her dead. Some would rather the king looked at them the way he looks at her."

"Well some ain't as pretty or as kind as her and ought to just piss off back to where they came from," the thin maid said. "I'll be glad when they're all gone again. They're lazy and rude. Fetch this, empty that...it's all they ever say, and me not even their own maid. That's just the ladies too. The men are worse. My arse still hurts from where that Deerhorn prick slapped it when I was trying to make his bed."

"You should have slapped him back," the big woman said.

"I would have but he looked like he could smack me from here to the other end of the palace."

"He can," I warned her. "Stay away from the Deerhorns, especially the sons."

"Thanks. I will." She pointed along the corridor. "Take this all the way. Turn right, then left, then right again. Go down the steps, through the arched doorway—"

"The second one," the thin maid said.

"No, the third. Then it's right, right again and left. Why?" she asked with a crooked grin. "Who're you meeting there?"

"Quentin, and it's not like that."

Both women chuckled. "We believe you," the bigger woman said. "If it were the captain, I'd have my suspicions."

"He has a lot of lovers?" I dared ask.

"Don't know. I meant you ain't the first one who's tried to find her way to his room in the night. Problem is, his chambers are next to the king's. It's impossible to sneak in without a dozen servants seeing."

"You tried, eh?" The thin woman chuckled and nudged her companion in the ribs with her elbow.

I continued on my way but became hopelessly lost when the corridor darkened. The torches in this part were not lit. I was surrounded by cool stone walls, a flagstone floor and wooden ceiling that creaked as someone walked above me. That's it! I'd forgotten to go down the steps.

I was about to retreat when I heard someone speaking. "How did he know, Hammer?" the man asked. "How did he know women aren't allowed into the medical college in...where is it again?"

"Logios." I recognized Captain Hammer's voice, drifting to me from along the corridor. He was still far enough away, however, that I couldn't see him. "It's an old city in Dreen where all the colleges are located, and the libraries. Perhaps he read about it. There's a book on the history of The Fist Peninsula in the palace library. More than one, in fact."

Why would the king need to read up on Logios? Everyone on The Fist knew of the colleges and how they didn't allow women. I could believe that these men, who may not be native to the peninsula, would need to read a historical text on the area to know such a thing, but it struck me as odd that they thought their king in the same boat.

"He doesn't read books. I know that for a fact." I now recognized the voice as belonging to Theodore, the king's valet. "He's worried the poisoner meant to target him and not the Lady Miranda. Can you reassure him?"

"Not yet."

The voices became more distant and I realized they weren't coming toward me after all. I went in search of them. I thought I almost had them but as I rounded a corner, I saw Theodore's back as he walked alone through a doorway. There was no sign of Hammer.

I took the other door. A faint keening echoed along the narrow space. I couldn't tell if it was human or animal, but it was certainly disturbing. My heart raced and every part of me wanted to turn back. But I was a healer and that sound could have come from an injured or ill person. It was my duty to check. Besides, Captain Hammer must be up ahead and he was no danger.

I crept along the dark corridor, feeling my way with a hand pressed against the stone. The keening sounded again. At first it seemed as if it was all around me, but as it faded, I could tell that it came from ahead. I sucked in a deep breath in the hope it would calm my rapidly beating heart, then pushed on.

Soon the pitch dark lightened to a dull gray and finally the flames of a lit torch banished the darkness to the shadowy edges on either side of a closed door. A padlock as big as my hand hung from the bolt. It was open.

Beyond the door, wood scraped and a metal chain clanked, but the keening had stopped. There were no other sounds. The silence closed in, as thick as a winter fog.

I reached out but the handle turned. My heart leapt into my throat. I don't know why, but I ran off back up the corridor.

I got as far as the corner when someone grabbed me from behind. I tried to scream but a hand slapped over my mouth. A strong arm wrapped around my waist and pulled me back against a solid chest.

"You shouldn't be here, Josie," Captain Hammer said in a low voice that stretched my nerves to breaking point. "You shouldn't be anywhere near here."

CHAPTER 4

*C*aptain Hammer's breath brushed my hair and his whisper echoed through my body. "Don't scream. I'm going to let you go now." His hands moved away from my mouth, my waist, and his body no longer warmed my back.

I shivered.

"Are you lost?" he asked.

I nodded. It was all I could manage. My voice could not yet be trusted to remain steady.

"Follow me." He strode off without looking back.

I picked up my skirts and followed. By the time we reached a brightly lit corridor, my heart had stopped racing. "Who was in that room?"

"No one."

"I heard something."

He rounded on me. "What did you hear?"

"A sort of wail."

"Probably just the wind. The drafts in this part of the palace could sail a ship." He took off again and I realized we were heading back the way I'd come.

"I was trying to find the garrison," I said. "Can you direct me? Usually I'm very good at following directions but the maid's instructions were complicated."

"You've spoken to palace servants?"

"Yes. Why? Am I not allowed?"

He turned left into another corridor. "The garrison is this way. Why do you want to go there?"

"Max said Quentin has been asking about me."

"Persistently." He sounded annoyed.

I smiled at his back then, as the corridor widened, moved up alongside him. He didn't break stride.

"So what is in that room?"

"Nothing that concerns you. Any other questions, Miss Cully?"

"Call me Josie. And I have a million questions," I muttered.

He turned to look at me. "This is why your father didn't want you to stay, isn't it? Because he knew you'd sneak around the palace and find trouble."

"First of all, I am not sneaking. I was looking for the garrison. Secondly, have I found trouble?"

"That depends."

"On what?"

"On whether Lady Miranda dies in your absence."

I slowed but he kept walking. He was utterly serious. "She's out of danger," I said, catching up. "She won't die now unless the poisoner gets to her again, but Max is there to stop him."

"Or her. Are you sure she's out of danger?"

"I know you'd prefer to have my father's reassurance, but I do know when someone is on their death bed or not."

"I believe you."

I blinked at him but refrained from asking if he really did believe me or was just saying so. I had a feeling Captain Hammer wasn't a man who said one thing when he meant another.

He pushed open a door and the sounds of quiet chatter welcomed me into the large room beyond. Ten men dressed in palace guards' uniforms sat in chairs, some positioned at the long central table, others near the fireplace. As with the service corridors, the walls weren't plastered, painted or carved like Lady Miranda's apartments. It was as bare as a crypt.

"Josie!" Quentin set down the boots he'd been polishing and sprang up. He went to embrace me then thought better of it and patted my shoulders instead. He couldn't stop grinning. "I'm so glad to see you! So, so glad. Come, sit down. You must be exhausted."

"Not at all. There's nothing to do except watch Lady Miranda sleep."

"Lucky you."

The captain ordered some of the men to relieve Max and the other guards. They plucked off belts hanging from hooks by the door, each one with a sheathed sword attached, and filed out.

Quentin pulled his chair around and directed me to sit. I did, somewhat self-consciously. All the men had stopped playing their card games or eating supper and watched me as if they'd never seen the likes of me before. I smiled at Sergeant Brant, the only other face I recognized. He tipped his chair back, balancing it on hind legs, and folded his arms over his chest. He looked broader without his doublet, the muscles of his shoulders straining his shirt seams.

"So she lives," he stated.

"Despite the unqualified daughter of the local doctor creating the antidote," I said, unable to resist the barb.

Quentin and at least one other guards snickered. "Ignore Brant," Quentin said. "He's an arse."

Brant shot to his feet and grabbed Quentin by the front of his doublet. "You're getting cocky. That got something to do with the pretty girl in the room? Haven't you ever seen one before?"

Quentin swallowed audibly.

"Let him go," Hammer said. He poured ale from a jug into a tankard and handed it to me, then poured another for himself.

Brant snatched up his own tankard and drained it. Quentin flattened his rumpled doublet and managed a limp smile. "Tell me about the poison, Josie," he said. "Brant said your father knew straight away what it was. How?"

I described the symptoms and my father's research. I told them how we'd tested the different combinations of ingredients for the antidote on Lady Miranda's vomit. Several looked revolted. One even gagged.

"Your father is good healer," one of the guards said in a thick accent. Like most of the men, he was broad, but he was also tall, taller even than Hammer, whereas the others were shorter. I'd never seen the likes of him before in Mull, with his ropey blond hair falling past his shoulders and the line of dot tattoos across his forehead. I may never have seen a man from the Margin but the hair and tattoos were a giveaway. Despite Glancia butting up against the south eastern edge of the Margin, it was rare for anyone from either side to cross the border. The Margin folk believed strongly in family tribes staying together. So why had this man left his home, and how had he come to work at the palace?

When he flashed me a grin, I realized I'd stared too long and looked away.

"That's Erik," Quentin said. "He's not as frightening as he looks."

"His looks don't scare me," I said. "I'm intrigued, that's all."

Erik arched a brow. "Intrigued? What word is this?"

"It means curious, interested. But not scared."

"Then you are not like others."

At my questioning look, Hammer added, "The visiting servants and nobles take one look at him and change direction to avoid him."

"We're not used to Margin folk here," I said. "The palace servants aren't afraid of you?"

"No," Erik said. "Are you healer too, Josie? Like your father?"

"Yes…and no."

"She hasn't studied medicine," Brant told him.

"Women aren't allowed to go to the colleges," Hammer clarified.

"No?" Erik's brow wrinkled with his frown, drawing the dot tattoos together. "Why?"

The guards all looked to me, even Hammer. "Because it's just the way it is and has always been," I said, lamely. A lecture on the unfairness of a patriarchal society seemed out of place amidst all these men. Still, their ignorance was somewhat refreshing. Part of me wished they'd never learned of the college's rules.

"What's the medical college like?" Quentin asked. "Can anyone apply? Do you have to be a certain age?"

"Any man over the age of eighteen can apply. Any man from The Fist Peninsula, that is," I added, watching him closely.

"Does the applicant have to prove he's from The Fist?"

"A letter of introduction from his village's sheriff or the local lord will suffice."

Quentin slouched into his chair. "Bollocks."

"Thinking of a career change?" Brant asked.

"Not anymore," Quentin muttered.

"You've got to find something else to do. You're the worst guard I've ever seen."

"How many you seen?" Erik asked.

"He's the worst guard *here*," Brant clarified. "By far. He can't ride a horse and he looks like he'll faint whenever he gets hit in the training yard, which is all the time. Him being a guard...it doesn't make sense."

"You think any of this makes sense?" Quentin shot back.

"Enough," Hammer snapped.

Brant glowered at his captain then rested his folded arms on the table. He leaned forward and muttered something under his breath that I couldn't hear.

"How much longer will Lady Miranda have to remain in bed?" Quentin asked.

"A few days," I said.

"Will there be any lasting effects? Scarring? Disfigurement?"

"It's a poison, not a disease or injury. She'll look as she always did."

"Beautiful." Quentin smiled. "The king will be pleased that she won't lose her looks."

"A pretty face does not make a good woman," Erik said.

Brant snickered, revealing a missing top tooth that I hadn't noticed before. "Spoken like an ugly man who can't get a beautiful woman."

"Beautiful women come to me many times. Them that do not fear me." Erik grabbed the bread and tore off a chunk. "Big is best, they say."

"They say that *before* they've seen your pizzle stick."

"Enough!" the captain roared. "Josie isn't interested in hearing you two lugs voice your ignorant opinions."

"Aye," Quentin chimed in. "She's far too clever for the likes of either of you, so stop beating your chests and showing off in front of her."

"Showing off? To her?" Brant looked at me and laughed.

At least Erik blushed, saving me from complete humiliation.

Quentin offered me some cheese from the board but I refused. "More ale?" he asked. "Are you cold? It may be summer but it's often cool in this room. We're used to it and haven't bothered with a fire tonight, but I can make a small one if you like."

"I'm fine, thank you," I said.

"Merdu, Quentin, you're worse than a puppy," Brant muttered.

"Thank you, Brant, I always knew you thought of me as adorable."

Everyone except Brant chuckled. "Shut up, you annoying little turd."

Hammer sighed and appealed to the ceiling. I wondered if it was always like this.

The door opened and Max entered with five other guards. He greeted me with a lift of his chin. "You found it, then. I thought you might get lost."

"I did."

The newcomers helped themselves to ale and food then took up seats around the room. "Find out anything today, Hammer?" Max asked.

"No," the captain said. "It's most likely traitor's ease was sold off-market to the poisoner, as Doctor Cully thinks."

Quentin leaned toward me. "The captain was in the village investigating Lady Miranda's poisoning all afternoon."

"I had no luck," the captain said.

Brant balanced his chair on its back legs, his toes just touching the floor. "You expect the guilty person to simply wave their hand in your face?"

"I didn't say my investigation was complete."

"So where will you go next?"

Hammer didn't answer.

"What was poison in?" Erik asked. "Food? Drink?"

"The maid said Lady Miranda ate and drank nothing after the main evening meal," I told them.

"There were no plates or glasses in her rooms when I went in," Hammer added.

"You wouldn't have been the first there."

"I wasn't. Hilda the maid was already with her, as were her parents. The maid sent a footman to fetch me so we can assume he was also in the room, albeit briefly."

"No one else?"

He shook his head. "It's possible the maid lied."

"I doubt it," I said. "She seems devoted to her mistress."

"She's a servant," Brant said. "Servants pretend to be devoted all the time. Don't we?" He swiped up his tankard and raised it in salute.

"Shut your mouth," Max muttered. "Your voice is irritating my ears."

"And your ugly face is grating on my nerves."

"I can't help it if you have delicate nerves."

"It's likely the poison was administered during dinner," Hammer said before the argument turned physical. "But no one else became ill, which means she was specifically targeted by the poisoner. That narrows down our suspects to those who had access to her and those with a reason to kill only her."

"Not the king." Quentin blew out a breath. "That's a relief."

"We must find out who sat either side of her at dinner," Max said.

"Brant, you and I will question the servants who were in the dining room before, during and after the meal," Hammer said to his other sergeant. "I want to know the movements of every single one of them."

Brant nodded.

"Do you know Lady Miranda, Josie?" Hammer asked. "Or her family?"

"Only by name," I said. "The Claypools had little reason to come to Mull before now. Hilda, the maid, suggested several of the higher families are jealous of Lady Miranda's rapid rise at court. She said the Claypools' new apartments are coveted by others who think they have more right to be there."

"It's not the apartments themselves," Hammer said. "It's what they symbolize—the king's regard. They all want it."

"They all want the riches he can bestow on them," Brant added.

"We've already searched the rooms of the women who are Lady Miranda's closest rivals," Quentin told me.

"I'm sure that went down well." At his raised brows, I added, "They think themselves above the law and not bound by the same rules as the rest of us."

"Perhaps under the old king, but not Leon," Hammer said. "My investigation has his support."

The front legs of Brant's chair returned to the floor with a thud. "Then allow us to use *every* method at our disposal to get to the truth. Questions will only result in lies unless we—"

"You'll do as I say, Brant. Is that understood?"

"But—"

"No."

Brant snatched up his tankard and, finding it empty, poured more ale from the jug.

Every method? I dared not think about it.

"You should ask the other nobles about the Claypools and Lady Miranda in particular," I said to Hammer. "Perhaps there's another reason why she was poisoned that has nothing to do with jealousy over the king's favor."

"Good idea," Max said. "Bringing all the Glancia nobles together under the one roof could have ignited long-festering rivalries."

"Land," Erik said, nodding. "We will speak with other tribes."

"Families," Brant corrected. "They don't seem to be called tribes here."

What an odd thing to say. I looked from one face to the other, but they were all serious, even Brant. None seemed to think it odd that King Leon didn't already know about the rivalries between the noble families of his own kingdom.

"The king ought to be aware of any land disputes," I said.

No one met my gaze. Not a single one.

"I know he didn't come from the noble set, and he hasn't been king long, but surely his advisors have informed him of all relevant grievances."

"His Majesty doesn't trust his advisors," Brant said. "They're all greedy and corrupt, according to him. Same with the dukes and other lords."

I couldn't quite fathom it. King Leon had inherited the throne a few short months ago, under unusual circumstances, just as

Glancia faced its darkest hour. Its very existence had been under threat. The old king's only heir had died over twenty years ago, without children. Or so the world thought. Days before his own death, Old King Alain declared his grandson had been found. The thing was, no one knew there was a search for him, and many had initially suspected Leon tricked King Alain, until they heard the full story; the story that banished all doubts from the minds of Glancia's ministers and lords.

Leon's father, King Alain's son, had visited Freedland and fallen in love years ago. The couple had married in secret because the son was afraid it would make Alain angry if he knew he'd married a commoner—and a Freedlandian at that. It was true, of course. Not only would King Alain have been furious, but the nobles and ministers too, and the marriage would have been annulled. Leon claimed his father loved his mother and wouldn't wish to disown her, particularly after learning she was with child.

Sadly, King Alain's son died, and so Leon grew up in poverty, not knowing he was of royal Glancian blood. Alain's son, however, had written a document before his death, naming his wife and child. He'd entrusted the document to the High Priest in Tilting, instructing it to be read in the event of his death.

Unfortunately for Leon and his mother, that had not happened. The High Priest forgot about the document. It became lost among the High Temple's records for years until another priest stumbled upon it. Realizing the importance of the document at a time when King Alain lay dying, and the Vytill king was circling, Leon was found and acknowledged. King Alain was said to be delighted to foil the plans of his greedy distant cousin, King Philip of Vytill, who wanted to fold Glancia into Vytill, as well as put the Glancian nobles back in their place before any of them got ideas of taking the crown for themselves. With his succession secured, King Alain died only days after meeting his grandson for the first time.

Despite this legitimization by the old king himself, rumors still swirled through the cities, villages and farms. The tale of Leon's rise to power was so unlikely, so fantastic, that whispers of magic passed between friends and neighbors. The whispers increased when the palace was built in mere weeks without a single builder seen coming or going.

"Is that why King Leon won't listen to his ministers when it comes to taking a wife from one of the other kingdoms?" I asked. "Because he doesn't trust them and thinks they'll force him into a bad alliance for their own benefit?"

"That would be a reasonable assumption," Hammer said.

"Why wouldn't he take a wife from Glancia when he's the king of *this* country?" Quentin asked.

"Because it's in Glancia's best interests to make an alliance with one of its more important neighbors," Hammer told him. "Marriage alliances keep the peace between kingdoms. No king wants to wage war on his daughter, for example, or his grandchildren."

Quentin nodded, thoughtful. "So why doesn't Leon want to marry a foreign princess? Are there none?"

"King Philip of Vytill has a daughter of marriageable age," Hammer said.

"And the Dreen princess will be of age in another year," I added. "There's nothing stopping a formal betrothal taking place now with the wedding to be scheduled for after her eighteenth birthday."

"But are either of them pretty?" Brant asked.

"Faces," Erik said with a roll of his eyes. "Did we not say a pretty face matters not?"

"*You* said. Clearly the king thinks as I do. Glancia has the most beautiful women of all the peninsula."

All the men frowned at Brant. "How do *you* know?" Max asked.

"I talk to the visiting servants instead of avoiding them. I ask them questions."

"And what do you tell them in return?" Hammer asked darkly.

"Nothing," Brant mumbled. "I tell them nothing. I've got nothing to tell, have I?"

An oppressive silence filled the room, weighing me down as if it were a tangible thing. It wasn't so much the silence that worried me, it was the look in each man's eyes. Something made these strong men deeply, desperately sad, and it had to do with their pasts.

"Where *are* you all from?" I asked carefully.

Some of the guards appealed to their captain, others stared at the table or into their tankards. Hammer's jaw firmed. He scrubbed a hand over it and I thought he would speak, but he didn't. The silence deepened.

"We don't know," Brant finally said. "That's the whole fucking problem."

"Sergeant!" the captain snapped.

Brant slammed the tankard onto the table and shoved his chair back. It clattered onto the flagstones. He glared at his captain and Hammer glared right back.

After a moment, Brant picked up his chair and sat again. "You might as well tell her, Hammer. I asked her father and he'll—"

"You did *what*?" the captain exploded.

"*You* said you were going to ask but you didn't."

"I've been busy looking for the poisoner."

"What about yesterday?" Brant sneered. "Or the day before? Or the day before that? Ever since you, Quentin and Max met the doctor, you've told us you would ask him. But you haven't. You put it off and put it off and put it off." He stabbed his finger in Hammer's direction with each repeated accusation. "What kind of leader are you? You're too cowardly to ask an old doctor a simple question."

The other guards squared their shoulders at the accusation, and both Max and Erik looked as if they'd gladly smash a fist into Brant's mouth to shut him up.

But Hammer merely looked down at the tankard gripped in both of his hands. His knuckles were white. "I did not give you permission to speak of this to anyone," he said quietly.

"I don't care," Brant went on. "I'll follow your orders when it comes to finding poisoners and keeping the inhabitants of the palace safe, but if there's a chance I can find answers about us, I will do it. For all we know, you are not our leader."

"Don't," Max said, his voice a sinister growl. "We all spoke an oath to obey Hammer. Even you."

"Well?" one of the guards asked. "What did the doctor say?"

"Wait." I held up my hands. "What question did you ask my father?" When no one responded, I added, "He'll tell me anyway."

They all looked to Brant, except for Hammer. The captain got up and strode to the fireplace. He leaned his forearm against the mantel and lowered his head.

"I asked him if he knows a cure for memory loss," Brant said quietly.

Being in a roomful of big, burly men looking as vulnerable as kittens was an unsettling experience. I couldn't laugh at them, despite the absurdity of Brant's words. He was not jesting or mocking me. He was utterly serious.

"Do *you* know of a cure, Josie?" Quentin asked in a small voice.

"No," I said.

Brant shot to his feet. "Of course she doesn't." He kicked over his chair. "Her father didn't, so why would she?"

I studied each of their faces, and finally addressed Hammer's back. "You've *all* lost your memories?"

Several of the men nodded. "Our memories begin three months ago," Quentin told me.

"When the palace was finished," I murmured.

"Not just us, but *all* of the palace's inhabitants," Max said. "Not a single one remembers their life before that day. We know our names and those of everyone else who works here. We know what our work entails and how to go about it. But that's all. It's as if…" He broke off and scrubbed a hand over his jaw.

Hammer turned around and those blue eyes captured me. "It's as if we didn't exist before that day."

CHAPTER 5

*A*ll of them had lost their memory? Every single palace servant? What an absurd notion. Yet the alternative explanation was even more bizarre—that magic had created them.

"Did you all eat or drink something at the same time?" I asked. "Perhaps you consumed a poison."

"Do you know of a poison that causes memory loss?" Max asked.

"No but I'll ask my father."

"I did," Brant said. "According to him, the only thing that causes memory loss is a severe blow to the head."

Quentin tapped his forhead. "No bumps."

Brant righted his chair. "It may be worth *you* asking your father about poisons, Josie. I don't think he believed me."

I couldn't blame Father for that. I couldn't decide whether to believe them or not either. Yet why would they all go along with the story if it weren't true? The humorless captain didn't seem like the sort to favor trickery. "The land here is low lying. Perhaps some sort of miasmic cloud carrying an air-born poison settled in the valley and you all breathed it in."

"Have you ever heard of such a cloud?" Hammer asked. "Or of another large group of people losing their memory like this? There are almost a thousand servants living and working here."

"And it seems unlikely they would all be affected," I agreed. "Tell me what you do remember."

"Only our first names, not our last," Quentin told me.

I eyed Hammer.

"It would seem the captain's parents named him after a blunt tool," Brant said with a grudging laugh. "Fitting."

"We do not know our home," Erik told me. "I did not know about the Margin until the new servants came. They all look at me like I am animal. When I finally ask Lady Miranda's maid why, she tell me the Margin folk do not come here."

"We didn't know anything about any of the nations on The Fist Peninsula," Max said. "We didn't know its history, geography, the politics or religion. Nothing. We were as ignorant as small children."

"That must have been unnerving," I said.

"That is an understatement."

"The captain and Theodore read in the library most nights," Quentin said. "They reported back what they learned to us. Do you know, Josie, the day we met you on the hill was the first time I'd seen anyone from outside the palace. I thought you the most beautiful woman I'd ever seen. Most of the maids are not as tall or elegant."

"Height and fair hair are Glancian traits," I told him.

"But not all Glancian women are as pretty as you." He blushed and looked away, missing my smile.

"You don't have a chance with her," Brant sneered, showing the gap from his missing tooth to full effect.

Ordinarily I would have bitten back at him but I didn't have the heart for it. Brant was as worried as any of these men. His bitterness was understandable.

"The Margin folk don't speak our language," I said to Erik. "Do you remember your native tongue?"

He nodded. "I speak it once and none knew what I said, so I did not do so again." He tapped his temple. "I know two ways to say things but only one way will be understood by others."

"The Margin tribes each speak a different language," I told him. "The rest of The Fist speaks a united one. I wonder how you learned it."

Quentin sighed. "We wonder about a lot of things."

I reached across the table and placed my hand over his. "This explains much. Thank you for telling me. Father and I will look through our medical texts to see if we can help get your memories back. I cannot promise to cure you but I will not rest until I've exhausted all avenues."

"You can discuss this only with your father," Hammer said. "No one else. Is that clear?"

"I don't see why you need secrecy."

"Whispers of magic already abound. If the ministers or nobles have any reason to think we are a result of magic, or that Leon became king under dubious circumstances, then our lives are in jeopardy. At the moment, they accept him as Glancia's king, but if they think magic put him on the throne, they'll no longer acknowledge him."

"No reasonable person believes rumors of magic," I told him.

"Your father does," Brant said. "Is he not reasonable?"

"He is a little superstitious. Be assured, I won't tell anyone. I promise."

Hammer held my gaze a moment then nodded.

"You imply that the king also has no memory," I said. "But that's not true, is it?"

"It's true," Max told me. "That's another reason no one must be told. Balthazar says that if the ministers think the king is unfit to rule because he lacks memories, they'll try to remove him from the throne."

I frowned at Hammer but he was once again staring into the unlit fireplace, his back to the room. "So he doesn't know about the document written by his father and found in the High Temple only a few months ago?" I asked.

"He does now, but not in those first few days," Hammer said. "We learned it from some documents found in his desk."

"At least *he* learned his background," Brant muttered. "He knows where he is from, who his parents were. We don't."

"What about the building of the palace?" I asked. "You say it had already been built before you, er, arrived, but have you since found out how it was built? Are there records of payments to builders?"

"None," Hammer said. "We've heard from the farmers and fish-ermen who delivered food to the kitchens that it happened very quickly."

"And that no builders were seen coming or going," I added. "What measures have you already taken to learn what happened to you?"

"None," Brant bit off.

"Research in the palace library," Max countered.

"What else can we do?" Quentin asked with a shrug.

"We can leave," Brant said.

Hammer turned around. "And go where? We don't know where we're from. We don't know if we have families. This is the only home we have. At least here we are not alone."

"We have to do something," Brant snapped. "I hate sitting here and doing nothing."

"We won't do nothing forever. But for now, we have a poisoner in the palace. We have to find out who it is."

Brant threw his hands in the air. "Why? What's the point? Why should we care?"

Hammer stalked across the room and slammed his hand on the table near Brant. I jumped but the sergeant did not. "Because the day I woke up, I knew three things," Hammer said. "My name, your names, and my purpose, and that purpose is to serve as captain of the palace guards. I have a feeling that's significant."

They fell silent and even Brant seemed to agree with him, albeit grudgingly.

"I should return to Lady Miranda," I said, rising. "Will you escort me, Captain? I don't want to lose my way again."

Quentin jumped up. "I'll do it."

"No." The captain's quelling glare forced the lad back onto his chair. Hammer strode to the door and held it open for me to go on ahead.

"Thank you, Hammer," I said, passing him.

"I prefer you call me Captain."

I blinked after him as he strode off. "But all the men call you Hammer when off duty in the garrison."

"You are not one of my men." He waited for me by one of the

torches. The flames cast patterns of shadow and light over his face that made it impossible to read his expression.

"Very well, I'll call you Captain." I regretted my snippy tone as soon as I heard it. Of course he wouldn't allow me the same familiarity that he allowed his men. Perhaps in time, however... "Hammer is an unusual first name and it doesn't seem to suit you."

His mouth softened. "Perhaps it's normal where I am from."

"Perhaps you have a sister named Wrench and brother named Saw."

He laughed softly, the first I'd ever heard from his lips. His pace slowed, allowing me to easily keep up with his long strides.

"Thank you for telling me your secret," I said. "I know it can't be easy to trust an outsider, but I want to assure you that my father and I are used to keeping details about our patients to ourselves, and this is no different."

He nodded. "Thank you for believing us. I wasn't sure you would."

"Why not?"

"You seem very practical, and this is…"

"Odd?" I glanced at him sideways.

"Very."

I smiled, a little relieved that he was talking to me with ease. "You may find your secret gets out," I told him. "The palace servants may talk to the visiting ones about their memory loss."

"They have been warned not to. They know the consequences of going against my orders."

Consequences? My step faltered and he caught my hand to steady me. His thumb stroked my knuckles and his gaze fell to my mouth.

"Be careful," he said. "If I send you home to your father with scraped knees he'll never allow you to return to the palace."

"True," I said in a small voice. I didn't know if I was attracted to him or afraid of him. I did know that I felt very aware of him, of his heat and size, the scents of horse and leather mixed with his masculine one, and the callused hand that still held mine.

"You do want to come again, don't you, Josie? To see that Lady Miranda fully recovers? And to talk to me?"

"Talk?"

"I can only learn so much from books."

Of course he meant that kind of talk.

I withdrew my hand, relieved that the spell he'd cast over me broke instantly. My father's warning rang in my ears—be careful of these people; we knew nothing about them. If they could be believed, they knew nothing about themselves.

I drew in a breath and chased the threads of our conversation until I found a safer place to resume it. "You didn't answer me in there when I asked if the king had also lost his memory."

He set off along the corridor again, his strides purposeful. "Max answered you."

I picked up my skirts and hurried after him. "Perhaps Max doesn't know the truth."

"And you do? By all means, enlighten me because I am sick of being in the dark." His biting retort came as a shock after the gentleness of his hand caressing mine.

A sensible woman would back down and walk meekly alongside him. But I wasn't always sensible, and I certainly wasn't meek. "I want to hear the answer from your lips, Captain. Has the king lost his memory too?"

"He assures me that he has."

"That's not the same thing."

"You're accusing your king of lying? That could be treason, although I'd have to look it up in the legal texts to be sure," he said bitterly.

"Stop being contrary. I am only trying to help."

"Thank you, but I doubt you can."

"I overheard you and Theodore discussing the king knowing things that he should not if he'd lost his memory too."

His strides lengthened even more, and I had to quicken mine.

"I don't understand you, Captain. You seem to want to confide in me then suddenly you don't. You seem to be willing to trust me then you don't give me proper answers when I ask a simple question."

"Haven't you heard? I am an enigmatic mystery. We all are."

"You are not funny, either."

He continued on and I trailed after him, feeling foolish and lost. I couldn't even find my way through the palace, let alone give medical advice for his memory loss. I didn't want to argue with him, either. I wanted him to trust me and confide in me so I could help him. Help them all.

We moved into the more populated part of the palace and passed maids and footmen carrying trays, some empty, some with sweetmeats, cake or wine for their masters and mistresses. Those wearing palace uniforms quickly stepped out of the captain's way. The visiting servants paid us no mind.

We emerged from the dark service stairwell into the bright ducal corridor that housed the Claypools and Gladstows. The guards stood to attention then relaxed a little when they recognized Hammer. He spoke quietly to them, and I went on ahead to Lady Miranda's sitting room.

Hilda lay asleep on the sofa, her mouth open. Lady Claypool sat in a chair by her daughter's bed, her eyes closed. I leaned over the patient and listened to her breathing. It was regular. Her color was natural too, and she no longer sweated. I made sure she was well covered then settled on a chair on the other side of the bed to Lady Claypool.

I caught the captain watching me from the doorway. He quickly looked away and left altogether.

I did not see him again until the morning, when he came to speak to Hilda. He silently beckoned her into the sitting room then closed the door. A few moments later, I heard her high-pitched voice.

Lady Miranda's eyelids fluttered.

I rose and joined the captain and Hilda. "Shhh," I hissed. "Please whisper or leave altogether."

Hilda buried her fists in her apron at her lap. "I'm sorry. I'm so sorry." Tears pooled in her eyes and she glanced past me to the closed bedroom door. What had Hammer said to her?

He stood by Hilda, his hands at his back, looking fierce and forbidding. It wasn't a good way to get answers from a timid maid.

"A moment outside please, Captain." I stepped past him into the corridor without waiting for his answer.

"Is Lady Miranda all right?" he whispered, closing the door behind us.

I nodded. "Are you questioning Hilda about the night of the poisoning?"

"Yes. Why?"

"Are you learning anything?"

"She says she can't remember." He glanced along the corridor. "Not in the way that we can't remember. She's muddled, that's all."

"Perhaps you're scaring her."

"How?"

"By being stern and grim."

He arched a brow. "Grim?"

"May I suggest a softer approach with the maids? You need to make them feel comfortable, unthreatened."

"How?"

I sighed. "Are you sure you're supposed to be a guard? Perhaps you were meant to be employed in building maintenance but lost your way and woke up in the garrison instead of the workroom."

"And you say *I'm* not funny."

Whether he meant it as a joke or not, I smiled anyway. His lips quirked. I counted that as a victory.

"Will you watch on as I talk to Hilda?" he asked. "Signal to me if I become too *grim*."

I went to reach for the door handle but he got to it first. I glanced up and fell into the deep pools of his eyes.

"I'm sorry I snapped at you last night, Josie. You're trying to help and there's no excuse for my behavior."

"You have a good excuse, as it happens. You must find the poisoner before he strikes again while trying to find answers to your memory loss. It's no wonder you're on edge."

"You're too forgiving." He opened the door and I passed him, very aware that his gaze followed me.

I sat with Hilda on the sofa while Hammer stood by the exit. The heavy curtains remained drawn and someone had lit candles but the room was still dim. The lack of light didn't ruin the elegance of the chamber. There was far too much gilding and color for it to ever be considered dull.

"Hilda, the captain is going to ask you some questions about the night of the poisoning," I said quietly. "I'll stay. Will you answer him as best as you can?"

"Aye, miss."

"Call me Josie. All my friends do."

A self-conscious smile touched her lips. "I'll do my best to remember what happened, Josie."

"Be assured, you are not under suspicion."

"I'm not? Oh, that is a relief." Her shoulders relaxed. "Go on then."

"Did anyone visit Lady Miranda that night?" Hammer asked.

Hilda nibbled her lower lip, leaving tiny teeth marks in the soft flesh. "She didn't want me to tell anyone…"

"Circumstances have changed," I urged her. "It might be important to finding the poisoner. Who visited her?"

"The king. He came after dinner but my lady didn't let him in. She's not like that."

"Did he give her anything?"

"Not then, but later a vase of flowers arrived for her." She nodded at the red and pink arrangement in the large white vase. "The note that came with them said he wanted to apologize for his poor manners and for assuming."

"Did Lady Miranda smell them?" Hammer asked.

"Aye. Why?"

"Did you smell them?"

"Aye." She gasped. "You think they were poisoned?"

"You didn't fall ill, so they weren't. Was anything else delivered to her rooms?

She shook her head.

"Did anyone else come to her rooms? Her parents? A friend? Another servant?"

"No, sir. No one. She has no friends here at court and she has no need of any other servants except me."

It would seem the poisoning hadn't occurred here after dinner. I looked to Hammer. "May I ask Hilda a question?" He urged me on with a nod. "Yesterday you told me there are some who see Lady Miranda as a rival for the king's affections and they're jealous."

"Aye," Hilda said.

"Who?"

She hesitated and for a moment I thought she might refuse to tattle. "Many people, I suppose. Lady Miranda is clearly his favorite and everyone has noticed."

"Are there any who are particularly nasty about her behind her back?"

She looked away "I wouldn't know…"

"I understand your reluctance to tattle, but this is important. I know the servants talk. They must be aware that Lady Miranda was poisoned and some must have suspicions about who did it."

"I've heard them say Lady Lucia Whippler is the king's next favorite and very ambitious she is too. Her maid doesn't like her, and that's damning if you ask me."

"Anyone else?"

"Lady Deerhorn's daughter."

"Lady Violette Morgrave? But she's already married."

Hilda leaned closer. "I heard she hates her husband. I can see why. She's young but he's old and fat and his rotten teeth give him bad breath." She screwed up her nose. "Her mother's maid says she overheard Lady Deerhorn telling Lady Morgrave how to go about seducing the king."

"Seducing him is one thing, but she cannot marry him if she's already married."

"Perhaps she won't be married much longer. Wait and see if her husband suddenly dies. If he's poisoned too, then you'll know your poisoner is Lady Morgrave or her mother."

It wasn't outside the realms of possibility. Lady Deerhorn was ambitious and vain. The only thing she would love more than her daughter being the king's mistress would be for her to become queen. She'd think nothing of a little murder to reach such heights. I remembered when Lady Violette married Lord Mograve. Rumor had it that Lady Deerhorn was against the match but her husband had been friends with the elderly count and insisted. The bride had cried throughout the ceremony.

"What about other enemies?" I asked Hilda. "Does anyone have any other reason to want Lady Miranda dead?"

She shook her head. "None. She's got friends back home, among the village folk, but not here at court. Not since it became clear the king favored her."

I glanced toward the closed door that led to the bedchamber.

"What about Lord and Lady Claypool? Are they involved in any disputes with other noble families?"

She lifted one shoulder. "I don't think so."

The door to the bedchamber opened and Lady Claypool poked her head through the gap. Her lips trembled before she schooled her emotions. "She's awake."

I gave her a reassuring smile. "Good. She has slept long enough."

Hilda pushed past me and knelt by the bed. "Oh, my lady, thank Hailia. The merciful goddess answered my prayers."

Lady Miranda rested a hand on her maid's arm. "Good morning, Hilda." Her voice was weak but clear. "Mama?"

"I'm here, my dear." Lady Claypool sat on the edge of the bed and took her daughter's hands. She pressed them to her lips and blinked damp lashes.

"How long have I slept?"

"Long enough, according to Miss Cully," her mother said.

Lady Miranda's gaze shifted to me. "The doctor's assistant. Yes, I remember. Do I have you to thank for my recovery?"

"My father," I said. "He should return shortly. May I check your vitals?"

Her mother moved aside so that I could feel Lady Miranda's pulse and listen to her breathing. "Does your stomach still pain you?" I asked, pressing it gently.

"It's quite all right now. How long have I slept?"

"An entire day and night." I checked her eyes. They were clear and focused. "The danger is over. The poison has left your system. You just need to rest now and regain your strength. Hilda, can you send to the kitchen for a bowl of broth, please."

"Shall I inform the king that you are well?" Hammer asked as the maid left.

Lady Miranda teased the ribbon of her nightdress between her fingers. "Can we delay it?"

Lady Claypool sighed. "My dear, he is the *king*."

Lady Miranda sighed too.

"Perhaps wait until my father has called," I suggested. "I wouldn't wish to declare you well when you are not."

She gave me a small smile of thanks but it faded when she

glanced at Hammer. He stood erect with his hands at his back, his jaw rigid. Lady Miranda's fingers resumed their tugging.

"You do understand my position, Captain," I said. "After all, I'm not qualified. It would be irresponsible of me to declare her ladyship well based on my uneducated opinion."

His eyes tightened at the corners. He could see straight through me. "I agree that it would be inadvisable to give His Majesty false hope," he finally said. "We'll wait until Doctor Cully has called. In the meantime, are you able to answer some questions, your ladyship?"

He asked her whether she'd consumed anything after dinner, and she claimed she had not. Nor had she received any visitors, except for the king and then a footman, who brought the vase of flowers. All her answers matched Hilda's.

"Did you eat or drink anything at dinner that no one else did?" he went on.

"I don't think so," she said. "We all ate from the same serving dishes and our glasses were filled from the same decanters."

"Did anything taste bitter?" I asked.

Her pretty brow creased. "The last glass of wine I drank had a strange aftertaste. Was that the poison?"

"It could be. Direweed has a distinctive taste. Was it earthy?"

"Yes." Her lips moved as if tasting it again.

"Who dined with you?" Hammer asked.

"The king, Lady Lucia Whippler, her brother Lord Frederick, Lady Violette Morgrave, the duke and duchess of Gladstow, and the duke and duchess of Buxton," she said. "It was an intimate affair."

"The two ducal families and the king's most trusted friends," Lady Claypool added.

"His favorites," Hammer countered. "The king doesn't trust easily and considers no one his friend. Did any of them handle your food or wine glass, Lady Miranda?"

She blinked slowly. "I don't know. They could have, when I left the room briefly. Do you think one of them did it?"

"It's a possibility. Most of those people have a reason to want you...removed. They're jealous of your rise at court."

Lady Miranda's fingers stilled.

"Isn't it more likely that one of the servants administered the poison?" her mother asked. "Perhaps someone paid a footman to slip it into her glass."

"It's possible. I'll question Lady Violette Morgrave and Lady Lucia Whippler first," Hammer said.

"Tread carefully, Captain," Lady Claypool said. "Those ladies' families are manipulative. If they feel threatened, they'll go to the king. He will not like his friends to be accused of murder."

"I'll be subtle."

I bit back my smile but he saw it. He shifted his stance.

"What about the duke and duchess of Gladstow?" he asked.

"What about them?" Lady Miranda said.

Her mother looked down at her lap.

"There are rumors of a feud between your two families that began many years ago," Hammer said. "Is there any substance to them?"

"We hardly know the Gladstows," Lady Miranda said. "Indeed, I'd never met them before we moved into this part of the palace. I think your rumor monger is trying to stir up trouble where there is none."

"Lady Claypool?"

"As my daughter said, we hardly know the Gladstows. I hadn't seen him in years and I'd never met her before this week." Lady Claypool rose. "I must inform my husband of Miranda's recovery. If you don't mind, I think she requires some more rest."

"And a bath," Lady Miranda declared with a wrinkle of her nose.

Hilda returned as we exited the bedchamber. She carried a tray with a covered bowl and a small jug and cup. Hammer put up a hand to stop her.

"The king has a taster," he told her. "He must be summoned."

"One of the dogs was given some in the kitchens," Hilda said. "It didn't fall ill."

"Even so. Find the taster."

"Aye, sir."

I plucked off the bowl's lid and sniffed it. It smelled of game and red wine. I dipped my finger in to the broth.

"Josie, no." I'd already licked my finger before Hammer finished protesting.

"It tastes fine," I said. "Delicious, in fact. No earthy aftertaste." I poured a little of the water into the cup but Hammer snatched it off the tray before I could.

He scowled at me over the rim of the cup as he sniffed the contents. Then he sipped.

"Well?" I asked as he set the cup down.

"It's plain water." He directed Hilda to go through to the bedchamber. To me, he said, "You shouldn't have done that." He held the door open for me and nodded at the guard standing in the corridor. I heard Lady Miranda thank Hilda and ask her to send servants up with water to fill the bath.

"The poisoner would be mad to strike now while you are on his trail and the palace staff are on heightened alert," I said, trying to keep up with Hammer as he strode along the corridor.

"We can't be certain of that. Perhaps the poisoner *is* mad. Next time, wait for the taster."

"That poor man. How did he become royal taster?"

"I wish I knew." Hammer pushed open the hidden door to the service corridor and allowed me to walk ahead of him. "You're right, Josie. About me not being subtle, that is."

I smiled. "I didn't say anything."

"You didn't have to. I saw the laughter in your eyes."

"I wouldn't dare laugh at you, Captain."

"Why not?" He sounded put out. "I can see that I don't frighten you."

"You're serious, that's all. Very serious."

"There is little to laugh about in this place."

"Oh, I don't know. I find Quentin quite amusing, and I suspect the only way to cope with Brant's bullish behavior is to laugh at him from time to time."

He stopped. "Do not laugh at Brant. Is that clear?"

"Y—yes. Of course. I'm sorry."

"Don't be. If anyone should apologize, it's Brant." He walked off again, trotting down the service stairs. I raced after him, wondering at the nerve I'd struck.

"If you don't like him, why do you keep him on your staff?" I asked.

"It's easier to keep an eye on him if I can see him. Not to mention that a palace servant can't leave. For good or ill, we are bound together by our memory loss. We must stay together until we know what happened to us."

We headed along the narrow, dimly lit corridors, passing busy maids and footmen. Outside, several servants stood in the breezeway between the buildings, chatting to one another in between performing their duties. Those servants belonging to the noble houses mingled, exchanging news and gossip about their employers, but the palace servants kept to themselves.

We entered the square building. The smell of roasting meat overwhelmed all other scents, and despite the open doors, it felt warmer than the palace. No wonder the servants chose to remain outside when possible.

Two maids filled pails from the fountain in a central courtyard, chatting quietly as they did so, while other servants rushed back and forth, carrying out their tasks. A procession of servants rolled barrels across the courtyard, most likely heading to a cellar. We passed a long dining room and several other rooms whose function I could only guess at—sewing and washing, perhaps.

We headed downstairs to the kitchen basement, a vast space with whitewashed walls and a vaulted ceiling the height of the entire building. We paused inside the door where heat and noise swamped us. There must have been more than a hundred staff at work at the tables or at one of the two yawning fireplaces. The young men turning the roasting handles looked no bigger than children as they stood behind screens that shielded them from the heat, somewhat unsuccessfully by the look of their sweating, red faces. Through a door on the far side, I spotted another kitchen where the activity seemed just as chaotic.

"Captain!" A stout, middle-aged man hailed Hammer from a long table where he stood looking over the shoulder of a woman kneading dough. "I've already spoken to Max and Brant so let me tell you what I told them. There was no poison in any dish that left my kitchen that night. My staff wouldn't dare."

Two women exchanged grim looks.

"Who took up the food?" Hammer asked.

"I don't know, do I?"

"Emanuel was senior server that night, sir," one of the women said. "Anton, Alexei, Paul and Victor were the under footmen."

"Where can I find Emanuel?"

"I don't know, sir."

"My staff aren't at your beck and call, Hammer," the cook said.

"I didn't ask them to be. But let's be clear, finding the poisoner must be everyone's priority, not just mine. Until he or she is brought to justice, every member of the palace household, from the highest visitor to the lowest servant, is under suspicion."

The cook straightened, extending his protruding stomach further. "Are you threatening me and my staff, Captain?"

"Informing you. The only person who should feel threatened is the one hiding something from me." He didn't speak loudly or through a clenched jaw, however the captain managed to put steel into his words nevertheless.

"Get those damned dogs out of here!" the cook suddenly shouted.

A man dressed in an apron shooed three long-legged dogs out of the kitchen. Hammer and I followed them. With a click of his fingers, the dogs came to Hammer's side, forcing me to walk behind. One dropped back to walk with me. I rubbed its ears and it drew even closer to my legs, almost tripping me. "This one likes attention," I said.

"They're bored," the captain said over his shoulder. "They're hunting dogs and the king doesn't hunt."

"Why not?"

"He's averse to bloodshed. He allows the grand huntsman and his staff to hunt only when it's necessary to supply the kitchens. It's not done for sport, something that the visiting lords are learning. They, like the dogs, are growing bored."

"Bored lords are never a good thing."

"So *I* am learning," he muttered.

"In what way?"

He took the stairs two at a time, but realized he was leaving me in his wake and slowed. "In a way that keeps me busy."

"Sir," hissed a woman from behind us. It was the same kitchen maid who'd given us the names of the serving footmen. "Captain, a word if you please."

"Go ahead," Hammer said.

The maid glanced over her shoulder then climbed the steps. She was a solid woman, albeit short, with a masculine jaw that caved in on her left side thanks to a lack of teeth. "I don't think any of our lads poisoned her. I know them all, and they're good men."

"Good men can be bought," Hammer said.

She shook her head. "Not when it's more important to them to find out why they're here." She glanced at me. "And to get back what they lost. They wouldn't risk it, sir. Not them."

The captain nodded.

"There's more." Another glance at me.

"Miss Cully can be trusted," Hammer said.

The maid didn't look too pleased but she didn't insist on speaking to him in private. "Lady Lucia Whippler and Lord Frederick Whippler dined with Lady Miranda that night."

"And?"

"That means they're suspects, doesn't it?"

"Everyone is a suspect."

Her gaze turned flinty. "Not to me."

"They're suspects," I told her since Hammer didn't answer. "Why?"

"I overheard one of the Whippler maids telling a footman from another house something about her young mistress and master. Something I think you should know. Something that might make you see them in a different way." The maid stepped up another step. Hammer moved down to stand beside me. "She said Lady Lucia and her brother, Lord Frederick, are lovers."

CHAPTER 6

"Incest." The kitchen maid licked her lips and her eyes flared. "What say you to that, Captain?"

"Did you overhear anything else?" Hammer asked.

"Lady Lucia's maid also says Lord Frederick gets jealous of any man that takes an interest in his sister."

"Such as the king?"

"Aye. They even argued about it. Lord Frederick didn't like her flirting with him. He went into a jealous rage."

Hammer stiffened. "Did he hurt her?"

"She calmed him down." The woman chuckled, revealing the bare gums on the left side of her mouth. "You can probably guess how, eh?"

"Thank you for the information," Hammer said. "Let me know if you hear anything further."

She returned downstairs while we continued up. Hammer left a message at a small office with the senior footman to send the men who'd served dinner to him when they were free. Then we headed out of the commons and back toward the service entrance of the palace. The dogs had run off and were nowhere to be seen.

"What do you think of the information about Lord Frederick and Lady Lucia?" I asked him.

"Interesting."

"Is that all? It's rather shocking." When I caught him watching me, I added, "Incest is not normal or accepted in Glancia, if that's what you're wondering."

"The fact is, it exonerates Lord Frederick rather than condemns him. He'd want to encourage Lady Miranda in her pursuit of the king, not get rid of her to make way for his sister."

"True. Perhaps that's what we need to do—eliminate one diner at a time."

"And how do you propose I do that?"

"With my help, of course, and that of the palace servants."

He frowned. "Go on."

"We need to listen to more gossip. Gossip has already taught us something about the Whipplers, so now we need to find out what we can about the others. It may help us create a broader picture of our suspects."

"*Our* suspects?"

"Let's discuss the plan in the garrison."

We didn't reach the garrison. A footman stopped us on the stairs and informed us that my father was with Lady Miranda. We changed course and headed to her rooms instead.

Lady Miranda's apartments were rather crowded. The king had learned of her recovery despite her hope for some time to herself first, and he waited in the sitting room along with the Claypools, Theodore, a guard and Hilda. I bobbed an awkward curtsy for the king, who watched with an amused gleam in his eyes. He seemed in good spirits.

"Doctor Cully asked you to go through when you arrived, Josie," Hilda said.

I knocked lightly on the bedchamber door then entered. My father stood by the bed, packing away his instruments. Lady Miranda sat propped up against the pillows, looking fresher after her bath. She was extremely beautiful with her long golden hair, dark lashes framing large eyes, and unblemished skin. She had the sort of ethereal beauty that sensitive men wrote poems in honor of, and masculine men fought over. I couldn't stop staring.

She greeted me with a smile. "Here she is," she said to my father. "I knew she wouldn't be far. She's looked after me so well while I've been ill. I'm so grateful to her, and to you for allowing her to stay with me, Doctor."

She was being rather too effusive, considering I'd not stayed with her the entire time. I eyed her carefully and she winked.

"Where have you been, Josie?" my father asked.

"In the service commons with the captain, trying to find out who may have poisoned Lady Miranda."

"The captain is capable of doing that alone. Why did he endanger you unnecessarily?"

"I...because of my medical knowledge. He needed me to ask if anyone had experienced any symptoms similar to Lady Miranda's."

From his scowl, I knew he didn't believe me, but he didn't press me further. "You seem to have fully recovered, my lady, with no ill effects." he said. "You should remain abed until tomorrow, but if you feel well enough to go outside, then the fresh air will do you good. I'll return tomorrow at midday to check on your progress."

"Send your daughter instead," Lady Miranda said in a tone that invited no disagreement. "I enjoy her company."

"If that is your wish," Father said with a slight bow. He picked up his bag and beckoned me to follow.

I trailed after him to the sitting room where the king looked past him toward the bedchamber.

"Well?" His Majesty prompted. "How is she?"

"Much better, sire," Father said. "The poison has been purged from her body but it has left her weak. While she isn't in danger from the poison, she needs time and rest to regain her full strength. Her prior good health means her recovery will be swifter than most. She's very fortunate. If she hadn't taken the antidote when she did, she would not be with us now."

Lady Claypool covered her mouth with her handkerchief and turned into her husband's chest. He gently rubbed her back.

"I am very grateful to you, Doctor," the king said. "Theodore will give you something for your troubles before you go. Now." He clapped his hands and beamed. "I think this calls for a celebration."

"Sire?" Lord Claypool pressed.

"An entertainment with music, dancing and wine. A bright and amusing event the likes of which this palace has never seen before. Something extraordinary, just as the Lady Miranda is extraordinarily beautiful. Theodore?"

"Yes, sire?"

"Send Balthazar to the Sky Salon to discuss arrangements. I'll meet with him shortly after I've spoken to Lady Miranda."

Theodore hesitated.

"What is it?" the king snapped.

"You're meeting with the ministers in the council room in ten minutes."

The king flicked his hand in a dismissive wave. "They can wait. Celebrating Lady Miranda's recovery is more important."

Theodore bowed. "Yes, sire. I'll inform Balthazar."

The king dismissed all of us, including the Claypools, and we left the apartments. In the corridor, Theodore gave my father a bulging pouch and Lord Claypool fetched another from his pocket.

"No, my lord," Theodore said. "It is His Majesty's honor and privilege to reward Doctor Cully. Lady Miranda's illness occurred under his roof, after all."

Lord Claypool's gaze flicked to the gilded ceiling rosette as if inspecting the roof in question. He re-pocketed his money. "I will not forget the service you have done my family, Doctor. You or your daughter. Lady Claypool and I are eternally grateful."

A door further along the corridor opened and a lady dressed in a voluminous lilac colored gown emerged. She beamed at us. "I thought I heard voices. Are the rumors to be believed? Is darling, sweet Miranda going to be all right?"

"Yes, your grace," Lady Claypool said.

It would seem this was the duchess of Gladstow, wife of the duke of Gladstow, one of the highest nobles in Glancia. "That is good news." The duchess took Lady Claypool's hands and continued to smile brightly. She was pretty and much younger than I expected, perhaps only my age. "We've been so worried! And do call me Kitty. Everyone does. When can we expect to see Miranda up and about?"

"Soon," Lady Claypool said.

"How we've missed her in the salons."

"Oh? I didn't realize you were friends."

The sapphires and diamonds in the duchess's rings caught the light as she clasped Lady Claypool's elbow. If she wore such jewelry during the day, what did she save for the evening? "We are set to become very close, I am sure of it. She is awfully pretty and young, and I know I can be of help to her as she finds her way at court as, shall we say, a *very* important lady."

"You presume too much too soon," Lord Claypool said carefully. "Miranda has only been here a week."

"Love is instant. When it shoots true, it shoots with accuracy. The arrow of love, that is. You know what I mean." She giggled. "What I'm saying so badly is that one only needs to see the way the king looks at her to know she is his favorite."

A gentleman emerged through the same door and stopped short when he spotted the Claypools. "Kitty," he barked. "Come."

The duchess's smile slipped. "Husband, I was just talking to the Claypools about the health of Lady Miranda. She's better. Isn't that marvelous?"

"Marvelous," he droned. He was considerably older than his wife, with the florid complexion of a man who drank too much. His doctor ought to warn him of the dangers of excess.

"Your grace," Lady Claypool said in greeting. "How nice to see you again after all these years."

The duke's broad, fat lips pursed as his gaze grazed her from head to toe, lingering on her face, still quite youthful considering the age she must be to have a daughter of eighteen. Beside her, Lord Claypool stiffened. He put his hand at his wife's back and she sidled closer to him.

"Yes," was all the duke said.

"How many years has it been?" Lady Claypool asked.

"Twenty-two."

"That long? I've lost track of time." She attempted a warm smile but it wilted when it wasn't returned.

The duke sniffed and turned away. "Come, Kitty. You cannot tarry here. You have important people to talk to."

"I do?" the duchess said. "Who?"

"The duchess of Buxton, for one."

The duchess wrinkled her nose. "She's so tedious. All she wants to do is talk about her children."

"She is an appropriate companion for you. Come, Kitty."

"Yes, Husband." The duchess didn't follow him immediately but addressed Lady Claypool. "Do see that Miranda rejoins society soon so that we once again have the pleasure of seeing her pretty face. I know Lady Violette Morgrave took a particular liking to her and is desolated by her absence."

She trailed after her husband. Lady Claypool took Lord Claypool's arm and headed in the other direction, her head high. I walked with Hammer and my father through the hidden door and into the maze of service corridors and stairs, mulling over the conversation between the illustrious ducal couple and the Claypools. While the duchess seemed interested in becoming better acquainted, the duke certainly didn't. Whatever the reason behind the rift, it had likely happened before she married the duke and he hadn't informed her of it.

"I'll need you to assist me when we get home, Josie," Father said as we exited the main palace building opposite the service commons.

"I won't be returning with you just yet," I said. "There's work to do here."

He rounded on me. "Your work is with me, in the village, not here. Not with these…" He glanced at the captain as he addressed one of his guards. "Our patients need you, Josie."

"But—"

"It's not up for discussion. Captain, a carriage if you please."

The captain sent his guard to fetch us transport. "I hope I haven't caused a problem by asking Josie to assist with my investigation," he said to my father. "I thought her knowledge of the poisons would help."

"She has no knowledge of poisons."

"I know a little about direweed, thank you," I snipped off.

"You strike me as a very capable man, Captain," my father said, ignoring me. "I'm sure you need her less than our patients do."

"All the pregnancies in the village are progressing smoothly," I said hotly. "I am not scheduled to see any of the expectant mothers today. Unless you wish me to attend some of your patients in your stead then I have nothing to do but mix up some medicines, something which you are quite equipped to do yourself."

My father's lips moved and I waited for the explosion of temper I knew to be brewing. He may not exhibit his temper often, but when he did, it was spectacular and I usually did everything in my power to diffuse it or run for cover. But I didn't want to diffuse it this time or run away. I wanted to battle it out with him.

"Thank you for your assistance this morning, Josie," the captain said before my father spoke. "But I can manage from here."

I wanted to throttle him for backing down and denying me the argument with my father. "I'll return tomorrow," I told him—them both. "Lady Miranda has expressly asked me to look in on her."

"And I have given my permission," my father said. "Tomorrow. For a brief time only." He walked off, expecting me to follow.

I sighed.

"Will he punish you for helping me?" the captain asked.

"He'll make me sit with him during his appointments and take copious notes which he'll then make me write out again and perhaps test me on later."

"You're smiling," he said, almost smiling himself.

"He calls it punishment, but I like doing it. I like to learn."

"I see I don't have to worry about you." He nodded over my head. "He's waiting. You'd better go."

I caught up to my father and we rounded the long pavilion together. He still looked cross, and I didn't particularly feel like forgiving him yet, but by the time we reached the guard waiting by a carriage on the grand forecourt, my own temper had cooled. Father was simply worried about me. I was luckier than most to have a father who indulged his daughter by allowing her to work for him. Most of my friends were already married, and not always to a man of their choice.

A footman opened the door while another assisted me then my father into the carriage.

"There are an awful lot of staff here, have you noticed?" I said as the door closed on us.

"Don't change the subject, Josie."

"I wasn't aware we were discussing something else."

"Stop being petulant. You know very well I gave you strict instructions to remain with Lady Miranda all night and this morn-ing, yet you wandered off around the palace with the captain. Who knows what might have happened!"

"Nothing, that's what. For goodness' sake, Father, the poisoner is after Lady Miranda, not me, and the captain has the utmost respect from everyone. He's one of the king's trusted friends."

He snorted. "Kings don't have friends."

This conversation would get us nowhere except in a mire of pettiness. If I wanted to change the subject, I had to engage his intellect. "I learned something interesting last night. Something Sergeant Brant discussed with you yesterday."

"You mean the memory loss? Come now, Josie, you don't believe him, surely."

"I do."

"It's impossible. There must be hundreds of servants at the palace. They can't all have lost their memory at the same time."

"A thousand servants actually, and why couldn't they?"

"Because I've never heard anything like it."

"That doesn't make it impossible, just improbable. Besides, you seem to believe in magic. Why couldn't that explain the memory loss?"

"It could." He circled his arms around the medical bag on his lap. "All the more reason for you *not* to wander about the palace. I told you before, there's something...wrong about it."

"Yes! Everyone has lost their memory!" I leaned forward and rested my hand on his arm. "Can you not think of any non-magical reason for it? A poisonous air, perhaps, or tainted water?"

He shook his head. "Not unless they were all hit on the head on the same day." He regarded me levelly and I was pleased to see that his anger had faded. "You really do believe them?" he asked.

"Why would they lie?"

He remained silent for the remainder of the journey. He went directly to his workroom when we arrived home while I found half a fish pie in the pantry and sliced it up for our midday meal. We ate in silence at the kitchen table, each of us reading medical texts, searching for any reference to memory loss. We only stopped because his first afternoon appointment arrived.

"Keep looking," he said to me as he rose to answer the door.

"What about mixing up the medicines? Or helping you in the workroom?"

"This is more important." He indicated the stack of books he'd piled at the end of the table. Some of them were ancient, their yellowing pages held together with thin leather strips. Those ones had no covers and were stored in boxes. I removed one and drew the smell of old paper into my lungs. These were my favorites, but I hadn't looked at them in years. I did know that they held no information about memory loss. None of the books did, but I indulged my father anyway and spent the afternoon re-reading several chapters.

"There's nothing in here," I announced when he joined me at the end of the day.

He rubbed his lower back and sat with a groan. "Fetch me something to drink, will you, Josie."

I filled a cup from the keg of ale stored in the larder and tackled the topic again. "What do we do now? Should we write to the college in Logios?"

"Merdu, no." He sipped the ale and sat back with another groan. "We'll leave the college out of this. They'll laugh at us."

"Or they might check the books we don't have access to."

"Their books won't contain anything about memory loss like this."

"Why not?"

He eyed me over the cup. "You know why."

"Magic," I said on a breath. I had no counter argument to that. As much as I thought him mad for suggesting it, how could I prove him wrong? "Why do you think magic is real? It can't simply be because you met people who believe. I know you. You require evidence, something you can see and touch, not blind belief. You won't even pray to Merdu or Hailia, yet you think the palace is magical."

"What other explanation is there for its existence? Now, no more questions."

"Just one. What do we do now?"

"*We* do nothing, and *you* are to stay away from the palace."

"I can't."

"Tomorrow is your final visit." He slammed the cup on the table. "Is that understood? You will check Lady Miranda then leave immediately. There's no need for you to linger."

Not unless she wished me to, and I was going to make certain that she did. "We still have to help find the poisoner."

"No we do not. It's a palace matter."

"But the poisoner most likely bought the poisons here in the village. We can help Captain Hammer find out who sold it."

"He doesn't need our help. He can ask the same questions as you or I."

"He has no knowledge of poisons. We do."

"*I* do. *You* are a novice when it comes to poisons."

I bristled. "Why are you being so difficult about this? Why are you refusing to help? Lady Miranda almost died. It's our duty to help if we can."

He drained his cup and slammed it down on the table, ending the conversation.

I tidied up then took stock of the larder. While we had all the medicines we needed for now, and the ingredients to make up more, we were woefully short on food.

"I have to go out," I said. "We only have a little cheese and nothing for tomorrow."

"It's late," he grumbled from where he sat at the table, nursing another full cup of ale. "The market's closed."

"The fishermen will still be around. Why don't we have some fresh cray? We have the money for it after the king's payment."

"That should be saved."

"For what?"

He inspected the bottom of his ale. "For after I am gone," he said quietly.

I closed my eyes and appealed to Hailia for strength. When Father became morose, he could stay that way for hours. It required a delicate touch to navigate him out of it.

"You won't die for years yet." I kissed the top of his head. "You're far too stubborn."

He smiled without humor. "Very well. Cray it is. Be home before dark."

Be home before dark—it was a common phrase now, not only spoken by my father but by parents all over the village. Before the Rift, Mull's main crime had been smuggling, as with all the villages dotted along the Glancia coastline. With the influx of trade and people, mostly men, after the Rift cut off The Thumb from the mainland, Mull had become more dangerous, particularly at night.

Sailors and dockworkers spent their money at the taverns then went in search of entertainment on their way home or back to their moored ships. Boredom and drunkenness were never a good combination.

I headed out with my basket into the long afternoon shadows. I thought about asking Meg to join me but she would be helping her mother to prepare supper at this time of day. Besides, she wouldn't want me to detour from my task to question the spice traders, and I wasn't up for another lecture so soon after my father's.

The market was closed so I called on Tamworth Tao at his small cottage. Originally from Zemaya, he now made his home in Mull but traveled extensively to source the herbs and spices he sold at his market stall. When he was away, the eldest of his five children took over with help from younger siblings. Tam's wife, a Glancia woman, was rarely seen around the village.

"I'm sorry to call on you so late," I said to Tam when he met me at the door. "I want to ask you about direweed and traitor's ease."

His gaze darted up and down the street. "I have already answered Captain Hammer's questions," he whispered.

"Yes, but I'm not sure he asked the right questions."

"He wanted to know if I sell those poisons. I told him I sell direweed to kill rats."

"And traitor's ease?"

He jerked his head and his plaited ponytail flicked off his shoulder. The small bells tinkled musically. "I do not sell it."

"Do you know who does?"

"No." He glanced up and down the street again. "You should go, Josie. Let the captain ask his questions."

"Just one more. What does traitor's ease look like?"

"A small yellow flower with a red center, but it is the root that's poisonous. It grows in warm, damp parts of Zemaya. It is rare. I do not have it. Now, please, I must go and so must you."

He went to close the door but I wedged my basket into the gap. "I think you know who sells it, Tam."

His dark eyes widened and his gaze once again darted around. "Hush, Josie."

"You're afraid of someone seeing me talking to you. Who? And why?"

"The poison seller, that is who, because your father is known to have attended the poisoned lady at the palace. It is also known that he identified the poisons and made an antidote."

"So?"

"So the poisoner will fear the guards coming for him now. Your father told the captain about traitor's ease, and the poisoner did not expect him to know about it. And if he did not expect then the poison seller did not expect either."

"That doesn't explain why you're afraid to be seen talking to me now, Tam."

"Everyone knows I supply your father for his medicines. That is a link between us." His gaze flicked past me to the street. "I cannot be sure but…but I feel as though I am being watched."

"If you're being watched, it means someone thinks *you* can identify the poison seller."

He gripped the door and swallowed heavily.

"You can either tell me or you can tell the captain that you lied to him," I said.

"I did not lie," he spat. "I do not know who has traitor's ease."

"But you can guess. Can't you?"

He muttered something in Zemayan. "Why will you not give up, Josie?"

"A lady nearly died, Tam. She's innocent and kind. It would be wrong of me to look the other way when I can help prevent another poisoning. It would be wrong of you too." I removed my basket from the doorway. "Do not expect our business anymore. We'll go elsewhere for our supplies." I turned to go.

"Wait, Josie. Do not do that. You are my best customer." He sucked in a breath between his teeth. "I will tell you all I know. It is not much." He once again scanned the street. "Last week, I waited at the pier for the ship that brings my supplies. I see another Zemayan, like me." He smoothed the plaited hair of his ponytail over his shoulder. "We talk and I learn that he is waiting for the same ship, bringing supplies from our homeland. When the ship's rowboat docks, we help the sailors unload the parcels onto the pier. Each is labeled with a name and the contents inside, for the customs officer to see."

"You saw the other Zemayan's name on a label?"

"A name was written in my language. Translated, it means No One."

"Very suspicious."

"What is more, one parcel does not feel right. The label says Powdered Crabtree Bark but the parcel is too heavy and hard for powder. The Zemayan claimed it, and other parcels too."

"Did the customs officer open the parcel and check the contents?"

"No. Customs are very busy. There is so much for them to do now and not enough officers. They cannot check everything. Even if they did and this man smuggled in traitor's ease roots inside the powder, would the officer know? I do not think so."

"What else can you tell me about your mysterious countryman, Tam?"

"Nothing. I have not seen him before or since. If he is wise, he has already left Mull."

I had to hope not. He was the only link to the poisoner. "Thank you, Tam. I appreciate you talking to me."

"Do not tell anyone I tell you this. And do not tell the captain I lied to him."

"You don't need to fear him. He won't seek retribution for it."

"There is magic in that palace, in him. Powerful magic. Do not assume to know what magic thinks." He shut the door in my face.

Well, that was an odd encounter. Tam was always so friendly toward my father and me, never rude. As he said, we were his best customers. If not for that, he wouldn't have told me anything about the Zemayan at the pier. This behavior was most unlike him. Fear changed people.

I settled the basket in the crook of my elbow and headed eastward. The briny scent of the bay grew stronger as I turned the corner and I could hear the gulls calling, although I couldn't yet see them. Tam's words rang in my ears, none more so than his suspicion that he was being watched. Surely he was mistaken. That brief encounter with a stranger at the pier shouldn't have triggered alarm in the man known only as No One.

Perhaps it hadn't at the time. Perhaps it wasn't until after my father's involvement in Lady Miranda's recovery that the poison seller had begun to worry that Tam might be asked to identify him. I hoped me talking to Tam wouldn't seem suspicious.

I quickened my step. At the corner, I checked behind me. A man stood well back, leaning against a wall as if he'd been there the entire time. But he had not. I'd passed that building only moments before.

I took a few more steps before once again checking over my shoulder. The man followed. *Merdu*!

Fortunately I came to the end of the street and the open space of the harbor concourse. The builders had finished for the day but their voices could still be heard spilling out of the Anchor and the more disreputable tavern, The Mermaid's Tail. The harbor itself seemed eerily quiet. The cranes cast shadowy fingers over the water, and crates and carts had been locked up in the warehouses. There were few people about.

I glanced behind me again but the man was no longer there. I hurried along one of the piers, past small boats waiting for a crew to row them back to the watchful mother ships in deeper water. Gulls circled the masts of the fishing boats moored at the pier's end. When one of the seamen tossed a fish into the air, the gulls dove for it then squawked in protest when the biggest caught it and flew off. It was the sound of my childhood. My mother used to bring me here when the fishermen returned. Of course, she would arrive much earlier to choose the best of the catch. I might need to fight off the gulls for the smaller fish.

"Good afternoon, Gill," I said.

"Josie!" Gill Swinson looked up from the crate of dead fish he'd been about to pick up, and removed his cap. His deep wrinkles folded into a pattern etched by fifty years at sea. "How is my favorite healer?"

"I'll tell my father you said that." I grinned. "Is there anything left? A cray?"

"It's late for marketing."

"All our crayfish are sold," his son called out from where he emerged from the nets at the back of the boat. "Sorry, Josie. I hear you spent the night at the palace. What was that like?"

"Not as interesting as you'd think. I only got to see the service area and Lady Miranda Claypool's rooms."

"She the one that got poisoned?"

I nodded.

"Terrible business, that," Gill said. "Imagine a poisoner at the palace, eh?"

"And who knows what else," his son said. At my questioning look, he added, "I hear the servants are a strange lot. They keep to themselves. One of the Deerhorn maids reckons they won't say where they came from."

"I found them quite friendly." I sounded a little snippy so softened it with a smile. "You can take it from me, the palace and its servants are not at all strange. Nor is the king."

"You met him?"

I described the king and palace to them. When I finished, Gill gave me a crayfish from another crate. "Take this for your troubles. Only one ell."

I smiled and held out my basket. He deposited the cray inside and I paid him.

"That was meant for the palace," his son whined.

"Josie is the king's healer," Gill told him.

"Do not say that to my father," I said in all seriousness. "One other thing. I have a question for you both. Have you ever seen a Zemayan here, aside from Tam Tao?"

They shook their heads. "Only Tam," Gill said. "But we're out all day. You should ask at the taverns." He angled his chin toward The Mermaid's Tail. "That's where most newcomers end up at one time or another. Wait for morning though. It's not safe for a pretty woman once they've started drinking."

"I will. Thanks for the cray."

I left the concourse and the noisy taverns behind, quite certain I was being followed by the same man as before. I couldn't make out his face, but it was obvious from a distance that his skin wasn't the color of a Zemayan's.

I doubled my pace and ducked around corners, crossed courtyards, and hurried down narrow alleys. A quick glance over my shoulder confirmed he was still there and closer than before.

I ran. My basket bumped against my hip and my skirts snapped at my ankles but I didn't slow. I turned every corner, no matter where it led, hoping he wouldn't follow. Every inch of Mull was familiar to me, although some areas I hadn't been to in years.

I recognized the area known as The Row as soon as I entered it. The air was fouler, the smell of excrement and sweat oozing from the packed dirt beneath my feet. People looked out from the buildings, if the lean-tos and derelict structures could be called that. Most were made of wood and canvas scraps sewn together. The few stone walls along the street struggled to hold up sagging roofs, and in some places, failed altogether. It didn't stop the residents from making their homes within the confined, hollowed-out spaces.

People slept on the streets, even now in the late afternoon. Children didn't seem to notice, playing beside the sleeping bodies in the dirt. They stopped to watch me pass, their vacant eyes and thin limbs telling the story of their desperate predicament.

Another glance behind me confirmed I was still being followed. I picked up my skirts with my free hand and rushed further along the main street, the original Row, but quickly diverted at the first intersection. The buildings were closer here, the stench stronger. The children wore little more than rags, their feet bare, and their hungry eyes watched me as if I were the source of their next meal. There wasn't an adult in sight.

Or so I thought. The unmistakable grunts of coupling came from behind makeshift curtains hanging over what could be considered doorways, but were merely openings in the walls. One of the curtain flaps was flung wide and a man lurched out, fumbling with his breeches. He saw me and grinned. His tongue slithered over blackened, broken teeth.

"You there!" he hailed me. "How much?"

I rushed on but the street suddenly ended. My heart stopped. I was surrounded on three sides by hovels, and behind me, the man following still advanced. I could clearly make out his face now with its black goatee beard and sharp cheeks. More men had emerged from behind the curtains, and women too. Some simply watched on, but others advanced, sensing sport.

My heart kicked back to life, hammering against my ribs.

"She's a ripe one," one of the men said, licking his lips.

"Oi!" a woman shouted at me. "This is our turf and we don't share."

"Especially with no fancies," cried another woman. "You got to pay to come through The Row. So what you got in that basket, eh?"

"I...I don't want trouble. That man is after me." I indicated my pursuer. He paused, uncertain.

"He's a man, ain't he?" said the first woman. "What d'you expect? Flowers?"

That set off the other women in fits of laughter, but the men still came, their intentions clear in their hungry eyes.

"Give us yer basket," said one.

"Give us your cunny," said another.

My pursuer stood behind them, watching. Waiting. Perhaps he thought it best to let the locals deal with me and keep his own hands clean. I swallowed but the fear remained, a tight, hot lump in my throat. They would deal with me, all right. No authorities would pass in time to rescue me here. The sheriff's men had given up on The Row. I had to fend all these people off on my own.

Or succumb and hope they spared my life.

Another quick look around confirmed there was no way out except past them. And there were too many to outrun.

I was trapped.

CHAPTER 7

"*C*ome 'ere, sweetheart," sneered one of the men. "Stop moving off." He lunged and grabbed my shoulder. His fingers dug through my clothing and into my flesh.

I screamed then threw my basket, cray and all, past him. He and the others dove on it, tearing it apart like ravenous dogs. It bought me precious moments.

"Is there another exit?" I asked the cluster of children nearby. "There'll be a coin in it for you."

One of them pointed at the canvas structure leaning up against the end of the street, its frayed flaps open in invitation. I plucked my purse from my skirt pocket and tossed the girl an ell. The adults looked up from the destroyed cray as if they'd smelled my money. I opened the purse, pulled out all the coins and sprayed them from one side of the street to the other, the purse too. Children, men and women pounced, blocking my pursuer from getting to me.

I passed through the canvas tent and prayed to Hailia that the girl hadn't lied. The tent covered a gaping hole in the wall of a building. I plunged through the hole and into a dim, stuffy room stinking of urine. It was empty. Better still, there was another door on the far side.

The next room was even darker. It was also occupied. I could just make out the shape of a woman sitting in the corner, her legs outstretched. A small child lay beside her, his head resting on her lap. As my eyes adjusted, her desperation came into focus. The boy hardly moved despite being awake.

Behind me, I heard the rabble draw closer, their scavenging finished. "Where is she?" one of the men shouted.

"Get her!" cried another. "Before she escapes!"

Escape. There must be another exit but I couldn't see one, only walls and pieces of wood nailed together to cover holes. The woman sat near a makeshift bed and I could now make out another bed on the opposite side of the wall. I man lay there, asleep or dead.

Outside, the shouts grew louder.

"I'm a healer," I quickly told the woman. "I'll give your boy the medicine he needs for free if I get out of here alive and unharmed. Please, help me."

Boney fingers pushed aside a plank of wood nailed at one end to the wall, revealing a hole. "In there," she said. "Go. I'll tell them you went that way." She nodded at more wooden planks on the other side of the room. They must hide another hole, another exit.

With my heart hammering in my throat, I pushed the planks further aside and climbed through. "You'll find me one street back from the market precinct, under the sign of Hailia's hands. Come tomorrow." I let the wooden panel slide shut and steadied it so that it wouldn't swing.

"Where is she? Where did she go?" a voice on the other side demanded,

I didn't wait to hear the response. A prick of light pinpointed the exit and I raced toward it, only to trip over the uneven surface and land on my hands and knees. It felt like I'd removed some skin, but I didn't pause to check. The light came from a crack between two boards. I pried them apart and peered out. Seeing no one waiting for me, I climbed through and blinked in the fading sunlight.

I recognized the children playing in the dirt beside a sleeping man. I'd circled back and was once again on The Row's main thoroughfare. I picked up my skirts and ran.

I didn't stop until I reached home. The sign of Hailia's cupped hands swung gently with the breeze. That same breeze brought with it the soothing, familiar scent of the sea. I breathed deeply. Halia, it felt good to be home. Safe.

I sucked in two breaths and concentrated on letting them out slowly to steady my nerves before pushing open the door. "I'm home," I called brightly to Father. "The fishermen had nothing left tonight. Everything's earmarked for the palace."

No answer.

The front door had been unlocked but we rarely locked up the house during the day when one of us was home. Sometimes our patients let themselves in. The door to my father's workroom stood ajar, but no sound came from beyond, not even a snore.

My blood chilled. I pushed on the door.

My father sat at his desk, bent over a book, his spectacles perched on the end of his nose. He didn't even look up.

"Father," I said heavily.

"I heard you," he said. "No crays, all sold to the palace. Don't know why they can't just magic up some fine food for themselves."

I spluttered a laugh and felt my insides unknot. "Apparently magic food doesn't taste as good."

He looked up at that and smiled. "Very amusing." The smile faded. "Are you all right? You look…" He waved a hand to encompass my length. "Disheveled and hot. Have you been running?"

"Why would I run? It's warm outside and the wind is whipping across the bay, that's all."

"Didn't you leave with a basket?"

"No." The lies came easily. But I had to lie to save my father from worry. If he knew I'd been chased into The Row and worse, he would never let me leave the house again. "What are you reading?"

"A book on poisons. I need to refresh my memory on the more obscure ones. If traitor's ease has made its way here, perhaps others will too, and I want to be able to identify them."

"So do I."

He hesitated then got up and pulled the second chair closer. "Supper can wait. I'm not hungry anyway."

* * *

I MANAGED to hide my skinned palms from my father but not the woman who came to the door the following morning. It may have been semi-dark inside her home the day before, but her hollowed cheeks and distrustful eyes were instantly recognizable. She was alone.

I invited her into the kitchen, where I gave her what was left of the bread. She squirreled it away beneath her ragged shawl. As I poured her a cup of ale in the larder, I whispered to my father that I'd met her on the concourse, scavenging for scraps.

He patted my shoulder. "You're a kind soul, Josie."

Guilt pinched my chest. I wouldn't be giving her charity if she hadn't helped me.

"Tell me your son's symptoms," I said once my father left us to see to a patient. "So I know what medicine to give him."

The woman—Dora—described the rash and fever, and I knew there was little to be done except allow the disease to run its course. It wouldn't kill a healthy child, but a malnourished one might not pull through. I gave her medicine to keep the fever in check as well as give her hope. Sometimes hope could be a more important medicine than the ones we sold in bottles.

"Don't drink the water from any wells in The Row," I added. "I know it's further to walk, but you must draw from the cleaner wells in the village's center." I hoped her thin arms and shoulders could manage a heavy pail over the extra distance. "Your son will need food, too. Good food. Luckily fish is cheap in these parts. Fruit is necessary too, or vegetables."

Tears welled in her eyes and at that moment, I realized she could be younger than me. Too young to be a mother all alone in The Row. "I'll do what I must to get enough money to buy them," she said through cracked lips.

I glanced around the kitchen and spotted a fine jug painted white and blue that we kept for good occasions. Father rarely glanced up to the top shelf and probably wouldn't notice it missing if he did.

I stood on my toes and plucked it off. "Sell this and buy him some proper food."

Her fingers twitched and she adjusted her shawl, not taking her eyes off the jug. "Are you sure, miss?"

THE PALACE OF LOST MEMORIES

"Quite sure. Take it to the Buy Or Swap shop. Peggy'll give you a good price."

"She'll think I stole it."

"Tell her I gave it to you for a service you did for me. No need to tell her what. She'll come and check with me if she still doubts you, but she won't be able to resist having that in her shop."

Dora clutched the jug to her chest. "Thank you, miss. You're kind. I'm sorry what happened to you yesterday. We ain't all like that."

"I know. Tell me, did you recognize the man who was following me?"

She shook her head.

"Have you ever seen a Zemayan in The Row?"

"Aye. Sometimes." She described him to me, but the braided hair and coloring were typical of all Zemayan men and she couldn't be more specific.

I saw her out and settled down to more reading while my father attended his patients. I wrote up his notes for him between each one, so knew precisely what ailed them, then picked up his books on poisons.

By the time the palace carriage came to collect me, I had a thorough understanding of the most common poisons found on The Fist, and their antidotes.

"Straight there and straight home again," Father said to me through the carriage window.

I waited until the coach moved off before I replied, "I'll stay for as long as I'm needed." I waved. He scowled back.

Captain Hammer met me inside the palace gate. He looked tall and important, standing there in his black uniform with the gold braid gleaming in the sunshine. He nodded at the guards who closed the gate and a footman opened the carriage door for me.

"Welcome back, Josie," Hammer said, taking my pack from the footman. "I'll escort you to Lady Miranda's apartments."

"Afraid I'll get lost again?" I said, striding alongside him.

"Just trying to stop you from wandering into the garrison and distracting my men."

"How is she?"

"I haven't seen her, but the king informs me she is looking

much better. He wants you to tell him if she's well enough to join him this evening for a musicale."

We passed the pavilion where faint music drifted from an open window. The musicians must be practicing in there. "I'll know once I've seen her."

"Of course."

"Have you considered that she might not want to leave her rooms until the poisoner is caught?"

"Lord Claypool has already told me he doesn't want her to leave her apartments. Whether that is Lady Miranda's wish or his, I can't be certain. I can't blame him," he added quietly. "If I were in his position, I wouldn't allow her out. It's too dangerous."

"You'll catch the poisoner," I said. "Speaking of which, I may have some information that will help."

We passed several servants in the breezeway between the pavilion and the service commons. A pretty maid leaned her shoulder against the wall, pushing out her chest, and fluttered her eyelashes at the captain. He didn't seem to notice.

"I'll tell you after I've seen Lady Miranda," I said. "In the privacy of the garrison."

Quentin rushed toward us from the palace servants' entrance. "Captain! The king is going for a walk."

"Escort Josie to Lady Miranda's rooms." Hammer handed him my pack and turned to me. "Wait for me in the garrison." He strode off.

Quentin slung my pack onto his shoulder. "What have you got in here? Rocks?"

"Mostly tools used for birthing."

He wrinkled his nose. "Is it as bad as they say? Giving birth, I mean?"

"I don't know, I've never given birth. And never fear, you won't have to."

He chuckled.

"Is the king afraid someone will attack him while he's walking in his own gardens?" I asked. "Is that why the captain had to go?"

"The captain goes everywhere with the king when the king leaves the palace. If he walks, the captain walks a few steps behind. He always has. It isn't because of the poisoner."

"Day or night?"

"No matter the time. Luckily, the king doesn't go out much. He doesn't hunt or ride, and he only walks occasionally. He's done more walking since the ladies arrived." He flashed me a boyish grin. "He wants to impress them with the gardens and fountains."

"I haven't been on the other side of the palace," I said. "Are the gardens quite beautiful?"

"Spectacular."

Quentin stayed in the sitting room while I saw Lady Miranda alone in her bedchamber. She was sitting at her dressing table when I arrived, inspecting her reflection in a hand mirror.

She greeted me with a smile. "Josie, how lovely."

"Good afternoon, my lady." I offered a curtsy and her smile widened.

"You don't have to curtsy for me, just the king and the dukes and duchesses. We lesser nobles barely even rate a nod."

"That's a relief," I said. "I'm hopeless at it."

"I can teach you, if you like."

"I don't think I'll have many more opportunities to perform one, now that you're well. I doubt I'll return to the palace again soon." I set down my bag and inspected its contents so she couldn't see my disappointment.

"What do I need to do?" she asked, rising. "Stand? Lie down?"

She was a similar height to me, which wasn't tall for a Glancian woman, but taller than most of the palace servants. She was far more graceful than me, however, seeming to glide across the carpet in her slippers and long blue silk gown. The sun streaming through the window picked out all the shades of pale gold in the loose braid of hair that fell to her waist. She settled on the bed as I directed and lay back against the pillows, her dark lashes framing big eyes and her skin glowing with health. It was easy to see why the king admired her.

I checked her pulse, her temperature, her eyes and inside her mouth. I asked her how she felt and more unsavory questions about her bowel movements. She answered them all without hesitation or pomposity.

"You're well enough to resume your daily routine," I told her.

Her gaze slid to her hands, folded on her lap. "Oh."

"Apparently the king wishes you to attend a musicale tonight. You're well enough to go." She slumped against the pillows. "Or I could tell him you require more time to recover," I added carefully.

She lifted her gaze to mine. "Would you mind? It's not really a lie. I do feel…"

"Tired?"

"Yes, lets call it that. And another day will give the others more time."

"Others?" I asked.

"The other ladies at court. It's only fair they have an opportunity to spend time alone with the king, as I have done. I did try to tell him that he shouldn't ignore them, but he said he didn't care. He laughed it off, in fact, and told me I should be honored that he's taken a liking to me." She didn't look honored. She looked like a mouse cornered by a cat.

"I think it's wise not to expose yourself while the poisoner remains at court," I said. "I'm sure Captain Hammer will catch him very soon, but until then, you should take particular care when near those you dined with that night."

"Yes." She studied her hands as she twisted them in her lap. "I could tell from the captain's questions that he suspects one of them."

"Do *you* suspect anyone in particular?"

"What an impertinent question!"

"I'm sorry, my lady. Forgive me."

"I don't mind. I like impertinent people. I find the impertinent ones are the honest ones who'll tell me what's what. This place is sorely lacking in impertinence," she muttered. "As to your question, Josie, the duchess of Gladstow was nice to me, as were the duke and duchess of Buxton. You can discount them, I think. I hardly spoke to the duke of Gladstow, but Lady Lucia Whippler, her brother, and Lady Violette Morgrave were sweet, although I've heard they use their sharp tongues to cut others down to size, particularly women. A wicked wit doesn't make them murderers, though."

"Among my friends, a wicked wit does not equate to a sharp tongue used to cut down rivals. We call that cruel."

"Everything is different here." There was that tone again, the resigned one, as if she wished she were anywhere but at court.

Miranda got up and padded to the window then sighed. "I'm not used to this, you know."

"Being poisoned?"

She laughed softly. "Rubbing shoulders with nobility. We live quietly at home. We're somewhat out of the way, you see, and my father's title is quite new and not very highly ranked, so we rarely have other noble families visit us."

"That must be lonely."

"Not at all. I have friends amongst the villagers; the governor's daughter and the doctor's daughters. Perhaps that's why I feel I can talk to you, Josie."

"Please do. I won't tell a soul anything told to me in confidence."

"Ever since arriving here, I feel as though I have been on display, my every move and utterance judged."

"By the king?"

"By everyone."

"You wish you'd never come?"

She didn't answer. She didn't need to. I could see it in the lowering of her chin and the slope of her shoulders. I could hardly blame her. She had been poisoned, after all. "It's not my parents' fault, you understand. They were given no choice."

"They weren't?"

She shook her head. "The king demanded every eligible daughter of Glancia's noble families be presented to him so he could choose a wife from among them. My father felt as though he couldn't refuse, and to be perfectly honest, I don't think he wanted to. He wanted to meet the king for himself and discuss national matters with him. Not that he's had many opportunities to do so."

"Why only Glancia women?" I asked. "Wouldn't a foreign princess be more politically acceptable?"

"That was one of the things my father wanted to bring up with the king." She leaned closer to the window. "There's His Majesty now. He's walking with Lady Lucia. Her brother, Lord Frederick, isn't far away, of course. He never is."

I couldn't tell whether she knew about their incestuous relationship. I didn't dare ask.

I joined her at the window but didn't see the king, at first. I was too stunned by the view of the garden, sprawled like an intricate carpet on the opposite side of the palace to the main gate and its forecourts. It was far more serene, with only a few nobles strolling around. My gaze followed the pathways woven through the lush sections of lawn like elaborate embroidery. Colorful flowers edged some of the paths, and topiary trees and potted plants dotted the landscape. The sun glinted off ponds and lakes. One was so large I couldn't see where it ended. I caught sight of the king, heading slowly toward a fountain in the center of the nearest garden. A woman rested her hand on his arm, her head tilted toward him as if sharing a secret.

Two footmen followed directly behind them, waving large fans to circulate the summer air. Even further behind walked the black clothed figure of Captain Hammer, and back again, another man kept in step with the ambling pace, a woman on each side. They were all too far away to make out their faces.

"I do hope she's making a good impression on him." It took me a moment to realize Lady Miranda was talking about Lady Lucia Whippler. "Although I'm afraid he might find her rather brash. She does so want to be noticed."

"You sound as if you hope he does notice her. Why?"

She eyed me closely. "I can see that you think me odd for not wanting the king's attention."

"I...I'm not sure. I don't know him, for one thing, but he's the king and you're a noblewoman."

"So I am supposed to want to marry him?" She sighed. "The thing is, *I* hardly know him either, Josie, and what I've seen so far..." She winced and shook her head. "Never mind."

"You can confide in me, Lady Miranda. I'll keep any secrets to myself."

"Call me Miranda. All my friends do, and I need a friend here at court." She turned back to the window. "As to the king, I find him quite immature and...changeable."

"Changeable?"

"Every time I think I understand his character, he does something that makes me doubt my opinion. The most extreme example was the time I was invited to his apartments to dine with him and four other guests. After dinner, we retreated to a salon that is quite close to his bedchamber and dressing rooms. One of the ladies, more brazen than me, entered his dressing room and wandered around, touching his things. She took a particular liking to a small cabinet of polished redwood inlaid with gold. When the king saw, he became furious and snatched it off her. He scolded her in front of everyone, reducing her to tears. I never saw her again, and it was rumored that he sent her and her family home in disgrace."

"What was in the cabinet that was so precious to him?"

"I didn't dare ask. His tirade frightened me, not just because of the vehemence but because it was out of character. He'd always been charming, if somewhat immature, but he was so *angry* with her for intruding."

"That is odd," I said. "Perhaps the pressure of becoming king is taking its toll. He's far from home, new to the role of kingship as well as to living like this and having people fawn over him. He wasn't raised to be royal. Adjusting must be hard."

"Indeed. I wouldn't wish it on a friend, that's for certain. The trappings are lovely, in a way, but he has some difficult decisions to make to steer Glancia safely into the future. The Rift changed so much, so quickly." She suddenly swung around to face me. "Josie, do you believe the gossip about magic?" It was difficult to tell whether she believed it or not, but she seemed keen to know my opinion.

"My father thinks it's possible, as do others in the village. I don't." I indicated the wall, the ceiling. "This looks very real to me."

"Ye-es, but...there's something strange about it, don't you think? Something not quite right, and it's not just that the palace was built so quickly. I can't quite put my finger on what it is, but I get the oddest feeling about the servants, and so does Hilda."

I shrugged and tried on a nonchalant expression. "I've only met a few of the guards, and they seem quite real to me too."

We talked some more as we watched Glancia's nobility passing time in the garden. Miranda pointed out the people she recognized, but I found my gaze wandering back to the king and the group trailing after him. It grew in size as more nobles were drawn into his wake. The scene looked so pleasant, so genteel and sophisticated, that it was difficult to reconcile it with the poisoning.

The group eventually returned to the palace and not five minutes later, I heard Quentin talking to someone in the sitting room, then he knocked.

"Excuse me, my lady," he said when Miranda opened the door between rooms. "The captain wishes to speak to Miss Cully in the garrison when she's finished here."

I said my goodbyes with a half-hearted promise to return to see her again soon. As much as I wanted to return, my father wouldn't allow it unless I were accompanying him.

"How is she?" the captain asked when Quentin and I reached the garrison. He removed his sword belt and hung it on the hook by a second door that led outside the palace. He must have arrived mere moments before us.

"Quite recovered," I said, scanning the now familiar faces that included Sergeant Max and Erik the Marginer, but not Sergeant Brant. "But..."

"Yes?"

"Would you inform the king that she needs more rest?"

"Does she?" Max asked, pulling the only spare chair closer and offering it to me.

"She wants some time to herself."

Erik handed a tankard of ale to me and another to Hammer, leaning against the mantel. "Why?" Erik asked.

"To..." I waved my tankard in the air, searching for the best way to tell these loyal men that Miranda had no interest in their king. "To enjoy the, er, peace and quiet of her rooms a little longer."

They all stared at me.

"She hates him, doesn't she?" Quentin said.

"Not hate, just..." Merdu, I'd got myself into a bind. I felt like I was betraying her trust. "Captain, please inform the king she needs more rest, and keep this conversation to yourself."

"You wish me to lie to him?" Hammer asked.

"Not lie, just..." I sighed. "Yes, I want you to lie."

"She shouldn't have put you in this position."

"I don't mind. I am her doctor, in a way, and it's my job to look after her wellbeing, not just her health."

"She is coward," Erik said. "She should tell the king she hates him."

"Not hate," I said again. "She simply isn't romantically inclined toward him."

"But he's the king!" Quentin cried. "She can't do better."

"Then why don't *you* flutter your lashes at him," Max said.

"I would if he liked men. And if I liked men too. Which I don't." He flushed to the roots of his hair. "I really don't. Not that I care if anyone else does. It ain't my business."

Erik laughed and slapped Quentin on the shoulder. "He would not like you in *that* way. I've seen your prick." He wiggled his little finger.

Quentin flushed even redder, and that only made Erik laugh more.

"Enough!" the captain barked. "Leave that kind of talk for when we're not in the presence of a lady."

"Clearly you've spent too long at court," I said. "I am not a lady, and I hear much worse in the taverns at Mull. But I think I ought to warn you that the sort of love you're discussing is not allowed in Glancia. It's unlawful, although I can't recall anyone being arrested for it."

"Thank you for the warning." Hammer glared at the others. "No more jokes."

"Yes, sir," Quentin mumbled.

Max crossed to the sideboard and checked the contents of a cylindrical tin. Quentin took advantage of the spare chair and sat down.

"Let Theodore tell His Majesty about Lady Miranda," Max said quietly to Hammer. "He's diplomatic."

Hammer crossed his arms. "And I'm not?"

"No," sounded a number of voices.

Max's severe features hardly changed, but I could swear he was warring with a smile. "Theodore will know the right words so that His Majesty thinks he's being kind by allowing her to be alone in her rooms another day."

"They won't be *her* rooms much longer if she continues to avoid him," Quentin said. "He'll lose interest and make her family pack their things and move back up to the attic rooms with the other barons."

Max turned around and, seeing Quentin occupying his chair, grasped the back and tipped it forward. Quentin tumbled to the floor.

"Merdu!" Quentin spat. "You fat-brained oaf, that's not nice."

"It's not nice to take someone's chair. Besides, I'm your superior."

Quentin folded his arms over his chest and lifted his chin. "I'll ignore the insult this time, on account of you being *much* older than me and Josie being present. I don't want to start an argument in front of her. She sees enough bloodshed in her work every day, she doesn't need to see it when she's off duty."

Erik cheered in what I guessed to be his native tongue. "Fight later, when she is gone."

Quentin's eyes rounded.

"No!" both Max and Hammer said.

"Bloodthirsty oaf," Max said to Erik. "I am not fighting the little turd over a chair. He'll lose, I'll be the villain, and Hammer will be forced to assign me to slops duty, leaving Brant as the only sergeant. Is that what you want?"

The tattoos on Erik's forehead drew together. "Bah! I yawn at you, Max." He then yawned loudly and long.

Max merely rolled his eyes.

"Very well," Hammer said to Max. "I'll find Theodore and tell him to inform the king that Lady Miranda isn't well enough for company yet." He set down his tankard and pushed off from the mantel.

"Just a moment," I said. "I have something I need to tell you."

"Walk with me to see Theodore. We'll talk on the way. I may also need you to convince Theodore of Lady Miranda's need for rest."

I picked up my pack and he opened the door for me. I had to step aside to allow two guards to enter. They were both solid men, one with a black goatee, the other without, but nevertheless both looked striking in their crimson uniforms. The uniform meant it took me a moment to register why the bearded guard looked familiar. At first I thought I'd simply seen him in the garrison the day before, but the uniform didn't seem right.

Then it struck me.

He was the one who'd chased me from Tam's house into The Row.

CHAPTER 8

"Josie?" Hammer said. "What is it?"

I stared at the guard as he passed, trying to think, to understand what it meant. If that guard had been watching Tam's house, did he know the poison seller that Tam had met at the pier? Was he watching Tam on his behalf?

And if he knew the poison seller, did the captain know him too?

The guard suddenly stopped and spun round. "You!" He wagged a finger at me. "You're her."

My lips parted in a silent gasp and I shrank away from him, away from the captain.

"Oh no you don't." The guard caught my wrist. "You're not going anywhere until you explain how you got away and what you were doing at Tao's in the first place."

"Unhand her, Zeke," Hammer barked. "What is this about?"

The guard released me. "Sir, this is the woman I followed from Tao's house. She could be the poisoner, or working for him."

"I am not!" I cried.

"Then why run away from me?"

"You're a stranger, a man, and you were chasing me! Any respectable woman would run off."

"I wasn't chasing you, I was following you."

"There's no difference."

"Yes, there is," several men chimed from the garrison.

Hammer ushered me back into the garrison and shut the door. He looked angry but I wasn't sure if it was directed at me or the guard. "Why did you visit Tao?"

"To ask him if he knew who imported traitor's ease from Zemaya," I said.

"I already asked. Since he imports herbs and spices, I thought it wise to place a watch outside his house."

"Tam isn't the poison seller!"

"He might be."

"He isn't," I said. "He's a good man. Did anyone suspicious visit him?" I asked the guard.

"Only you," the guard said.

I ignored the implication and turned to Hammer. He still looked angry. "I learned something from Tam, as it happens. Something I assume you did not, Captain, or you wouldn't have bothered setting a watch on him."

"Go on," Hammer said flatly.

"He told me of a Zemayan he met at the pier and the suspicious package he collected from a ship that came from Zemaya. It was labeled as powder but it was heavy, like the poisonous roots of the plant from which traitor's ease comes from. You should go to the taverns and ask about him. Tell them you're looking for a man from Zemaya, but not Tam Tao."

The captain stared at me a moment then nodded at Max. "Take a small team into Mull."

"Aye, sir," Max said.

"And you, Zeke, need to identify yourself next time you're spotted by the person you're following."

"But then they'll know we're onto them, sir, and lead us astray," Zeke said.

"If they see they're being followed, they'll lead you astray anyway, as Josie did by entering The Row."

"Where she lost you," Quentin said from the chair Max vacated a second time. "Well done, Josie." The entire group of guards scowled at him and he shrugged sheepishly.

Hammer held the door open for me and we once again set off through the maze of service corridors.

"You're angry with me," I said to Hammer.

He looked at me sideways. "Why did you go into The Row? That place is dangerous."

"I was lost. My head got turned as I ran and before I knew it, I was there. As it turns out, it was the perfect place to lose your guard. The lanes are as confusing as these corridors."

"You could have been hurt. Or worse."

"Now you sound like my father."

"Your father is a wise man."

"And I am a wise woman. I used that wisdom to find a way out safely and lose Zeke."

He grunted. "I'll punish him later."

"Don't do that. It's hardly his fault for losing me."

"Not for losing you, for not immediately identifying himself, and for chasing you into The Row."

"I thought he was following, not chasing."

Another grunt, but this time it held some humor. "Thank you for the new information. I'm willing to concede that neither me nor my men could have gathered that information from Tao. Like most folk in Mull, he doesn't trust us."

"That's almost gracious of you, Captain."

Another sideways glance and this time it was accompanied by a tilt of his lips.

We passed guards approaching from the opposite direction. They nodded at Hammer, who nodded back. Several maids also walked past but paid us no mind. Their uniforms did not sport the palace coat of arms on the left breast, unlike the next maid. She smiled at Hammer but it slipped when she spotted me.

"Why do they all look at me like that?" I whispered.

"Like what?"

"Like they hate me."

"I suspect they see you as an outsider and think I should be avoiding you. Only the guards, Theodore and Balthazar, know that you're aware of our secret. Not the other staff."

I didn't think that explained it but kept my opinion to myself. "Balthazar is the master of the palace?"

"Yes. He's close with the king."

"As are you and Theodore."

He thought about it a moment. "In a different way. Balthazar is older and the king listens to his advice, much like a son listens to his father."

"Whereas you and Theodore are more like friends or brothers?"

"Not quite, but our relationship with him is more informal than it is with the other servants."

Getting to Theodore meant leaving the hidden service corridors behind and entering the main part of the palace. We passed through room upon room of opulence, each painted a different color, some vivid, others in pastel. One room led directly into another and another, many with gentlemen or ladies talking quietly in groups, some playing cards, others fanning themselves by the windows. They watched us pass by as if we were the most interesting thing to have crossed their paths that day. I tried not to meet their curious gazes. Instead I took in the many paintings and tapestries, the chandeliers, some larger than me, the elegant furniture and lush carpets. The nobles must think me vulgar for staring but I didn't care. I might never see such grandiosity again and I didn't want to miss a single gilded flourish.

We found Theodore in a room of no discernable function except to advertise the king's wealth. The domed ceiling was divided into quarter sections around a fifth central one, each painted with scenes from the Holy Book. A chandelier with hundreds of tiny tear-shaped crystals hung on a long chain over a circular carpet of bright blue and gold. The carpet colors matched the patterned walls and fire screen. The room was mostly empty, except for two sideboards facing one another across the carpet and a series of low velvet-covered stools arranged around the perimeter. Theodore sat on one beside a closed set of gilded double doors. I could hear voices beyond, but not what they said. He rose and greeted us.

"Can we talk?" Hammer asked.

Theodore directed us to a large adjoining room containing a masculine desk positioned beneath a portrait of King Leon on a horse with dogs at his feet and a forest in the background. I recognized two of the dogs from the kitchen. It was a strange painting considering he didn't like to hunt.

Theodore left the door open and asked me to sit. He sat too, but Hammer remained standing by the entrance where he could see the entire sitting room and the door to the room where the voices came from.

"Lady Miranda is better," the captain announced.

"That is good news," Theodore said.

"But she would like some time to herself. She asked Josie to inform you to break it to the king in such a way that will not hurt his feelings."

Theodore slumped into the chair. "Ah. Doesn't she share his affections?"

I glanced between them, wondering how much of the conversation I could divulge to them without betraying Miranda's confidence. "She feels as though she doesn't know him well enough to have those sort of feelings yet."

"They've spent a lot of time together. How much more does she need?"

I simply lifted one shoulder.

"She has not allowed intimacy," Theodore went on without a qualm. "Perhaps that would change things."

"And how do you propose to broach that topic with her?" Hammer sounded amused but there was no outward sign of a smile.

Theodore looked at me.

"No!" I shook my head. "That is a conversation for the two of them. May I suggest you allow *her* to direct the king into her bed when and if she wishes? She seems to know her mind, on this matter and others."

"I don't understand...why does she not want to be with him?" Theodore seemed genuinely confused. "Setting aside the fact he is the king, there's nothing wrong with him. He's not as handsome as Hammer, for example, but he's not ugly. He's generous and kind, mostly good natured and even tempered. He's not overly masculine, I suppose, but that is not always a good measure of a man. The other ladies seem to desire him."

"Then perhaps he ought to look among them for a wife," I said.

"But he wants *her*." Theodore's gaze narrowed. "What are you hiding, Josie?"

"That's not fair, Theo," Hammer said. "She's simply passing on a message."

"Lady Miranda has clearly confided in her. I can tell by the way she won't meet my gaze."

I forced myself to stare at him.

"You should blink once in a while, Josie. It'll make you more believable." Theo tossed me a crooked smile to soften his words. "You can tell us. Hammer and I trust one another implicitly. Nothing you say to us will be passed on to the king. It won't leave this room. I simply want to understand."

Hammer was no help. He neither encouraged nor discouraged me; he simply waited. It was an interrogation technique that worked too well on me.

"She says she can't grasp his character, that he's changeable," I said. "She mentioned an incident where a lady touched a cabinet in his rooms and he became so furious that he ordered her and her family to leave the palace. Is that true?"

Hammer shifted his weight from one foot to the other. Theodore cleared his throat. "Yes," he said. "It is."

"What's in the cabinet?"

"Nothing of importance."

"We don't know," Hammer said, ignoring Theo's glare.

"Miranda witnessed the king's tantrum that night and I think it rather put her off him," I said. "She says he also acts immaturely sometimes. She doesn't seem like a woman in love, or a woman prepared to act like she is just to become queen." The fact she confided in me at all would suggest she hoped I would pass on her reluctance to these men. It was the act of a trapped, desperate woman.

Theodore pulled on his lower lip as he thought. After a moment, he slapped his hands on the chair arms. "What do we do, Hammer?"

"Give her time?" the captain suggested. "Perhaps she will change her mind."

For Hailia's sake! Were they this stupid because they didn't understand women or because they'd lost their memories and had forgotten how the opposite sex behaved?

"May I offer a suggestion," I said.

"Please do," said Theodore eagerly.

"Try to direct the king to a woman who *is* interested in him.

117

Do it subtly so he thinks he's making up his own mind. Seat him near suitable women, not Miranda, and keep him occupied in other parts of the palace, not near her. If he still won't look elsewhere, she might agree to you spreading a rumor about a fungal infection. I can tell you the symptoms if you like, to make it more authentic, but I would encourage you to discuss it with her first."

"You're diabolical." Theodore's eyes gleamed. "I'll speak with the king after his meeting. Any movement yet, Hammer?"

"No," the captain said.

"Good. The longer they're in there, the better. The advisors were growing desperate for this meeting. Apparently they had much to discuss."

"The king was avoiding them?" I asked. "Why, when he asked them here?"

"Asking them and wanting them are two different things." Theodore offered me a flat smile. "The king doesn't like meetings."

"Or his advisors," Hammer added in a mutter. Theodore glared sharply at him but Hammer paid him no mind.

So the king didn't like meetings, advisors or hunting. Luckily he liked beautiful women or I would have worried that every kingly trait had passed him by altogether.

"How goes your hunt for the poisoner?" Theodore asked the captain.

"We have several pieces of information, one of them thanks to Josie," Hammer said. "I questioned the footmen who served that night so now I know the seating plan, who got up from their chairs, and the general mood of the party."

"And?" Theodore asked.

"Lord Frederick Whippler sat on Lady Miranda's left and the duke of Gladstow on her right. Gladstow barely spoke to her, preferring to converse with the duchess of Buxton, but Whippler engaged her in regular conversation. He also cast several dark glares in the direction of the king, who found himself seated next to Lady Lucia Whippler."

"The dark glares were most likely because he was jealous of his sister flirting with the king," I said.

"I may not recall much of anything," Theodore said, "but even I know incest isn't natural. If the king knew... I actually don't know what he'd do."

"Will you tell him?" I asked.

Another glance passed between them. "Perhaps," was all Theodore said.

"It does make Lord Frederick less likely to want to poison Miranda," I said. "Without her, the king could very well turn his focus onto Lucia."

"Don't discount him yet," the captain said. "There may be another reason he wants to kill Miranda that I haven't yet discovered."

"Go on, Hammer," Theodore said. "What else happened that night?"

"Lady Lucia got up from her seat once, and draped herself over her brother's shoulders while he sat. He was sitting beside Miranda, if you recall, so Lucia would have had access to her food and wine. Lady Violette Morgrave also got up between courses, while Miranda was out of the room, and even sat in Miranda's chair."

"That's odd," I said.

"She mimicked Lady Miranda's way of eating and drinking, so one of the footmen told me."

"Mimicked or mocked?" I said wryly.

"How did the king react?" Theodore asked.

"He didn't seem pleased at first, but Lady Morgrave said something witty that sounded exactly like Miranda and the king laughed."

There was that word again—witty. The court's definition of it was very different to mine.

"Thanks for the report," Theodore said. "I'd offer to help with your investigation but I'll be busy diverting the king's attention toward a woman who will reciprocate his feelings."

"Preferably not one of the suspects," I said.

Theodore pointed at me. "Precisely."

"It's all under control," Hammer told Theodore. "I have men looking for the poison seller now. I'll send them out of Mull if I have to. Once we find him, we'll know who he sold the poisons to."

"Spare us the uncivilized details of how you go about getting answers," Theodore said, hands in the air.

Hammer's glare turned flinty before he looked away.

Theodore didn't notice. He was about to head past the captain when he remembered something. "By the way, the king wants an evening of entertainment to be held in ten days time."

"That'll keep Balthazar busy," Hammer said.

"He has complained incessantly to me already, but I think he secretly enjoys the challenge. I'm looking forward to seeing what he does."

"Ten days doesn't seem like a lot of time to prepare festivities fit for a king and hundreds of nobles," I said. Then again, this was the magnificent palace of King Leon—the palace that had been built in under three months, from the empty land to the final gilded ceiling rosette, and all without a workman being seen.

Theodore resumed his original seat on the stool by the meeting room door. We were about to exit the office too when a group of gentlemen and ladies arrived. Hammer pulled me back behind the open door.

"Look," he whispered, turning me to face the door jam. "Observe." I could see part of the room through the gap and the six new arrivals. I recognized Lady Deerhorn and her daughter, Lady Violette Morgrave, who still visited her parents from time to time since her marriage to Lord Morgrave. The rest were strangers to me.

"Is the blasted meeting still going?" whined a woman dressed in a gown the same color as her red-gold hair. With her hair piled high on her head and a long brown feather shooting from the top of the arrangement, she seemed excessively tall. Only one of the gentlemen was taller.

"That's Lady Lucia Whippler." Hammer's breath brushed my hair and his body warmed my back. I struggled to focus on the group of nobles in the sitting room, and not on his compelling presence. I drew in a deep breath, but it only filled me with the scent of him, sharpening my senses in the wrong direction.

It took Lady Lucia's prancing toward the meeting room to shift my focus forward. Theodore stood, blocking her way.

"I only wanted to remind the king that he promised to watch

our little theatrical," she said in a voice that could leave no listener uncertain as to who was the higher ranked of the two. "I wouldn't want him to miss it and break his promise."

"The king will be more than happy to watch your theatrical after his meeting," Theodore said with bland politeness. "I'll remind him as soon as he becomes available."

"Or I could remind him now. Move aside."

"The king cannot be disturbed."

"What is your name again?"

"Theodore."

"I shall be sure to tell the king who forbade me to enter."

"It is your prerogative to do so."

The expansive cleavage on display above Lady Lucia's tight bodice swelled. "I have never experienced such insolence from a servant before. If you were in my household, I would thrash you then dismiss you."

He indicated the door through which they'd entered. "If you wouldn't mind waiting elsewhere. Your voice has a way of piercing through solid doors and we wouldn't want to disturb His Majesty and his advisors."

The feather in her hair shook with her anger. "My lady," she snapped.

"Pardon?"

"You will address me as Lady Lucia or my lady. Is that understood?"

"Yes, my lady." He bowed low, much lower than necessary, turning deference into mockery.

Lady Morgrave smiled behind her hand. Her mother, Lady Deerhorn, pressed her lips together.

A tall, blond gentleman came forward and grasped Lady Lucia by the shoulders. "Lucia, darling, let's take this opportunity to rehearse one more time. I certainly need it." He steered her away then mouthed "Sorry" over his shoulder to Theodore.

"Her brother, Lord Frederick Whippler," Hammer whispered in my ear.

Theodore gave Lord Frederick a nod. Once they were all gone, he crooked his finger at us to join him. "That went well," Theodore said, eyes flashing in the direction in which the group had left.

"You should be careful, Theo," Hammer said. "She has some influence over the king and may acquire more if he turns his attentions from Miranda to her."

"He has better taste in women than that."

"She's his second favorite."

"That's because he can't see past the two over-inflated charms she manages to thrust in his face at every opportunity. Once he raises his gaze above her chest into her cold eyes he'll see her for the wasp she is."

"As long as he doesn't get stung first."

Theodore turned to me. "What did you think of her, Josie?"

"I think if her brother didn't divert her attention, she might still be here," I said. "She seemed determined to speak to the king."

"She can't keep away from him."

"She's worried he'll forget her if he goes more than an hour without seeing her," the captain added.

"Desperate," Theodore spat. "Let's hope the king smells it on her soon so we can direct him to a more worthy lady." He sighed. "Are you quite sure Lady Miranda won't change her mind? I do like her."

"I'm not at all sure what's in her mind," I said.

He was about to sit again when the double doors leading to the meeting room burst open and the duke of Gladstow stormed out. His pounding footsteps shook the crystal teardrops hanging from the candelabra on the sideboard.

"That upstart!" he said, loud enough for everyone in the meeting room to hear. "This is outrageous. What has he done to earn it? Fathered a brat of a girl on that whore of a wife, that's all."

"Gladstow!" the king barked from the doorway. "Do not walk away from me." The man I'd only ever witnessed as affable, looked as ferocious as a thunderstorm, ready to unleash a deluge over the duke's head. I'd not thought him terribly regal until now. He looked every bit the powerful ruler of a nation.

I inched away until I was back in the room with the desk. I hid behind the door again and watched through the gap. Neither man had taken any notice of me.

The duke halted but did not return to the king's side. They glared at one another from opposite sides of the room.

"Do not disparage Lady Claypool in such a manner," the king said. "She is the mother of an admirable, kind woman and you would be wise to hold you tongue."

The duke sniffed. "Claypool doesn't deserve an earldom. He's only a baron, and second generation at that. Merdu, he's practically a peasant!"

"If Lady Miranda and I marry, her father will become an earl, whether you agree or not. It's only right."

"Right? Ha!" Gladstow looked past the king into the room beyond where other men all stood, watching. "I think that requires some investigation of the legal texts before you can declare such a thing."

"I am the king," His Majesty said through a hard jaw. "I change the laws if I wish."

"No," Gladstow said triumphantly. "You cannot."

One of the advisors shuffled forward. "Discussion of marriage is too soon, surely."

"Precisely," Gladstow said. "Anything could happen. She hasn't even fully recovered yet. Besides, she might reject an offer."

"Why would she?" the king said, throwing out an ominous challenge.

Gladstow smiled a twisted smile. "She is her mother's daughter, a fickle, disobedient creature."

"Enough, Gladstow! You are on thin ice."

"I am merely stating my opinion, sire. There is no law against doing so. Indeed, that is the entire point of these meetings, to debate opinions. You cannot chastise me for that."

"I can and I will do more than merely chastise if you cross me again, Gladstow. Your position is not set in stone. Your title can be taken away as easily as it was granted to your forebears."

Behind him, several men gasped. Gladstow took a step forward but stopped. He'd gone pale.

"You can't strip me of my title," he said, although he did not sound entirely sure.

"The king can do as he wishes," the king said.

"Within reason. Some decisions must be voted by council before they become law." Gladstow nodded at the other men. "Didn't you know, sire?"

The king clasped his hands at his back. "Good day, Gladstow."

The duke gave a perfunctory bow and marched off. The other men followed, each bowing before exiting.

"Is that true?" the king said to Theodore after the others were gone. "What he said about some decisions requiring a vote?"

"I think so," Theodore said carefully. "I haven't had time to wade through all the legal texts in the library yet."

"Why not? What in Merdu's name do you do all day?" The king waved at the stool where Theodore had been sitting. "You could have been reading while you waited." He tapped his forehead. "You should always be thinking about how to serve me efficiently."

Theodore bowed. "Yes, sire."

I ought not be listening to their conversation. I should reveal myself and make up some sort of excuse for my presence. But I dared not make a sound. The king looked angry, and I didn't want to find out what punishment he meted out to eavesdroppers.

The king tugged on his lace cuffs and I thought the matter ended, but Hammer spoke up. "The library is not nearby. Theo would have been gone from this chamber for an unsuitable length of time. Time during which you may have needed him."

I held my breath, expecting the king to scold the captain as he had scolded the duke. But he simply continued to tug on his cuffs. "Yes. Well. There is that."

"If you told them you don't know all the laws and customs of Glancia, they might be more forgiving," Hammer went on. "There's no shame in it."

"Never show weakness to men beneath you, Hammer. They'll ridicule you then take advantage of you." The king's nostrils flared, making him look more like his portraits.

"I will research the laws applicable to the king's powers this afternoon," Theodore said. "Unless Your Majesty requires me elsewhere?"

"No. I'm expected in the amphitheater to watch Lady Lucia and Lady Morgrave act in a play scripted in my honor. Hammer will accompany me. Begin your research on the sovereign's powers of dismissal, Theo. Surely it's not true that I can't strip a duke of his title."

"It seems wise," Hammer said.

"Wise?" the king hissed. "What is the point of a king if he can't control his nobles? What if that duke tries to overthrow me?"

"I'm sure the laws will have special considerations for such an event."

"We'll know soon." King Leon looked down at his dark gray doublet with the white collar and cuffs and blue diamond shapes embroidered on the front. "I think I'll change into something less drab before the theatrical. You can go to the library after that, Theo."

I watched them leave but did not emerge from my hiding place until the captain assured me the king would not return. "He didn't see you."

"What would he have done if he had?" I asked.

"Beheading, perhaps."

I gasped and clutched my throat but lowered my hands when he smiled. "You have a twisted sense of humor, Captain."

"He wouldn't have done anything," he said in all seriousness. "I wouldn't let him."

"He's the king. If he wanted to beat me, he can do it, and you don't have the power to stop him. I don't know all of the laws surrounding his powers," I went on, "but I do know he can whip the local doctor's daughter if he wishes to."

"He wouldn't whip you or beat you, Josie, or anyone else. He hasn't got the stomach for it."

It was an argument I couldn't win so I let the matter drop. I wasn't convinced that the king wouldn't have beaten me if he'd caught me. It was his right to defend his property—including secrets—within his own palace.

We headed back through the palace, past lords and ladies seated exactly where they had been the first time we'd passed through. In a room larger than my entire cottage, a fat gentleman sat with his head tipped back, snoring loudly. Two ladies perched on the sofa opposite threw berries at him, trying to get them in his mouth.

"A footman can direct me out from here," I said to Hammer.

He slowed and eyed me sideways. "I'm sorry my joke offended you that much."

"It was a terrible joke but I'm not offended. You're supposed to accompany the king to the amphitheater."

"He'll be some time yet. Changes of clothing are not simple affairs."

"Where is the amphitheater?"

"It's set amongst the trees in the garden, just before Lake Grand. You can't see it from the paths."

"I saw the gardens from Lady Miranda's room. They're very pretty and interesting. Is there a herb garden?"

"The pottage garden grows herbs. Why?"

"I use herbs in medicines. I wonder what they grow."

"I'll take you one day and you can look around."

"I wouldn't want to upset the cook. He doesn't look like he'd want me wandering through his garden, picking his herbs."

"He's harmless. He likes to make himself out to be more important than he is in front of pretty Glancian women. Don't mind him."

"If you're sure it'll be safe, then I'd like to see the garden one day. My father can't object to herb gathering for medicines, and I don't need to tell him I'm coming here to get them."

The captain didn't respond for some time and I thought the topic finished until he said, "I won't go against your father's wishes."

"He worries unnecessarily."

"Would he object to me visiting you?"

My step slowed. "Why would you visit me?"

"Ever since you mentioned the illegality of men loving men and the disparity between the law and its enforcement, I've been thinking of other things I need to know that aren't written in books. Things that only a Glancian would know—one with a memory, that is."

"Oh. I see." *Of course* that was why he wanted to see me. I was a fool to think it was for any other reason.

The rooms we'd been traversing through suddenly opened up to an expansive landing, lushly carpeted with a double-sided sofa offering a place for the weary to rest before going up or down the stairs. The gilded relief of the king's initials decorated all the doors with the Lockhart crest above. The staircase itself was made of the same red, white and black marble that adorned the forecourt, the pilasters topped with golden domes. A gold statue of the king wearing a crown and holding a branch in one hand and a scepter in the other took pride of place in the center of the landing. It was large enough to be visible from the grand black and white tiled entrance gallery below.

"So what do you think?" Hammer asked.

"It's beautiful," I said on a breath.

He looked around the entrance gallery as if seeing it with fresh eyes. "I suppose. But I meant about you answering my questions."

"When can you get away from here?"

"Tomorrow afternoon, unless there are developments with the investigation that require my attention."

My father had two patients to visit in the afternoon, both of them too old and ill to come to us anymore. He would expect me to go with him, but I could make an excuse that I wanted to study his notes or make up some medicines. Lying was the only way to see the captain—my father would never agree to me meeting a man from the palace alone.

"Have you seen our beaches yet?" I asked as we exited the palace into the bright sunshine.

"Only from afar."

"Meet me at Half Moon Cove tomorrow afternoon. It's half a mile north of the village and only accessible via stairs."

"I'll be there, armed with questions."

He escorted me to the main gate where he signaled for a waiting carriage to collect me. The thrill of his hand touching mine as he assisted me into the cabin lasted until I left the estate altogether. It was replaced not only with a flutter of trepidation, but also the sense that my father was right and I was a fool for meeting a man I hardly knew whose past was shrouded in mystery, in a secluded place with only one exit back up the steep cliff.

CHAPTER 9

*P*alace guards were conspicuous throughout Mull that afternoon and evening. They paid particular attention to the Row, questioning its occupants about Zemayans. Every one of our patients arrived with the news and an opinion on what it might mean.

"Seems the guards are as subtle as their captain's name," Father said to me after the final patient left. He eased himself onto a kitchen chair with a groan.

I dipped a clean cloth into the basin of water and passed it to him. He patted it over his brow and the back of his neck. "You're working too hard," I said. "You should have allowed me to see the last patient. It was only a few bruises."

"Possible cheek fracture," he said. "And I didn't like the look of him."

I ladled broth into a bowl and set it before him. "You're judging your patients on their looks now?"

"How else am I supposed to judge the ones I've never met before?" He dipped his spoon into the bowl and tasted the broth. He pulled a face and inspected the bowl's contents. "It's watery."

"I wanted a change from fish, but prices of beef and mutton are outrageous. I only bought a little."

"Good girl. You're wise to save at the moment."

"Why?"

He pushed the bowl aside. "In my experience, if a man looks like a thug, he usually is a thug."

"We're still discussing that, are we?"

"That man looked like the biggest bruiser in the village," he went on. "I don't want you anywhere near him, Josie." That explained why he'd sent me to the kitchen as soon as he'd laid eyes on the man who'd filled our doorway. "Judging someone on appearances might not seem fair to you, but you've lived a sheltered life, and you don't know what bad men look like."

They looked like the men who'd followed me in The Row, but I didn't tell him that. I didn't say anything. He was in the sort of mood where it was impossible to reason with him.

"Mull is changing, and we must change with it," he said. "Or leave."

I paused, the spoon halfway to my mouth. Surely he couldn't be serious. "Mull is our home. We're not leaving. Stop talking nonsense and have your soup. If you're not going to let me help you every time a strange man walks in the door, you're going to need your strength."

He drew the bowl toward him then after a hesitation, dipped the spoon in. We didn't speak throughout the rest of the meal and only spoke afterward out of professional necessity.

The arrival of a man carried by another two interrupted our evening routine. The injured man was unconscious, his hair matted with blood. His two companions may have been able to walk, but they sported cuts and bruises on their faces.

"Josie, go to the kitchen," Father said, directing the men to take the unconscious patient through to his surgery. "Boil some water."

"I'll bring it in when it's ready," I said, turning to go.

"I'll fetch it myself. You stay in the kitchen." He shut the surgery door and that was the last I saw of the three men.

I heard the front door open and close an hour later and went to see how the patient fared. I found Father sitting at his desk, his hands bloodied, his eyes glassy with exhaustion.

A lifeless body lay on the workbench, the skin the color of the dead. I slumped against the door.

"This is why I don't want you roaming Mull at night," Father said quietly. "That man got into a fight at The Mermaid's Tail. It wasn't the punches that killed him, it was the fall. He hit his head on the edge of a table. There was no chance of recovery."

"Poor man. His poor friends."

"They say they hardly knew him. He was just another newcomer to Mull, like them, who found employment on the dock. They didn't even know where he was from originally."

"That's terribly sad. He may have a family waiting for him to return."

"It's not our concern now. They'll inform their foreman tonight. Someone will come for the body in the morning." He pushed himself to his feet. "Help me clean up."

"I can do it." I squeezed his arm. "Go and wash up then go to bed. You need rest."

He nodded but didn't leave. He looked over the body with professional disinterest. "It's men like him who've ruined this village. Men like him are the reason I don't want you out after dark anymore. Mull isn't safe."

I watched him go, his shoulders more stooped than usual. It wasn't the workload that weighed him down, it was seeing his home change almost overnight. He no longer recognized the sleepy village he'd settled in with his new wife. At least he didn't mention leaving Mull again.

* * *

THEY TOOK the body away the following morning while I was at the market looking for reasonably priced food. I settled on eggs and a selection of salad vegetables. Meat was too expensive and the fish were small, all the best ones having gone to the palace.

I spotted Tam Tao at his stall but didn't speak with him. I had no need of exotic herbs or spices. Meg joined me on the walk home. The basket slung over her arm looked as pitiful as mine and we shared our complaints about the prices.

Father greeted me at the door with a scowl when I got home. "You were gone too long."

"Stop worrying," I said. "For Hailia's sake, I simply got talking. You know what I'm like." I held up the basket. "We have eggs."

"I'm sick of eggs." He pressed the heel of his hand to his chest and his jaw clenched.

"Father? Are you ill?" I set the basket down but he turned away before I could get a better look at his face. "What's the matter?"

"I'm just worried about you." He strode off to the kitchen. "I don't want you out on your own."

I picked up the basket and followed. "So you've already made clear."

"I mean during the day too, now," he said from the larder.

"What?"

"Not until we leave."

"Leave!"

He picked up a jar, read the label, and returned it to the shelf. "Between the poisoning at the palace, the guards poking about, the newcomers to the village, the fights, the high prices...Mull isn't the place for us anymore." He picked up another jar, read the label, and returned that too.

I caught his hand before he plucked a third jar off the shelf. He wouldn't look at me but he didn't pull away. "Is this about the man who died?" It shouldn't be the sort of thing that worried my father. He'd seen death many times. "Has something happened?"

"Only go to the market with Meg or her mother from now on." He scanned the jars then picked up the one containing dried catspaw flowers. He opened it and smelled the contents. Satisfied that he'd got the right jar, he pushed past me.

"Why do you need that?" I asked.

"A patient came in this morning complaining of an erratic heartbeat. I thought I should prepare some catspaw if he returns."

"Who was it?"

"No one you know." He took the jar to his workroom.

I followed and watched as he emptied two flowers into the mortar and ground them with the pestle. "It's for you, isn't it?"

"Stop fussing," he chided without looking up. "Fetch some hot water."

I spent the next little while in the kitchen avoiding him and thinking up ways to leave the house without worrying him. I'd lie if necessary. Meg would certainly need to be involved. I wasn't going to miss my meeting with Hammer.

Luckily I didn't need Meg's help. Father went out in the early afternoon. He didn't take his medical bag, nor did he have any scheduled patients to visit, but he refused to tell me where he was going. At least he looked better than he had earlier.

"There's something I must do, Josie," he said as he left. "Someone I must see."

"This had better not be about leaving Mull because I'm not going anywhere," I said to his back. When he didn't answer, I called out, "When will you return?"

"In an hour."

An hour wasn't long enough. The round trip to Half Moon Cove would take up most of that time. I glanced at Meg's house across the street. No, too easy for him to check. Instead, I wrote him a note and left it on his desk. "Jamilla complaining of pains. Gone to check." He was unlikely to follow up on an expectant mother. He left those patients to me.

* * *

HAMMER WAS WET. The ends of his hair had begun to dry but the rest of it was damp and messy, as if he'd ruffled it to shake off the drops. His shirt clung to the contours and ridges of his body, leaving nothing to my imagination. My imagination could never have done him justice, however, not even in my wildest fantasies.

He spotted me and approached along the beach. "Why are you staying back there?" he asked.

So I could admire you without being noticed, I wanted to say but didn't dare. My cheeks heated and I looked down only to see that his feet were bare. "You've been swimming," I said stupidly.

"And I didn't drown."

I looked up, straight into his gaze. His eyes were the same color as the water behind him. I blinked, dazzled by the sun and the sky and the man looking back at me, more relaxed than I'd ever seen him. More handsome too.

"I wasn't sure if I could swim," he said. "Seems I can."

"You didn't know if you could swim until you went in? Captain, that was foolish. There's no one here to save you."

He walked back along the sand toward some large boulders at the southern end of the beach. "You're here now."

"What makes you think I can swim?"

"You strike me as a very capable woman."

Well this capable woman couldn't catch up to him. I stopped and removed my shoes before they filled with sand.

He stopped too and waited for me. "You've lived in Mull your entire life. I'd wager you came to this spot and swam with your friends when you were supposed to be studying your father's books."

He was wrong. I had stayed home and studied when my friends lied to their parents and snuck out on sunny afternoons. I'd been to Half Moon Cove many times with my mother before she died, but not too many since. With her, I'd paddled in the shallows and collected shells or seaweed that washed up on the shore, and used them to decorate our sandcastles. But years later, when my friends experienced their first kisses behind the boulders, I'd been at home, learning what to do in the event of a breached birth.

"I can't swim," I said, striding past him.

I'd almost reached the boulders when he caught up to me. "I overstepped. I'm sorry, Josie."

I winced at the heaviness in his voice. He'd been relaxed, cheerful even, and I'd ruined it. I turned on a sunny smile. "There's nothing to apologize for. So how well do you swim?"

"Moderately well."

"Since you're modest, I'm going to assume you swim like a fish."

He picked up his boots and sat on one of the boulders. "Am I modest?"

"You're not boastful."

He considered that but didn't make his thoughts known to me. He dusted the sand off the sole of one foot.

I sat on the sand, my hands behind me, and stretched my legs out. "It must be strange to learn who you are all over again."

His movements slowed. All the sand had been removed and he seemed to be simply going through the motions. "I feel as though I know who I am, in a way." He shook his head. "It's hard to explain."

"Try."

He put his foot down, getting it sandy again. "I know I want to find the poisoner. I want him or her to pay for their crime, and I want Lady Miranda to feel safe again. I want everyone at the palace to feel safe."

"You have a strong sense of justice then," I said. "And protective instincts. That must be why you became a guard."

"If I had a choice in the matter."

"You don't think you did? Sorry. Stupid question. If you haven't always been a guard, then you must have done something else that involved physical work before the palace was built."

He frowned. "Why do you say that?"

"The calluses on your hands, the muscles...everywhere."

He shifted his weight and folded his arms. He must have realized that it only made the muscles bulge so he unfolded his arms and dragged a hand through his hair instead. It would seem he was a little self-conscious but I didn't mention it. I was already blushing fiercely and if I became any redder I wouldn't be able to blame it on the sun.

"What else do you know about yourself?" I asked.

"I want answers," he said.

"That goes without saying."

"Not just to the poisoning and memory loss, but to...everything. I want to know why the people from the Margin don't cross over the border to Glancia or Dreen. I want to know how many earthquakes The Fist gets. I want to know why women aren't allowed into the colleges, and why Freedland is called Freedland."

"It became a republic forty years ago," I said, glad I could answer at least one thing. "The people rebelled against a tyrannical king. There was a lot of bloodshed but they succeeded and formed a council to rule their country. They changed the country's name to reflect their new freedom. What else do you want to know?"

He shrugged. "So many things. I want to know why Lady Lucia and her brother cling to one another."

I was about to make a rude quip but he seemed utterly serious. "Love?" My answer surprised even me. I drew up my knees and rested my chin on them. Could they love one another? Or was it simply pleasure? Or did they need one another the way flowers and bees did?

"I want to know a lot of things," Hammer said so quietly that I tilted my head up to look at him.

The sun was in my eyes and I had to squint, but he turned to look at the sea before I could make out his expression. "Ask me anything," I said.

He opened his mouth then closed it again. He rested his elbow on his knees and seemed transfixed by the gentle lapping of the waves. "Was the last Glancian king a good king?"

So he wanted to discuss dull affairs. Very well. It was necessary for King Leon to know the state of his kingdom, I supposed. "It's said that King Alain didn't care about the kingdom in his final years. Either he was old and weary or simply didn't care as he had no heir. Or so he thought. Vytill's King Phillip was rumored to be preparing to take over, and the two Glancian dukes were also said to be plotting independently of one another."

"Buxton and Gladstow?"

"The very same. As the highest ranking nobles, they had a good claim on the throne. They couldn't have succeeded though, not even if they joined forces. Apparently Vytill's army is large and well trained." I swept my palm across the warm sand, smoothing it flat. "King Leon appeared at the right time. If he hadn't, Glancia could be at war now."

He said nothing, simply continued to stare at the water.

"What does the king say is his earliest memory?" I asked.

"Waking up in the palace one morning, months ago, the same as the rest of us. The palace was completed. He knows nothing of its origins, and nothing that came before it. He doesn't recall how he became king, although he has since read about it from the documents found in his desk."

"Do you believe him?"

He gave me a sharp look. "It would be a cruel person who withholds information like that from people desperate to learn more about themselves."

"That doesn't answer my question."

He straightened and turned back to the expanse of water hemmed by cliffs on two sides and the crescent beach on a third. It wasn't a good place for smugglers to offload their wares. It was too close to the village, for one thing, and too easy to get trapped by the cliffs. I wondered if Hammer knew those things the way I did, the way other residents of seaside villages instinctively knew them.

"What else do you know how to do aside from swimming?" I asked. "Perhaps we can narrow down your origins. Being an able swimmer means you most likely came from somewhere along the coast or a river."

"Or lake."

"You've already put some thought into it."

"We all have. We've discussed it many times. All the staff have speculated. There are some interesting similarities and differences between us. Not just in our appearances, I mean, but other things. Most of the guards know how to fight." He smirked. "Except Quentin. Many of the stable hands say that working with horses felt natural to them. The cook knew how to cook, the gardeners knew about plants, herbs and seasonal variations, although something about the Glancian weather seemed wrong to them."

"So they're not Glancian natives."

"I don't think I am, either. I'm too dark to be Glancian but too tall to be Freedlander. I learned that thanks to you, the first day we met in the forest, and confirmed it after reading a book from the library."

"You don't have Dreen features, either. You could be Vytill, I suppose." I sighed. "Sorry. I haven't been much help."

"Talking to you about it is help enough. We needed outside suggestions. None of us know enough about...about anything to solve this."

"I don't know enough either," I said with a shake of my head. "I feel so useless. I'm sorry, Captain. I won't give up, but I don't have much hope of finding answers. Is there anything else that might give me a clue? Anything at all?"

He shifted his weight and his gaze briefly met mine before slipping away. I had the odd sensation that this was the reason he'd asked to meet me today, but now that the time had come, he hesitated.

"Go on," I said. "I won't tell a soul. Not even my father."

"I would have asked him but he doesn't seem to believe our memory loss."

"So it's a medical matter?"

"In a way." He glanced at the top of the stairs, built into the side of the cliff. "I have to remove my shirt."

"I'll try not to swoon."

The edges of his lips twitched before he turned away, presenting me with his back. He lifted his shirt slowly, inch by inch, as if he still wasn't entirely sure he wanted to take it off. The skin of his lower back was smooth, taut, punctured only by the ridge of his spine. But from the middle up, it was an entirely different story.

The scars stretched from one side of his broad back to the other. They were mostly horizontal, none vertical, and all of them straight. They were pink, raised, ugly things, and didn't belong on this handsome man's body.

I counted them, not because it mattered how many there were, but because it helped me focus on the patient, not the man or on the pain he must have felt at the time the scars were inflicted. In this instance, his memory loss was a blessing.

There were twenty.

"Josie?"

I drew in a deep breath and let it out slowly. He needed me to be a doctor now, not a sheltered girl from Mull who'd never seen such scars before.

I didn't need experience to know what made them. Even so, I touched one after the other to see how hard the skin was, how high they were raised, and simply because I wanted to touch them. I couldn't explain why.

"You've been struck by a switch or length of rope," I said in a voice that was steadier than I expected. "It didn't have sharp protrusions like nails or thorns." I pressed my palm to his back and smoothed it over the densest scarring and up to where the highest scar lashed his right shoulder. His skin was warm.

He drew in a deep breath and held it.

"You've been whipped," I murmured.

He let the breath out slowly. I had only confirmed what he already knew, or suspected.

"Can you tell when they were inflicted?" he asked.

"They're several months old. Less than a year, certainly not more. It's difficult to be more precise, as everyone's skin heals at different rates."

He lowered his shirt but did not turn around. I was grateful. The healer in me knew what to say, but the woman did not. What did one say to a man who'd been whipped twenty times yet couldn't remember it?

"Thank you," he said.

"You already guessed."

"We didn't know how old they were."

"We?"

"I'm not the only one with scars like this, but I have the most. Max and Brant have a few, as do some of the other guards. As far as I know, the rest of the staff don't have any, but we haven't discussed it with everyone, only those we know best."

"It's hardly a casual conversation starter."

He brushed the sand off his feet and put on his boots. "I'd better go. The king won't leave the palace without me escorting him, and he likes to walk around the gardens in the late afternoon with his favorites."

"Is he afraid of an assassination attempt in his own garden? By whom?"

"By anyone. He's a fearful man. It took some convincing for him to invite the nobles into the palace, and for the first week afterward, I had to follow him everywhere *inside* too."

"He must trust you. I wonder why."

He lowered the boot and arched his brows.

"I mean, I wonder how he knew to trust you if he has no memory."

"You trust me and you don't know me well. You wouldn't have met me here if you hadn't. For future reference, don't meet strange men on a cove accessible only by a steep staircase and water, particularly since you can't swim."

"You're only a little bit strange," I said, hoping to earn a smile from him and failing. "I suppose I trust my instincts, and they're telling me you're not going to hurt me. The king must have good instincts too. Unless he remembers you from his past." And unless he was lying about his memory loss, I wanted to say, but I held my tongue. The extent of King Leon's memory loss was a sore point for Hammer, yet I knew he had doubts. He must. But he'd made it clear he wouldn't discuss those doubts with me.

"Your instincts may be good, but you should still be careful," he said. "I hear there was trouble at one of the taverns last night."

"A man died in my father's surgery. He couldn't save him." I shivered. Even though I'd seen death before, I wasn't used to it like my father. I couldn't imagine ever growing used to it.

I felt Hammer's gaze on me but couldn't meet it. I changed the subject instead. "Your men are crawling all over Mull. They're the talk of the village. Have you learned anything new about the poisoner or who sold him the poisons?"

"Not yet."

"Could the man you were chasing through the forest have something to do with it?"

"It's possible."

"He wasn't an escaped servant then?"

He blinked at me. "I don't chase the servants."

"Your men fetched the maid who came into the village."

"Fetched, not chased." He tied up his bootlaces. "She was confused. She was better off being around people with the same condition as her. Where else can she go?"

It was a fair point, and the guards had been gentle with her. "Is she well now?"

"Better."

"If you want my father to look at her—"

"She's fine. Thank you for your concern." He was in command again, the stern captain of the palace guards, not the vulnerable man who'd lost his memory. "That man in the forest wasn't a servant," he went on. "If he was, we would have known his name."

"I suppose. He can't be the one who sold the poisons to the poisoner either. Tam Tao described the man on the pier as Zemayan, and he didn't look Zemayan. I suppose he was just a poacher or vagrant passing through, hoping to find something to eat from your kitchen garden."

"Vagrants and poachers don't ride good horses."

He had a point. "So who do you think he was?"

139

"A spy, but I don't know who for. We found him sneaking around the palace grounds. When I questioned him, he gave evasive answers. He escaped before he could be escorted away."

He put out his hand and I took it and stood. His thumb stroked mine before letting go. Or perhaps I'd only imagined the stroke.

He picked up his doublet and removed something from the pocket. "For your time," he said, offering me some ells.

I turned and marched off. "I'm not accepting payment for this." I wanted to say more, but I couldn't tell him that I came in a non-professional capacity. I came in the hope to learn more about him, as a friend.

He drew alongside me, still holding the coins, and opened his mouth to speak.

"Do not insult me again," I said before he insisted I accept the money.

He pocketed the coins. "I don't know when we'll meet again. If someone in the palace becomes ill or is injured, I'll send for your father. Perhaps you will come to assist him."

I glanced at him but he wasn't looking at me. He focused on the stairs straight ahead.

"Yes," was all I said. I wished it would be as simple as waiting until we were needed, but I suddenly doubted I'd ever see the captain again. If my father had his way, we would leave Mull, and I would never see the palace inhabitants again. I'd never see Meg and my other friends, and my patients would have to give birth without my presence.

Surely Father couldn't have been serious about leaving. Surely it was all talk stemming from his fears. If not, he'd have a fight on his hands. I wasn't leaving Mull.

We climbed the stairs in silence and he offered me a ride back to the village, albeit reluctantly. "I don't want to get you into trouble with your father," he said.

"I'll walk. Thanks anyway."

I watched as he mounted in an easy, practiced move and rode off. He knew how to ride. He couldn't have become that proficient in just a matter of months. Yet another piece to the Captain Hammer puzzle.

I walked quickly home, turning over the things I'd learned

about him and trying not to picture his scarred back. I'd send a jar of ointment to the palace but I couldn't imagine the men rubbing it into one another's backs, even if they did know it would help the skin to heal faster. Perhaps they each had a maid who'd do it for them. Perhaps Hammer did.

Yet another thing I didn't want to picture.

I was hot and thirsty by the time I arrived home. "I'm back," I called out to Father in the surgery. The door was ajar but he didn't answer. He might simply be busy, lost in his work, or he might be giving me the silent treatment as punishment for leaving the house when he'd asked me not to.

The kitchen showed no signs that he'd entered it during my absence. I filled a cup with water from the pail by the door. It was almost empty. I wondered if Father would allow me out to the well to fill it or insist on coming with me. This was getting ridiculous, and I would tell him so.

"Father," I said, pushing open the workshop door, "I don't—" I stopped, the words dying on my lips.

He lay slumped over the desk, notes and books scattered around him. His hair was dangerously close to the heat box, but the lumps of peat had burned away. How long had he been asleep? I didn't recognize the contents of the dish he'd been testing, some of which had spilled onto an open book. Behind the burnt smell was a sweet, sickly odor.

"Father? Father, wake up." I shook his shoulder but he didn't move. "Father!" I gave him a more violent shake and his hand slipped off the desk. The fingers brushed the floor. I tilted his head to the side and pushed his hair off his forehead to get a better look at his face.

It was the same color as the dead man who'd been collected that morning.

CHAPTER 10

The rest of the day passed in a blur. I must have fetched Meg's parents, because I remembered her mother steering me to the kitchen and trying to feed me. Her husband took charge of the body and the following day, I buried my father beside my mother.

Then I cried. I'd never cried so much in my life, not even when my mother died. At six, I hadn't really understood that she wasn't coming back. At twenty-four, I knew the finality of death. For the first time in a long time, I prayed to both Hailia and Merdu, and hoped that the afterlife was a real place and I would one day meet my parents there.

I stayed with Meg's family for two nights but on the third day, I insisted on going home. While they were pleasant enough, I knew they struggled to feed an extra mouth, and Meg's brother looked at me in a way I'd not noticed before. For a youth who'd always treated me like another sister, and an annoying one at that, his new attentiveness was unnerving.

Despite being grateful to be home again, the house had an awful emptiness about it. No patients came. They'd all given me their condolences at the burial ceremony, but none had returned for scheduled appointments.

"Give them time," Meg said a few days later as we sat in the kitchen. "They'll return when their aches and pains become too much or they run out of medicine."

I shook my head. "There are too many like Perri Ferrier. Besides, it doesn't matter if they don't mind being treated by a woman, I can't treat them anyway. I'll be thrown in jail if I do."

"I'm sure it's just a warning first, then a fine before they jail you. But yes," she added heavily, "it's illegal. You'll have to rely on your midwifery and selling medicines."

We both knew neither task could support me. Perhaps as the population grew, and more women joined the men, there might be more births. Until then, I'd have to supplement the fees with my father's savings. That meant searching for them, which meant going through his things. I couldn't face that yet.

"I can't believe he's gone," I said, choking back tears. I thought I'd used them all up, but it would seem I still had more to shed. "One day he's chastising me and the next...silence."

"Not even a warning," Meg said with a shake of her head.

I sat back with a thud. "There had been a warning." I cast a glance toward the larder. "He'd been looking for catspaw."

"What's that used for?"

"Heart problems. It helps stabilize an irregular beat. It's not a cure, though. Nothing can cure disease of the heart. Hailia," I murmured. "I suspected the catspaw was for him but didn't press him. How could I be so stupid, Meg? How can I be so selfish as to not notice when my own father was ill?"

She drew me into a hug. "You're not selfish, Josie. You're the least selfish person I know."

I shook my head. "Not that day. That day, I wanted to get away from him. I met with Captain Hammer at Half Moon Cove."

Her eyes widened. "Well. I see." She nudged me and smiled. "No wonder you won't look twice at my brother."

"It's not like that. He had a professional question to ask me."

"Then why not come here and ask your father?"

"It's difficult to explain."

"No, Josie, it's not. It sounds to me like he likes you."

I sighed. I couldn't tell her without divulging the palace secrets, and I wouldn't do that. Not even to Meg. She'd have to think what she wanted to think. I only hoped she didn't spread rumors through the village about Hammer and me.

"You will encourage him, won't you?" she asked, peering closely at me.

"What do you mean?"

"Now that you're all alone, you need someone to take care of you."

It was so absurd I would have laughed if I didn't feel so sad. "I'm not going to marry just because I'm alone."

"Why are you so against marriage?"

"I'm not. I don't want to marry just anybody though. Besides, I hardly know him." He hardly knew himself.

"You're talking about love again." She sighed and touched the wine-colored birthmark creeping up from her neck, over her jaw to her right ear. "Not all of us expect love to strike but I'm sure it will strike you—if you allow it to."

I put my arm around her and kissed the mark but said nothing. I'd offered her sympathy and words of hope many times over the years, yet she still believed herself ugly. It might not be such a problem if she weren't so desperate to marry, but after watching all of our other friends wed in recent years, she'd probably take the first man who asked.

"Ivor Morgrain has been very attentive to you," she said with a wicked gleam in her eye.

"I don't want to talk about Ivor."

"I'm sure you don't. Not after secretly meeting with the delectable captain of the palace guards at Half Moon Cove."

"Meg..." I shook my head. "I'm not in the mood."

"Of course. I'm sorry. Let me fix you something to eat. You're looking thinner than usual." She hugged me then entered the larder. She returned with some dark bread and shriveled apples. "Honestly, Josie, you can't eat this."

"I haven't been to the market since he died."

"I'll go for you in the morning." She set the bread down and began slicing it while I fetched her some money for the market.

I found a few ells in the tin where we kept enough for daily supplies and handed it all to her. "For tomorrow," I said. "I'll be fine in a day or two. I just don't feel like seeing people right now. I've had enough of sympathetic words to last a lifetime."

She skewered a slice of bread on the end of the knife and held it out to me. "Let me know when you are ready, and I'll come with you. Anyone who dares offer you sympathy will have to deal with me."

I smiled, despite myself, and gave her a hug.

* * *

THE FOOTMAN DRESSED in crimson palace livery standing on my doorstep looked familiar. It wasn't until he gave me a thorough inspection that I remembered seeing him in the palace's service corridors the night I'd become lost searching for the garrison. I hadn't trusted him that night and didn't want to be alone with him in a dark place. Now, I had nowhere to escape to. My father's warnings came back to me all at once.

The footman licked his lips. "The goddess shone down on Glancia when she made its women."

"Can I help you?" I asked.

His wet lips stretched into a smile, revealing an overcrowded mouth full of crooked teeth. He stepped forward. I moved to close the door in his face, but he thrust his foot into the gap. "Don't do that, miss. I have a message for the doctor. Is he in?"

"You can pass your message on to me."

His top lip lifted with his sneer. "Even the low-born ones act all high and mighty here." He sniffed. "Tell your father he's wanted at the palace urgently."

"Why? What's happened?"

"He's needed."

"Is Lady Miranda sick again?"

"Don't know."

I opened my mouth to tell him I'd go with him, but closed it again. I couldn't go. I wasn't qualified to treat anyone unless they were giving birth. While some villagers might not care about qualifications, the king's advisors and the nobles certainly would. I couldn't hide behind my father anymore. As his assistant, my presence in the sickroom was acceptable. Without him, it was not.

"Who sent you?" I asked the footman.

"Theodore."

"Please inform Theodore that my father died last week. He'll have to ask the finance minister's doctor for assistance, if he's still at the palace."

The footman was shocked into stepping back, allowing me to close and lock the door. I pressed my forehead against it and listened to the sound of receding hoof beats.

A very short time later, I opened the door to another knock. I was relieved to find Captain Hammer on the doorstep, not the footman. His cheeks were flushed and his hair windswept, but it didn't take away from the air of solemnity he brought with him.

"I'm saddened to hear about your father," he said. "We all are."

"Thank you." I opened the door wider but he hesitated.

"I don't want to intrude."

"You're not. I could do with the company. The house is so quiet and...oh, you probably have to get back to the king."

"Soon," he said, stepping past me. His hand went to the hilt of the sword strapped to his hip, as if it were a natural, ingrained reaction. When he realized what he was doing, his hand dropped to his side. After a moment, he clasped both hands behind him.

"Ale?" I asked, leading the way to the kitchen. "Or a tisane of mildwood to calm your nerves?"

His footsteps changed rhythm and I smiled to myself. I really shouldn't tease him when he was feeling ill at ease.

"Ale is fine. I can't stay long." He watched as I filled two cups then sat at the table when I sat. "I didn't know," he said simply. "I would have come sooner."

"I don't expect you to know, but thank you."

"Was his health failing?"

"His heart must have been. The morning of his death, he was taking catspaw for an irregular heartbeat. He never mentioned anything out of the ordinary to me, though." I stared into the cup, cradled between both hands. "It's so typical of him not to worry me, but I wish he had. I may not have been able to cure him, but I could have stayed here and been with him when he..." I bit down hard on my wobbling lip, determined not to cry. A tear escaped anyway. I dashed it away and drank deeply.

Hammer shifted on the chair, drawing his feet under it, and leaned forward. "I'm surprised to find you here. I thought you would be with relatives."

"I have none. I stayed at a neighbor's house for two nights, but I don't want to impose on them any longer. Besides, I had to face being on my own sooner or later."

He frowned. "You're going to remain here? Alone?"

"Of course. This is my home. Where else would I go?"

I was glad he let the matter drop. Perhaps his lack of memory meant he didn't know that young, unwed women rarely lived alone. The world accepted widows living on their own after their husbands died, but daughters of marriageable age moved in with relatives, no matter how distant. I could not name a single woman in a similar position to me. No matter. I would simply be the first.

"Is there anything I can do while I'm here?" he asked, looking up at the roof as if he expected to find it needing repairs. "Heavy lifting? Chopping firewood?"

"Thank you, but no. I've managed with an elderly father for years. Meg's brother—my neighbor—helps with anything I can't do myself."

"I see I don't have to worry about you."

It was nice that he did worry. "You have enough on your plate, Captain. Speaking of which, what happened at the palace that required my father's attendance?"

"Lady Lucia Whippler fainted while walking around the garden."

"How is she now?"

"She was resting in her room when I left to come here. The finance minister's doctor looked at her and suggested she simply got overheated. He prescribed bathing her feet in cool water."

"Were her feet swollen?"

"I don't believe so."

"Then bathing them won't achieve much." I looked out the window to the overcast sky. "I haven't been outside today but it didn't seem all that warm when I opened the door to you."

"It's not. It's pleasant and Lady Lucia walks with the king every day, when it's sometimes much warmer. She has never appeared to suffer from the heat before."

"Particularly on a mild day?"

"Precisely."

In my experience, women who fainted for no apparent reason usually had one thing in common—pregnancy.

"The king wasn't satisfied with Doctor Clegg's diagnosis and wanted your father to look at Lady Lucia," Hammer went on. "His Majesty trusts—trusted—your father after he successfully treated Lady Miranda."

"He must have been disappointed when Theodore told him of my father's death."

He concentrated on his cup before drinking.

"Captain? What did the king say?"

"The king can be selfish. He can't often see beyond his own needs."

I took that to mean he wasn't entirely sympathetic, but more frustrated that my father was no longer at his service. That didn't strike me as a good quality for a king to have but I held my tongue. Hammer was too loyal to want to hear my opinion. "What did he say?" I asked again.

"He told Thoedore to send for you. Theodore refused, telling him you're grieving. His Majesty then sought me out. I also refused to send for you."

"You came though."

"I wanted to make sure you're all right."

"You didn't have to."

His fingers stroked the cup. After a moment, he lifted it to his lips and drained the contents.

"But thank you," I said. "I appreciate it."

He set the cup down and stood. "I must go."

"I'm coming with you. Give me a moment to gather my things."

"No, Josie. You're grieving."

"That doesn't mean I can't be useful. I'm bored here, Captain. There's nothing to do except think, and right now, I don't want to think. Besides, I believe I know what might be ailing Lady Lucia."

His brows rose. "You do?"

"I'll need to see her to be absolutely certain."

"What is it?"

"I can't tell you," I said, heading to my father's workshop. I glanced at the desk and tried not to picture the way I'd found him that day, slumped forward, surrounded by his books and apparatus. I swallowed the ball of tears clogging my throat and picked up my pack. It already had the things I needed for this visit and I indicated to Hammer that I was ready.

"Do you suspect poisoning?" he asked as he opened the front door for me.

"No, but I will need to see her to completely rule it out." I locked the door and displayed the GONE FISHING sign.

Hammer waited for me by his horse. I would have to sit in front of him. I clutched my pack to my chest but handed it to him when he held out his hand for it.

"If her ailment is a threat to the king's safety, I'll have to insist you tell me," he said. "Patient confidentiality may be important to your profession, but saving the king's life is important to mine."

I smiled. A baby would not threaten the king's life, and his reputation would only be bolstered if it were his. Kings were lauded for their virility, even if their children were born out of wedlock. Commoners, on the other hand, were reviled. I may need to reassure Hammer and the king that he had nothing to fear if the test proved positive. They might not be aware of society's double standards.

Hammer assisted me onto the saddle then settled behind me. I was very aware of his presence and the stares from my neighbors. I nodded at Ivor Morgrain as we passed him walking along my street. He carried a clutch of wild flowers but it wasn't until he flung them onto the ground that I realized he was on his way to see me. Perfect timing. I did not want to be alone with Ivor. I'd already refused his offer of courtship last year, telling him my father needed me. I could no longer use that excuse.

"A word of caution, Captain," I said. "I am not a qualified doctor and should not be attending a patient. This visit needs to remain a secret."

"Doctor Clegg reminded the king that you can't attend patients. The king insisted, however, and the doctor graciously backed down. It was Theodore and myself who wouldn't allow you to come at this time."

"I must still insist on keeping my visit a secret. If the doctor thinks I'm reaching beyond my midwifery duties, he's within his rights to have me arrested."

"Arrested!" His breath brushed the nape of my neck. "For treating a patient in the palace at the king's request? That's absurd."

"It's the law."

He scoffed. "Be assured, King Leon wouldn't allow you to be arrested on his account, no matter what the law states."

"Even so, let's not put the king in a difficult position. If someone asks why I'm there, we shall say I'm calling on a maid who needs a midwife."

"That will only get the tongues wagging."

"Very well, we'll say I've come to visit…Quentin?"

"That will suffice. He has been asking to go to the village to see you. It's very annoying."

I laughed softly. "He's harmless and simply curious about medical matters. He wants to learn."

"He is inquisitive, but I don't think medicine is entirely to blame for his interest in you."

I turned to look at him better but he was focused on the road ahead. "Quentin is sweet, but I don't want to encourage him."

"Then don't call him sweet to his face. He'll take it as a compliment and never leave you alone. What about the man with the flowers?"

The question came so suddenly and unexpectedly that I couldn't think of an immediate answer.

"You saw him?" I said, somewhat pathetically.

"I couldn't fail to feel the sharpness of his glare. Do I need to smooth things over with him and reassure him that I'm simply transporting you to the palace?"

"Merdu, no. Let him think what he likes. Hopefully that'll put an end to his attentions. He has called on me three times this week alone and we ran out of conversation on his first visit." The flowers were a new development, though.

"As you wish," was all he said.

I was able to relax a little as we left the village and curious stares behind. I still felt self-conscious having the captain so close, but I tried to ignore him and simply enjoy the fresh air and the patchwork of farmlands and forest. I'd been inside far too long, wallowing in self-pity, when I should have been appreciative to be alive. Tomorrow, I would call on those who'd attended the funeral to thank them. I'd visit my father's patients and reassure them that I would help them if it were an emergency as long as they kept quiet about it. That led to thoughts of finding a new doctor for the village. Perhaps I would write to the college in Logios and request them to send a newly qualified one. I must also see to my own patients, two of whom were drawing close to their time.

"You think Lady Lucia is with child," Hammer said.

I'd been so lost in my thoughts that his words startled me. "What makes you say that?"

"It's the only reason you can give for coming to the palace with your medical bag. And you said yourself that you didn't want to put the king in a difficult situation by illegally seeing a patient. You're not the sort of person who wants to cause trouble for others."

"I might be. You don't know that."

"I'm a good judge of character, Josie." He sounded amused.

Our arrival at the palace earned us a few raised brows and curious stares from the other servants, but mostly they were too busy going about their work to notice. Indeed, it was the palace servants and not the visiting ones who took the most interest. I felt their gazes on me even after we passed by.

Unlike Miranda's rooms, there were no guards posted in the corridor outside Lady Lucia's. Like Miranda, she was housed on the first floor in a sizeable bedroom, but she did not have her own sitting room. Miranda must still be the favorite.

Hammer knocked on the door and a call of "One moment," came from the other side. It was several moments before we were invited in.

The patient sat up on a large bed, her long hair cascading around her, as bright as the golden palace gates. Her skin had a good color and her eyes were quick as they assessed me and then Hammer.

"Who are you?" asked her brother, standing beside the bed.

"Miss Cully will assess Lady Lucia's condition," the captain said.

"The doctor has already seen her. He has prescribed rest. You're the captain of the guards, are you not?"

"Captain Hammer. If you'll come with me, sir, Miss Cully needs to see the patient alone."

Lord Frederick bristled. "I'm staying with my sister."

"No, sir, you are not." Hammer stood aside to indicate Lord Frederick should go ahead of him.

Lord Frederick took his sister's hand. Knowing the rumors about them, I found I couldn't tear my gaze away from those linked hands. That's how I came to see his thumb caress hers. "I don't understand," he said. "Why does Miss Cully need to see my sister alone?"

"Isn't Cully the name of the doctor who attended Miranda?" Lady Lucia asked.

"I'm his daughter." I focused on the small dent on the tip of her otherwise fine nose in the hope the concentration would stop any tears from welling. "My father passed away last week."

That took the puff out of Lord Frederick's chest. "We're sorry for your loss, but I must protest again. You can't assume your father's role."

"I don't intend to."

Lady Lucia clicked her tongue and muttered, "For Merdu's sake. My brother has already told you, an actual doctor has prescribed rest. I was doing just that until you two barged in. Kindly leave or I'll inform the king that you've overstepped. I'm sure he'd be interested to learn you've been impersonating a doctor."

"I am not impersonating a doctor," I said hotly, "I am doing my duty as a midwife. I have reason to believe your fainting spell was a symptom of your delicate condition."

"My what?" It was blurted out with such fervor that the word delicate couldn't be applied.

Her brother's jaw dropped. He turned huge eyes onto his sister. "Lucia?" he whispered.

She withdrew her hand and crossed her arms. "I am not with child. Leave, Freddie, so this woman can go about her business and prove it."

"Sir," Hammer prompted when Lord Frederick continued to stare at his sister.

I set my pack on the dressing table and removed the jar of Baby's Breath salts. By the time I pocketed it, the men had left. "Lift your nightdress, my lady," I said.

She clicked her tongue but did as directed. "This is a waste of time. I'm still having my monthly courses."

I checked her abdomen and asked for a urine sample that she grudgingly obliged to give me. She retreated behind a privacy screen and I studied the room while I waited. It was elegantly furnished with thick curtains and rug. The view over the gardens was similar to the one afforded Lady Miranda. I looked out then returned to the opposite side of the bed. Something poking out from beneath the valance caught my eye. I knelt down and lifted the blue silk brocade to get a better look. A pair of men's shoes had been neatly placed under the bed alongside a folded shirt and pants.

"What are you doing?" Lady Lucia snapped.

CHAPTER 11

"You prying little wretch," Lady Lucia snapped. "How dare you spy on me!'

"I'm not spying," I said, surreptitiously removing the jar of Baby's Breath salts from my pocket as I stood. "I dropped this on the floor. It rolled under the bed."

Her nostrils flared and her eyes narrowed, turning her from beautiful to deadly in a moment. I eyed the chamber pot in her hands in case she decided to throw it at me.

She marched past me and set the pot on the dressing table beside my pack. "You're all the same here," she said with a sniff. "Impertinent and opinionated with no respect for your betters. You're not normal."

"I am not palace staff."

I added a pinch of Baby's Breath salts to the urine in the pot as she settled back on the bed with all the grace of a woman used to reclining all day. The salts did not change color.

"You're not with child," I said.

"I know that but you wouldn't listen. Freddie!" she called. "You can come back in."

The words were hardly out of her mouth when her brother barged through the door. "Well?"

She shook her head.

He sat heavily on the bed. "Thank the goddess."

My gaze connected with Hammer's, but he showed no signs of interest in the conversation.

"There is still the mystery of your fainting spell," I said to Lady Lucia. "Can you describe how you felt—"

"I am not speaking to you about it," she said. "The doctor has already seen me."

"She was hot, that's all," Lord Frederick said, rising once more. He really was quite handsome, but in an elegant, fine-boned way. He was all golden hair and coltish limbs with eyes that matched his sister's for quickness. "She's fine now."

"I'll inform the king," Hammer said.

"The doctor already has."

"Wait, Captain." Lady Lucia sank back against the pillows and arranged her hair around her shoulders. "Tell the king I am still feeling poorly. His company would cheer me enormously, and my health will benefit from his presence. Please suggest that he join me in here instead of taking a turn about the gardens."

Her brother squeezed her hand but she either didn't notice or pretended not to.

Hammer bowed then asked if I was ready to leave. Without being able to ask more questions, there was no point in staying. I had all the answers I needed anyway.

"Don't say a thing yet," Hammer said before I could speak in the corridor outside Lady Lucia's room. "We'll talk in Balthazar's office."

The master of the palace's office was situated in the northern wing, close to the garrison. Or possibly a little away from it. Perhaps. It was certainly on the ground level, that much I knew. Like the garrison, it was a room with a function other than decorative. The desk was covered with paperwork, ledgers and books, and there were more on a set of shelves. A colored map of the palace and its grounds covered an entire wall. The detail was very fine with each of the outbuildings and gardens labeled in neat script. The only other noticeable feature was a portrait of the king behind the desk dressed in somber gray and black, holding a quill pen in one hand and a document in the other.

Hammer closed the door. We were alone. He indicated I should sit then took up a position by the sideboard. "She's not with child?"

"No."

"So what caused her to faint?"

"Her need for attention. Specifically, her need for attention from the king."

He tilted his head to the side. "It was all an act?"

"I believe so, but without examining her at the time, I can't be certain. It's not hot out, so I doubt she fainted from the heat. The doctor didn't mention her bodice being laced too tightly?"

He shook his head.

"Her ankles weren't swollen, she's alert, and her skin has a healthy glow. As far as I can see, there's nothing wrong with her now. There's no reason for her to stay in bed."

"Except to have the king worry about her."

"And spend time with her alone instead of with her rivals."

He poured a glass of wine from the jug on the sideboard and handed it to me then poured another for himself. It seemed like a natural thing for him to do, despite being in another man's office.

"Did you notice their exchange when Lord Frederick returned to the room?" I asked. "While she was certain about the outcome, he wasn't. That means he knows she's been with someone. The question is, is that someone the king?"

"It's not the king."

"How do you know?"

He hesitated then said, "Between Theodore and myself, we know every move the king makes. He hasn't been alone with Lady Lucia."

How strange to have intimate knowledge of someone, yet not be considered their friend. "I saw clothing under the bed," I said. "Men's clothing, neatly folded beside a pair of shoes."

"She's entertaining someone?"

"More than entertaining. I'd say he's moved in with her."

"If I were a betting man, which I may be, I'd put my money on Frederick. If the rumors are true, he probably assumed he was the baby's father, if she was with child."

I couldn't meet his gaze. I couldn't be as detached as him in the face of such a scandal. "Lord Frederick was more attentive than any brother to his sister that I've known," was all I said. I may not have first hand experience of sibling relationships, but I'd seen the way Meg's brother treated her and it wasn't with the affection and kindness Lord Frederick showed to Lady Lucia. "Will you inform the king?"

"Not yet. If she becomes his favorite then I will to save him from embarrassment, but the badge of favoritism still belongs to Lady Miranda."

I wasn't surprised. The difference between the two women was as clear as night and day, and I knew both of them only a little. "Is Miranda happy to be his favorite? She didn't seem too sure of him when I last saw her."

"It's difficult to tell. When I see her, she's reserved, quiet. She keeps her thoughts to herself and when the king does insist on her opinion, it's measured. I can't tell if she's giving her own opinion or the one she thinks he wants to hear."

He didn't describe the woman I'd met. Miranda had seemed forthright enough to me. "Does the king agree with your assessment of her?"

"He seems to adore her. He's frustrated that she won't...give more of herself."

"You're not referring to her opinions, are you?"

The door opened and an elderly man limped in followed by Theodore. Theodore paused upon seeing us but the old man simply made his way to the desk, his walking stick thudding on the floorboards in a laborious rhythm.

"Make yourself at home, Hammer," he said.

The captain set down his cup and filled another with wine. "Balthazar, this is Miss Cully."

"I know." Balthazar finally reached the chair on the other side of the desk and sat with a deep exhale. The lines on his face—of which there were many—drew together in a wince of pain before spreading again. He was much older than my father, with a set of black eyes that fixed on me with an intensity that could strip paint.

"So this is she," he said, accepting the cup of wine from Hammer. "The woman who can't be a doctor and knows all our secrets."

"Not all," I said.

"Of course not. Not even we know all our secrets." He gave a dry bark of a laugh. "What do you think of that, Miss Cully?"

"Call me Josie. It doesn't seem right that I refer to you by your first names while you call me miss."

He placed the cup on the desk. His hands were as wrinkled as his face but the fingers were long and agile as he picked up a pen. "Is there a reason for your presence in my office, Hammer, or are you simply availing yourself of my wine?"

"Your wine is excellent," Hammer said, lifting his cup in salute. "Better than we have in the garrison. But Josie and I came here to talk in private. We've just come from Lady Lucia's room. She's not ill."

"Is she with child? Is that why the midwife has come?"

Theodore shook his head. "She can't be. The king hasn't..." He glanced at me and blushed.

"The king hasn't," Balthazar repeated, "but if Hammer's source is right, the brother has."

"He has," Hammer said. "He still is." He nodded thanks to me for that piece of information. "But she's not with child."

"Then why did she faint?" Theodore asked, taking a seat. Hammer remained standing by the sideboard, holding the cup loosely by his fingertips.

"I don't think she did," I said.

"She's acting ill for the king's attentions," Hammer told them. "So we believe."

"She's that desperate?" Theodore shook his head. "Desperate enough to poison her rival too?"

"She may have abandoned that plan now that Lady Miranda is being closely guarded. The king's taster is also sampling her food."

The scratching of Balthazar's pen filled the silence. He appeared to be lost in concentration. Hammer and Theodore exchanged glances and the silence stretched thin, finally breaking when Balthazar spoke without looking up.

"I have work to do. The festivities are only two days away and there's still much to be done. These things don't organize themselves. I'm sure you both have work to do that doesn't involve gossiping in my office."

"We're not gossiping," Theodore said. "We're trying to find the poisoner."

Balthazar finally looked up from his ledger. "I am not sure of many things, gentlemen, but I am sure of one. You won't find the poisoner in here. Josie, it was nice to meet you. You seem quiet. I like that, but I want you to leave, and take these oafs with you. I can't get anything done with their constant jabbering."

I expected one or both of them to retort but they did not, not even in jest.

I stood as Balthazar turned to the map on the wall. He squinted so hard his eyes almost disappeared into the wrinkles. "You should have some spectacles made," I said.

He grunted and continued to study the map.

I summoned some courage and forged ahead. "That map is beautiful. The detail is very fine. Did you draw it?"

"It was already here," he said absently.

"I wonder who made it. A very skilled cartographer, I expect. Certainly no one from Mull could do it. There are no records of its commission among all this paperwork?"

He picked up the pen and dipped it into the inkwell. "I take it back. You're not at all quiet."

"I'm simply curious. Your predicament is a strange one and the palace and all the things in it are a mystery. In my profession, mysteries need to be solved if patients are to survive."

"Your profession as a midwife, you mean?" he asked as he wrote. "I would have thought there was very little mystery in how and why babies come into the world."

Beside me, Theodore shifted his weight from one foot to the other. He gave his head a slight shake. Hammer didn't move. He watched Balthazar very closely.

"Hammer, see that Josie is escorted from the palace," Balthazar said. "We wouldn't want her getting lost again."

"Again?" I prompted.

"When you went looking for the garrison the night you were supposed to remain in Lady Miranda's rooms, you got hopelessly lost."

"How do you know about that?"

He finally looked up from the ledger and fixed me with that unnerving stare again. "I know everything that happens here. Now if you don't mind, I have work to do."

Theodore took my arm and tugged me toward the door. I followed him out, Hammer at my heels.

"What are you doing, Josie?" Theodore hissed when Hammer closed the door. "Don't anger him."

"I wasn't trying to anger him," I said. "I thought he might have answers about the palace."

"He doesn't."

"Have you considered that he might be lying to you?" I asked. "Or perhaps the king is? Or both?"

"Balthazar is above suspicion," Theodore said. "There's no evidence he's lying, and I have every reason to believe he has also lost his memory. He's merely a recalcitrant old man with a fierce temper and a lot of work to do. He doesn't suffer fools. Trust me, it's best to stay on his good side. When he loses his temper, the entire palace quakes."

"He makes the Rift seem like a mere tremble." Hammer indicated I should follow Theodore.

"He's not the only one," Theodore muttered.

I let the matter drop. Neither man was going to engage in speculation with me. Their loyalty was a credit to them, but I hoped it didn't blind them. To be fair, there was nothing to indicate Balthazar knew more than the rest of the staff. The king, on the other hand, seemed to be lying. He knew about women not being allowed into the Logios colleges, for one thing.

Or was I allowing my imagination to run away? It was entirely possible. Hammer was right when he said it would be a cruel person who withheld information from them, and he was in the best position to know the king, along with Theodore.

Yet I couldn't shake my doubts as I followed two of the king's most trusted staff through the underbelly of complex passages. Theodore paid me from a purse tucked into his pocket and veered off down one corridor, while Hammer and I took a different route that led outside. We emerged from the palace to find dusk had settled. Two footmen lit the torches between the palace and kitchen commons to light the way for the staff. Smells of roasted meats filled the air. My stomach rumbled, reminding me I hadn't eaten a proper meal in days. Grief was only partly to blame. I needed to economize now that the patients no longer came. Until I found my father's savings, I would not be enjoying a feast the likes of the one I smelled.

"Max," Hammer said, greeting his sergeant as he trotted up to us. "What's wrong?"

Max joined us, a little out of breath, and nodded a greeting to me. "I've been looking everywhere for you, Captain. The king wants to go for a walk."

"Damn it," Hammer muttered. It was the first time I'd seen him annoyed by an order from the king. "I'm taking Josie home."

"I'll do it."

Hammer tapped a finger on the hilt of his sword. "Let me speak with him."

"He's in the forecourt by the fountain."

Hammer marched off and Max followed. I trailed behind, not entirely sure what I was supposed to do. We rounded the long pavilion that acted as a division between the staff commons and the forecourt. Even though the torches had been lit behind us, it was like stepping from dusk into daylight. Dozens upon dozens of torches blazed around the forecourt perimeter and on every balcony, their flames picking out the gold on the balustrades. Looking at the palace, bathed in a golden glow, it was easy to believe why rumors of magic hadn't abated. It was a breathtaking spectacle, the likes of which I'd never imagined.

The cluster of ladies and gentleman near the fountain acted as a beacon to the king's location. Some were in conversation with him, others simply seemed to be hovering in the hopes he'd notice them. As we drew closer, I recognized two of the ladies in his sphere—Miranda and Lady Violette Morgrave.

Hammer strode up to them and bowed to the king. "Sire."

"There you are, Captain," His Majesty said. "I've been waiting for you." He held out a hand to Miranda. "Shall we?"

"One moment, sire," Hammer said. "A word, please."

A flicker of panic passed over the king's face. They moved away from the nobles toward us, close enough for me to hear the worry in the king's voice when he asked Hammer if something had happened.

"Miss Cully came to the palace to check on Lady Lucia," Hammer told him.

The king looked at me. "Is she all right, Miss Cully?"

"There appears to be nothing wrong with her now," I said as I curtseyed. "Whatever caused her to faint has passed, but Doctor Clegg advised her to rest."

"Then rest she shall have. Is that all, Hammer?"

"I was about to escort Miss Cully home. It's growing dark and she should not go alone."

"That hardly requires your personal attention. One of your men can do it. Max!"

Max bowed. "Yes, sire."

"Take Miss Cully to wherever she wishes to go. I can't spare the captain." He cast a glance over his shoulder at the two ladies. They curtseyed in unison, like puppets on a string. Miranda lowered her gaze but Lady Morgrave did not. She gave the king a coy smile.

"Miss Cully has just suffered the recent loss of her father," Hammer went on. His voice sounded strained to me, but the king gave no indication he heard it. "She shouldn't enter the house alone at night, and—"

"Max can do it, Hammer. He's built like an ox. No one will dare cross him" He clasped the captain's arm and leaned closer. "I understand, but *my* need of your protection is greater."

"Allowing me to go with her would show how much you appreciated her for saving Lady Miranda's life."

"She didn't save it, her father did." The king softened his words with a smile for me. "You were an excellent assistant, Miss Cully, and I ordinarily would allow the captain to take you home, but not today. It's a fine evening and Lady Miranda would like to take a turn around the gardens. You understand, I'm sure."

"Of course," I said, curtseying again.

He smiled. "Good." He went to walk off, but stopped. "Oh, Miss Cully, I am very sorry about your father."

"Thank you, Your Majesty." He'd turned away before I finished speaking.

Hammer watched him go with a glare so icy I thought the king might shiver.

"Captain?" Max asked. "Your orders?" How curious that he didn't follow the king's orders without question, but waited for his captain's.

"Make sure you escort her inside," Hammer said. "Check the entire house before you go."

"Please do," I said, batting my lashes. "I don't think we have rats, but it's always good to be thorough, and it'll make me feel so much better to have a man as strong as an ox to protect me from them."

Both men stared at me. "Is she teasing us?" Max asked Hammer.

"Yes," Hammer said.

"Did we deserve it?"

"I have no idea but I think if we ignore her, she'll stop."

Max frowned at his captain. "I can't ignore her. I have to take her home."

Hammer's short laugh came from the depths of his chest, and caused Max's frown to deepen. Hammer clapped his sergeant on the shoulder then joined the king.

Max offered to take my pack and we were about to walk off when Miranda broke away from the group.

"Josie," she said, clasping my hand in both of hers. "I overheard the exchange. I wasn't aware of your father's passing. I am deeply sorry for your loss." The shine in her eyes produced a response from my own and tears welled again. "I owe him my life. If there's anything I can do for you, please just ask."

"Thank you, my lady."

"Miranda, remember?" She smiled then kissed my cheek. She smelled of spring flowers. I hoped I didn't smell of Baby's Breath salts and Lady Lucia's urine.

She rejoined the king and they walked slowly toward the palace's main entrance to reach the formal gardens on the other side. Lady Violette Morgrave walked on his left, laughing at something he said. Behind them, Hammer kept pace and behind him, several more nobles followed. It was quite the procession.

Max sent one of the guards roaming the forecourt to organize transport for me. The guard passed Quentin coming through the front gate with two others. Quentin spotted us and grinned. Then his grin vanished.

He hugged me wordlessly. I felt his sob ripple through his

body. "Don't cry," I said, patting his back. "Or you'll make me cry too."

He pulled away and swiped at his cheeks with the back of his hand. "Sorry," he choked out. "I'm so sorry, Josie."

I drew him into another hug and he clung to me until Max coughed.

"Compose yourself, man," Max barked. "You're a palace guard. Have some respect for your uniform."

"Yes, sir." Quentin nodded and wiped his nose on his sleeve.

"You're no better than a little girl," said Sergeant Brant, joining us with Erik. They must have all been on duty outside, but none seemed to be particularly keen to resume patrolling.

Erik clasped my shoulder. "My heart broke for you, Josie."

"Thank you, Erik."

"We were all sorry to hear of Doctor Cully's passing," Max said simply if somewhat awkwardly. "Men, you have work to do. I suggest you do it."

"There's nothing to do," Quentin said with a lift of his shoulders.

"The point of patrolling isn't to be doing anything, it's to be seen. Our presence reassures people, particularly now that it's getting dark."

Quentin looked around and spread his arms out. "We *are* seen."

"*His* presence won't reassure anyone," Brant said with a snort. "Come on, Erik, some of us don't shirk out duties."

"What is shirk?" Erik asked.

"Can't I stay here and talk to Josie?" Quentin whined as they walked off.

"Josie's leaving," Max said. "I'm escorting her home. She's living alone now and shouldn't be entering an empty house after dark."

Brant and Erik returned, causing Max to mutter under his breath. "Alone?" Erik asked. "You have no family, Josie?"

"None," I said. "But it's quite all right. I'm well known in Mull. No one will harm me."

"Even so," Max said.

"You and the captain both seem to forget that babies have no concept of day or night. They arrive when they want to arrive—

and rarely to a schedule. I will have to leave the house at night if required."

From the look on Max's face, he hadn't thought of that. He cast a glance at the palace's main entrance through which Hammer had just disappeared.

"I'll take her home," Quentin piped up.

"And get out of standing on your feet all night?" Brant grabbed my pack off Max. "I'll do it."

Max snatched it back. "You're on patrol."

Brant drew himself up to his full height. He towered over Max. "You don't outrank me."

Max grabbed my arm and marched me away. He didn't stop until we were outside the palace gates. Finally he let me go and looked back to the forecourt. The other guards had dispersed.

I let out a breath, not quite sure why I'd been holding it. "Thank you, Max. I don't want Brant taking me home. I can't explain why, there's just something about him I don't like."

"I didn't do it for you, I did it for me. Hammer doesn't like Brant either, and he'd tear me to shreds if I let you go home with him."

"Why doesn't he like Brant?"

The carriage rolled up and Max never did answer me.

* * *

I SPENT the following morning checking on the two expectant mothers closest to their due date then returned home via the market. The money from my previous day's visit to the palace bought enough food to last several days, but there was little left over. I resolved to spend the afternoon searching for the savings my father always spoke about.

My plans changed when I arrived home to see a palace carriage waiting at the front of my house and Erik giving one of my neighbor's children a ride on his shoulders. The girl squealed with delight and clung to his thick ropes of hair as if they were reins.

"Perhaps you should be working in the schoolroom, not the garrison," I said, smiling.

He crouched and the girl slid down his back to the ground.

"Good horsey," she said, tugging his hair then running off to her mother, who scowled in the doorway.

"The mother is angry," he said heavily.

"She's probably a little worried about you. She wouldn't have seen a Marginer before, and you're very big."

"Big is not scary."

"Are you sure? Have you never met anyone bigger than yourself?"

"I do not know."

"Oh. Right. You don't remember. Sorry." I indicated the carriage. "Is everything all right at the palace?"

"A dog is dead."

I wasn't sure if I'd heard him correctly and asked him to repeat it. He placed his hands in front of him like paws, stuck out his tongue, and panted. He followed up the pantomime with a bark. I hadn't misheard then. "Come, Josie. Come to palace."

"But why? If the dog has already died, what can I do?"

He glanced at the coachman, perched on the driver's seat. "Check for poison," he whispered.

I hadn't thought of that. "I see. Let me get some things first." I exchanged my pack for my father's medical bag and rejoined Erik at the door where he waited. "Did the captain insist I come?"

He nodded. "He tells king it is best. The king agrees."

"Does Doctor Clegg know?"

He nodded at my neighbor's door. "He looked like her when Theodore tell him king wants poison expert."

Hopefully since it was a dog and not a person, I couldn't be fined for giving medical advice. I wasn't entirely sure of the extent of the law. If the king sent for me, then I ought to be safe, the dog notwithstanding.

Instead of taking me to the palace gate, the carriage stopped at the stables on the long approach road. Erik ushered me through the colonnaded entrance. I hardly had time to take in the high vaulted ceiling and what appeared to be a large indoor arena when we were once again outside. Erik strode across the courtyard, unconcerned by the dozens of horses being put through their paces under the watchful eye of the stable staff. I hugged the bag to my chest and followed.

The building on the far side of the courtyard housed individual stalls, most of them occupied. The smell of horse was stronger, as well as an undercurrent of leather. The staff wore the dun colored uniforms befitting outdoor servants, all with the House of Lockhart coat of arms embroidered onto the chest.

"Is it much further?" I asked Erik. "Only this bag is growing heavy." We must have passed a hundred stalls already, all housing more than one horse, and we'd not even traveled half the length of the building. If the buildings on the east and west of the courtyard also contained stables, I calculated close to a thousand horses.

Erik took the bag from me then continued on until he reached the last stall. A guard on duty by the door nodded at Erik then left. Erik pushed open the door and set my bag down beside the body of the dog. It was one of the hunters I'd seen in the kitchen.

"Did he die here?" I asked.

Erik remained by the door, his steady gaze on the corridor, his stance evenly weighted. He was standing guard, I realized. "Commons courtyard," he said.

Near the kitchen then. "Did he ingest anything?"

"Ingest?"

"Eat or drink?"

"I do not know."

I knelt by the animal and opened its jaw. The stench of vomit tumbled out along with the regurgitated contents of its last meal. I buried my nose and mouth in my elbow, drew in a breath, and resumed my task. Beneath the smell was another familiar one. It was sweet. Too sweet.

I knew where I'd smelled it before.

I fell back and gasped for air, but that only filled my nostrils with a riot of odors. I scrambled to my feet and raced past Erik to a door that led out to the training courtyard. I sucked in several deep breaths, preferring the smell of dung over the stink of vomit and poison.

"Josie?" I recognized Hammer's voice and looked to see him and Quentin striding toward me. "Josie, are you unwell?"

I put a hand to my rapidly beating chest. It felt tight, my face hot. I nodded to reassure him but couldn't yet form the words to speak.

Hammer's face appeared before mine, very close. He peered into my eyes and pushed back the hair from my forehead. His action was gentle but his hands were rough from the calluses.

"You're flushed," he said. "Quentin, fetch a cup of water and a damp cloth. Erik, return to your post."

I closed my eyes as they ran off and concentrated on my breathing instead of the captain's worried eyes. A firm hand gripped my elbow and an arm circled my waist.

"Sit down out of the sun." Hammer directed me to a bench under the eaves and crouched before me. "You shouldn't have come if you're unwell."

"I'm not unwell."

Quentin returned and handed me a cup of water. I drank it all. "Erik said you ran out of the stall," he said. "Do you feel sick?"

Hammer took the cloth from him and sat beside me. He pressed the cloth to my forehead then against the back of my neck. It was blessedly cool. Neither man pressed me for an explanation, but the worry did not leave their faces.

"I did feel sick," I told them, "but not from an illness. The smell coming from that dog's mouth…"

"Was vile?" Quentin filled in.

"Familiar. I noticed it in my father's room the day he died."

Silence. Then Quentin swore.

The pressure of the cloth on my neck eased. I lifted my gaze to Hammer's. His eyes were huge. I'd managed to shock him.

"You think he was poisoned?" he asked.

I nodded. "I'm certain of it."

CHAPTER 12

"*D*id you find evidence of poisoning on your father's body?" Hammer asked.

I shook my head. The dog and Lady Miranda vomited, but there was no sign of discharge from my father's mouth or nose, yet the smell couldn't be mistaken. "The poisoner must have cleaned up."

"To make it look like he died of natural causes," Quentin said with a nod. "Clever."

"And Lady Miranda?" Hammer asked. "Did you smell the same smell on her?"

"No," I said. "It's possible that by the time we reached her, the smell had dissipated since the discharge had been removed to the bathroom. Or a different poison may have been used on her."

"I don't understand," Quentin said. "Why did the poisoner kill your father? He didn't know the murderer's identity."

I tried to think of the things my father said on the day of his death, what he'd done and where'd he gone, but I could think of nothing that implied he knew the poisoner's identity.

"Describe the room to me when you found him," Hammer said. "How did you find him? Was anything out of place?"

I could hardly recall any of it beyond my shock and sadness. "He was slumped over his desk. There were some books within his reach, but I didn't notice which ones." I closed my eyes against the rush of tears and fought not to cry. It was not the time for tears, it was the time for clear thought. It didn't help my concentration when Hammer folded my hand into his.

"Take your time," he said, his warm voice washing over me.

"The heat box was nearby. I remember because I worried about his hair burning. The contents of a dish had burned and the smell lingered. It almost hid the smell of the...of the poison."

"Do you remember putting away the books?" Hammer asked. "Could you find them again?"

"My neighbor tidied up."

"I'd put money on them being books about poisons," Quentin said. "Seems like Doctor Cully knew he'd been poisoned and was trying to make an antidote for himself."

"But ran out of time," I finished for him. "Merdu. I cannot believe it. My father was poisoned. But why?"

"He must have learned something that could identify the poisoner," Hammer said. "Did he act differently that day? Did he seem anxious?"

"He was always anxious lately, but even more so after Lady Miranda was poisoned." I blinked watery eyes at him. "He knew even then, didn't he? He knew who poisoned her but he didn't say. Why wouldn't he tell you?"

"Perhaps he only suspected and didn't want to accuse anyone without proof."

"Even so, he should have mentioned his concerns to you. I cannot believe he would withhold something so important."

"He had a daughter to protect, and a livelihood. He wouldn't want to jeopardize either for people he didn't know."

I thought back to the day I'd gone out to meet Hammer at Half Moon Cove, and come back to find my father dead. The strangeness of that day was etched into my soul, a memory that would be with me forever. I'd been happy seeing Hammer on the beach, and sickened by the scars on his back, then overwhelmed by immense sorrow upon finding my father. It was difficult to wade through the tumult of emotions to remember the conversations I'd shared with Father.

"He went out that afternoon," I said. "That I do remember. He didn't take his medical bag and wouldn't tell me where he was going."

"You think he confronted the killer?" Quentin asked.

"It doesn't seem like something he would do. He was a cautious man, full of fear." With good reason, it would seem. "His heart had been bothering him, but now...I wonder if that was a clue as to the type of poison that was used on him." A small sob escaped and I lowered my head. "It would mean he'd been poisoned more than once, or perhaps that it was slow acting." I wish I knew more. I felt woefully unqualified.

Hammer put his arm around me and drew me into a hug, his chin resting on the top of my head, his thigh against mine. The only man I'd been this close to before was my father. It should have been thrilling and exciting, but I simply felt comfortable.

"Captain," came a raspy, deep voice. "I need that stall."

Hammer's arm retreated and he stood to address a man with a pointed gray beard and ginger hair. Quentin took his place on the seat beside me.

"Grand equerry," he whispered. "He's in charge of the stables."

"You'll have the stall back soon," Hammer said to the grand equerry. "Miss Cully, do you need to look at the body again?"

"I want to collect samples of the discharge," I said rising.

He nodded. The grand equerry wrinkled his nose. "Why? What's this about?"

"Your stall will be available again soon," Hammer told him. "Miss Cully, if you please."

I walked with him back inside, Quentin following.

"You're going to test the discharge?" Hammer asked me as we approached Erik on guard by the stall.

"I'd like to create an antidote for the poison in case the poisoner uses it again. To do that, I need to identify the type of poison first. It could take some time though, without Father's guidance."

"I'll help," Quentin piped up. "I can leave with her now and act as her escort, Captain."

"You will not be her escort," Hammer said. "I will."

Erik smirked at Quentin.

"You can assist Josie with her tests this afternoon," Hammer went on.

"Ha!" Quentin barked in Erik's direction.

"You only help her because you are not good guard, like me," Erik said.

Quentin flicked dust off Erik's sleeve and smiled up at the Marginer. "Or because I am not going to worry Josie's neighbors when I'm left alone with her."

Erik frowned. "I do not frighten all." He tapped his chest. "Not when I am horsey."

"Horsey? Have you lost your mind as well as your memory?"

I used a knife to scrape some of the contents from the dog's mouth into a jar. Hopefully it would be enough.

Hammer signaled for Erik to wrap the poor animal in a hessian cloth and remove it. "I'll have a carriage prepared for you, Josie."

"And me," Quentin said.

"You'll ride. You need the practice."

The three of us crossed the courtyard and returned to the avenue, only to be hailed by the king, alighting from a sedan chair carried by two of the burliest men I'd ever seen. No less than a dozen sedan chairs stopped behind him and their passengers stepped out. Miranda waved at me. I curtseyed.

"Captain Hammer, just the man I needed to see." His Majesty approached us but he only had eyes for Hammer. It was as if I weren't even there.

"How can I help you, sire?" Hammer said.

The king checked that none of the other nobles were nearby. He didn't seem to care that Quentin and I could overhear him. "I need to go hunting."

"You hate hunting."

"Yes, but it's necessary. The gentlemen need some sport and the ladies…" He heaved a sigh. "The ladies are at each other's throats. They need constant entertainment or they'll snap one another's heads off. There's only so much theater, opera and card games one can take. Balthazar convinced me that a hunt will tire them out. He sent the grand hunstman and grand equerry a message to prepare horses, dogs and whatever else we need. But *I* need *you*."

"I'm busy at present," Hammer said.

The king bristled. "You are not too busy to obey your king's orders."

"I'll have six of my men accompany you. Six of them are better than one of me."

The king turned his ear to Hammer as if he'd not heard correctly. "Are you defying me, Captain? You do recall what happens to people who refuse my order?"

Hammer's fists closed at his sides but he otherwise didn't move a muscle. Quentin, however, swallowed audibly and I found I couldn't swallow at all. I didn't dare draw attention to myself.

"You won't confine me to the cells," Hammer went on. "If you do, you'll never leave the palace again."

The muscles in the king's jaw flexed and his nostrils flared. "What has got into you lately?" he snarled through gritted teeth. "You've become defiant."

Hammer simply stood like an impenetrable tower, looking down on his surroundings with cool indifference. He must be very sure of his value to the king to defy him like this. "I'm doing my job," Hammer said. "The poisoner has attacked again."

"What!" the king exploded. "Why didn't you say? Who has been poisoned?"

"A dog. It's dead. I didn't mention it because I didn't want to alarm you." Hammer's gaze slid to the cluster of nobles who'd all looked up upon the king's outburst. "I didn't want to alarm anyone."

"You should have mentioned it to me."

"I'm mentioning it now, sire, after only just learning that it was indeed poison that killed the dog. Miss Cully confirmed my suspicions."

The king looked at me for the first time. "I see. Do you have an antidote for this poison, Miss Cully?"

"I'm returning home to make one now, Your Majesty."

He pressed a hand to his stomach. He looked a little pale but I resisted asking him how he felt. "Good. See that she has every-thing she needs, Captain. Hopefully this latest development will speed up your investigation. It's taking far too long to bring the culprit to justice. What have you been doing all this time, anyway?"

"Gathering evidence," Hammer said.

"Gather faster."

"It's not as easy as that," I said, immediately biting the inside of my cheek. Hailia, why couldn't I keep my mouth shut?

The king slowly turned his icy glare onto me. "You have something to say, Miss Cully?"

I cleared my throat. I'd already dug a hole for myself, now I had to climb out of it with as much dignity as I could without making it deeper. "The captain is working as hard as he can, sire. I may not know him well, but I do know he won't allow the poisoner a moment of freedom if he can help it. When you employed Hammer as the captain of your guards, you chose well." There. Hopefully giving him some credit would make amends for my loose tongue.

The king's features softened. He grunted a laugh. "It seems you have another admirer, Captain." He looked to his nobles, now watching with interest. "On second thought, I don't think I'll be needing your services, Captain. A hunt in the open with weapons seems like a bad idea given the circumstances."

"Very wise," Hammer said.

"Ride alongside my chair back to the palace."

Hammer bowed. "Yes, sire."

The king strolled to the sedan chairs and gave the nobles the news that he no longer wished to hunt. It was initially met with long faces that quickly lifted as they realized it was in their best interests to think the king's decision to stay indoors was precisely what they wished too. A discussion of the weather ensued.

Hammer signaled to a groom to bring him a horse. "Wait for me here in the stables, Josie. Quentin, stay with her."

He strode off before I could tell him I would be fine, or that I wasn't another of his admirers, that I was merely defending him as anyone would.

"Come into the shade, Josie," Quentin said as we watched the king's sedan chair leave. Some of the other nobles followed in theirs, including Lady Lucia. She was one of the first to trail after the king, and her brother behind her. It would seem she'd decided to be well again.

Some of the sedan chairs had already departed, empty, leaving the remaining nobles stranded unless they decided to walk. Only Miranda set off toward the palace on foot while the other ladies gave orders to stable boys to find them transport back to the palace gate.

"I ought to warn her about the latest poisoning," I said to Quentin.

"Wait, Josie. I'm supposed to protect you."

"Then you'd better walk with me."

I intended to give Lady Violette Morgrave, Lady Deerhorn, and the duchess of Gladstow a wide berth but changed my mind. It was clear from the way they watched Lady Miranda that she was the object of their discussion. I slowed to an amble as I drew closer.

"I don't know what he sees in her," Lady Morgrave said with a purse of her lips. "She's pretty enough, but so are dozens of women. She's not at all witty."

"She's sweet and has a sense of humor," the duchess of Gladstow said, her face bright and open. "I like her."

Lady Morgrave and her mother, Lady Deerhorn, exchanged glances. "You're just saying that because you want to befriend the king's favorite," Lady Deerhorn said.

"I'd like to be her friend. Truly I would. But what would I gain from the king by being her friend?"

Mother and daughter exchanged another knowing glance that the duchess of Gladstow didn't notice, or chose not to.

"Unfortunately, my husband has forbidden a friendship between us," the young duchess said. "He's been rather beastly about it, and he won't tell me why." Her eyes suddenly lit up. "But he's not here, is he?" She picked up her skirts and raced after Miranda.

"Why has the duke forbidden their friendship?" Lady Morgrave asked her mother.

"It's rather a scandal," Lady Deerhorn said with a smug smile. "The duke was set to marry Lady Claypool, before she married Lord Claypool. Apparently he'd been madly in love with her ever since they were children. Their families were in agreement, and arrangements were set in motion for them to wed when they came of age. Rumor has it that she was content with the match until she met a more handsome and more interesting man than the future duke of Gladstow."

"Who can be more interesting than a duke?" Lady Morgrave asked with a laugh.

"Lord Claypool, apparently. He may be only a baron, but he was an extraordinarily handsome man in his youth and very charming."

"Well, well. How intriguing. No wonder Gladstow loathes the Claypools."

"He's not used to losing," Lady Deerhorn said. "Do you know, I think this is the first time they've seen one another in all these years. I've noticed he won't even look at her, and he walks out of the room every time Claypool enters it. It must gall him to see their daughter is the king's favorite."

The question was, did it gall him enough to poison her?

They lowered their voices so I could no longer hear them. I picked up my pace and met Miranda and the duchess of Gladstow, now walking together along the avenue. I enquired after Miranda's health.

"Much improved, thanks to you and your father," she said with a warm smile.

"Are you the doctor's daughter?" the duchess asked. "I only just heard about his death. I am sorry for your loss. He did a marvelous service for Miranda."

"Thank you." As much as I wanted to ask Miranda if she was more enamored of the king now, I couldn't with the duchess there. "His Majesty seems very attentive," I said instead.

We all gazed up the avenue to where the king's sedan chair made swift progress toward the palace.

"Not attentive enough to offer me his chair." Miranda didn't seem all that perturbed by his lack of consideration. Indeed, she sounded a little relieved.

"Why did he rush off like that?" the duchess asked.

I merely shrugged. I'd changed my mind about warning them. It was for Hammer to decide if Miranda needed to be told about the dog.

The duchess linked her arm with Miranda's. "I wonder if the hunt will go ahead," she said. "I do hope so. I adore riding, don't you, Miranda?"

* * *

IT WASN'T until we arrived at my house that I had a chance to tell Hammer what Lady Deerhorn had said to Lady Morgrave about the Gladstow-Claypool rivalry. He thanked me for the information but gave no sign that he found it important.

"Do you plan on telling Miranda and the others about this latest poisoning?" I asked as I unlocked the door.

"The king said he'll warn her the danger is not over," he said. "He doesn't want anyone else told for fear of panic."

I wasn't sure if that was wise, but kept my mouth shut. Palace security was Hammer's responsibility. If he thought the king was wrong, I no longer had any doubt that he'd tell him so. The king's threats didn't seem to perturb him.

"I didn't know the palace had prison cells," I said, pushing open the door.

He put a hand out, barring my entry. "Stay here. Quentin, with me."

They checked the house and announced it was clear of dangers before allowing me to enter. I went straight to my father's workroom and looked over his tidy desk. Books had been shelved, papers stacked, and the dish that had been burning over the heat box was nowhere in sight.

"Are any of these books out of order?" Quentin asked, indicating the shelves.

"I couldn't say. My father had no order to his books. My neighbor might remember which ones he put back and where. I'll ask him."

"I'll do it," Hammer said. "You and Quentin stay here and test the sample."

"You don't have to return to the palace?"

"The king will remain indoors for the rest of the day and most likely tomorrow. My men are on guard both within the palace and the commons. Only kitchen and serving staff are allowed in the kitchen until further notice."

"For once, the cook agrees with the captain's measures," Quentin said. "He hates people wandering in and out, picking at the food. Dogs too. Without him yelling so much, I hear it's a better place to work."

"There seem to be quite a few senior staff with tempers," I said.

"Are you including me in that assessment?" Hammer asked.

"I'm yet to see you lose your temper, although I worried that you were close today with the king. It was unfair of him to accuse you of not trying to find the poisoner when you're supposed to guard him every moment he leaves the palace."

He stepped closer and lowered his voice. "I owe you thanks for your defence of me."

"It didn't do a lot of good. You managed to deflect his temper without my help."

"Even so, I'm grateful, but I want you to be more cautious in future. The king is volatile. I'd prefer you to avoid his notice."

He was right, of course, and I needed to restrain myself. The thing was, I'd not been prepared for my own outburst. The only conflict I'd ever experienced was with my father, and I'd always stood my ground with him if I thought he was being unfair.

"It's not that easy," I said.

"So I've noticed."

"I do tend to open my mouth when I shouldn't."

"That's not what I meant." He turned away. "I'll speak with your neighbors while you perform tests."

"Wait a moment. You were going to tell me about the palace cells."

He hesitated in the doorway and rested his hand on his sword hilt. "There's nothing to tell."

"Are there prisoners in them?"

"Of course," Quentin said. Hammer glared at him over his shoulder and Quentin swallowed loudly. "Not many. Very few, really. Maybe one or two. Or three."

"The prisoners are not your concern, Josie." Hammer strode out, leaving me feeling like I'd been rapped on the knuckles for my impertinence.

Quentin helped me set up the heat box then placed a small amount of the dog's discharge into a dish. We noted down the smell, color, and texture of the discharge after the heating process then checked the results against the handwritten notes in one of my father's books.

"Here," I said, pointing to a page. "The poison is a combination of these three ingredients. It's different to the poison used on Lady Miranda, although it does contain traitor's ease. No direweed though, which explains why it didn't have the same earthy smell. The sickly sweet smell comes from the cane flower which affects the heart. It means he was poisoned twice. The first time wasn't enough and merely gave him chest pains. That's when he used the catspaw. The second dose, ingested later, was fatal." I scanned the rest of my father's notes but there was no antidote listed, not even any suggestions on what to try. "Damn."

"What is it?" Quentin asked.

"We have to test different combinations of ingredients to find the right amounts to neutralize the poisons. The problem is, there are dozens of ingredients with the right properties. There's nothing here that helps us narrow it down."

"That means thousands of possible combinations to test." He sighed. "We'll be here for some time."

"*I'll* be here for some time. You and the captain have to return to the palace."

Hammer returned and crouched by the bookshelves. "Your neighbor said he returned three books to the left side of the lowest shelf. He can't recall which pages were open."

"I have one here," I said, indicating the notebook.

He passed me the other two, both slender volumes, and I flipped through the pages. "These are very specific about a particular group of plants. My father must have known the solution to finding the antidote was in these books."

"That's good." Quentin tapped the ends of his fingers with his thumb, counting. "Instead of thousands of combinations, we'll only have hundreds."

"Less. I have only a few of these ingredients to hand."

We set to work, testing and re-testing small portions of the discharge using ingredients from the larder. Hammer left again to question my neighbors and returned at dusk.

"Several saw your father leave the house that day and return some time later," he said. "None spoke to him. According to one, his countenance didn't invite idle conversation. He looked in earnest and keen to get home."

"Did he look ill?" I asked.

"None mentioned it."

"So the fatal dose was administered after he got home." I looked around the room, picturing how the scene had played out. The front door was rarely locked so that patients could come and go. My father was perhaps in here, working, when the poisoner entered. Had they forced him to ingest the poison or had he done so willingly, unwittingly? I wished I'd looked closer at his body for signs of force.

I pressed a shaking hand to my throat as bile rose.

"Josie?" Quentin asked. "You look sick."

"I'm fine," I said, adding another lump of peat to the heat box.

"You should eat," Hammer said. He left and I heard pots clattering in the kitchen. A few minutes later, he returned holding a carrot in one hand and a knife in the other. "There's not much food in your larder, but a lot of medicines, herbs and spices."

"I haven't been to the market lately," I said without meeting his gaze.

He didn't immediately respond or leave and I had the sickening sensation that he'd learned something of *my* movements from his enquiries and knew that I'd been to the market only that morning. The carrot had been one of my few purchases.

"Josie, if it's money—"

"It's not." I turned back to the dish and added a pinch of amani powder.

"I'm sure I can make something from what's there."

"You can cook, Captain?" Quentin asked.

"I'm about to find out."

"There's no need," I said. "Thank you, but I don't want you experimenting on me. Either of you. Now, if you don't mind, I have work to do and you both have to get back. I'll send word of my results tomorrow, if I have any."

Hammer pointed the carrot at me. "Make sure you eat tonight."

"Don't tell me what to do, Hammer."

"You promised to call me Captain." He walked off.

"What's got into him?" Quentin muttered.

* * *

BETWEEN PERFORMING tests and tossing in bed, I got very little sleep. I awoke early and decided to take a break from work and question my father's friends. There were few he would have considered a friend who weren't also neighbors, so the list was short. None had seen him the day he died, or the days leading up to his death. None could tell me if something troubled him.

I returned home only to be stopped by an elderly neighbor who lived three doors up from Meg. She was rather reclusive and only left the house to go to the market twice a week. She told me she hadn't answered the door when Hammer knocked the day before as she hadn't been expecting visitors. Like my father, Mull made her fearful these days.

"I hear that guard was asking about your father the day he died," she said. "I should have spoken to him yesterday but..." She shrugged. "I saw someone go to your house that day, Josie. I was sitting in my window here, and I saw your father come home. Then someone else came. I couldn't see his face," she went on. "He wore a long cloak with a hood. Nobody wears a cloak in this weather unless he's up to no good."

"He?"

"Figure of speech. I couldn't see what they wore under the cloak." She invited me in for refreshments and a longer chat, but I declined.

"I have work to do. Thank you for the information. I'll see the captain gets it."

"Why does he want to know, anyway? Didn't your father die of a heart problem?"

"Probably." I didn't want to worry her. If she thought a poisoner was targeting respectable citizens, she would never leave her house.

I finally had a breakthrough with my tests in the early afternoon and immediately set out for the palace on foot. The road was busier than usual, and I hitched a ride on a cart laden with crates full of ribbons and flowers. The driver told me it was for the revels the following night.

I hopped off at the gate and he continued on to the service entrance further along. The guards on duty recognized me. One of them escorted me to the garrison, but Hammer wasn't there. Sergeant Brant sent a young guard to fetch him while the other returned to his post at the gate.

I was left alone with Brant. He sat at the table, hunkered over a slab of bread that he tore apart with thick fingers.

He pushed another chair out with his booted foot. "Sit."

I sat and pulled my medical bag onto my lap. He watched me as he shoved bread into his mouth until no more could fit, then wiped his mouth with the back of his hand. His stare was so unnerving that I had to look away, yet I could still feel his gaze roaming over me. My skin prickled with the heat of it.

"Hammer says we were whipped."

His voice startled me. I hadn't expected him to address me, let alone about something so personal.

"It's my professional opinion that you were," I said.

"Professional opinion," he scoffed. "You're not a fucking doctor."

I didn't bother answering. Men like him didn't want to hear reason and truth.

He tapped his chest. "I wasn't whipped. Nobody would dare."

I hugged my bag tighter.

"Got any ideas why we can't remember yet?" he asked.

"How can I when I'm not a doctor?"

He pushed to his feet, scraping the chair legs across the bare floor. "You've got a mouth on you. Lucky for you, I like that." He pressed his knuckles to the table and leaned forward until his face was mere inches from mine.

I leaned back. He had foul breath, but I wasn't going to tell him how to get rid of it. The man didn't deserve free advice. He might also take offence, and I suspected that an offended Brant was an angry one.

He refilled his cup from a jug then filled another and handed it to me. "You look hot and bothered. Drink this."

It took me a moment to recover from my surprise at his kindness then accepted the drink. "Thank you."

He crossed his arms and watched me. I felt compelled to drink it all, even though the ale was stronger than I was used to. When I finished, I glanced at the door but it remained closed. What was taking Hammer so long?

"You like him, don't you?" he asked.

"Pardon?"

"Don't play dumb. You like Hammer."

"He seems like a good man."

He leaned forward again. "I said, don't play dumb." He turned his chair around and straddled it, his forearms resting on the chair back. "Hammer warned us not to tell you about the cells."

I blinked at him. I must have looked foolish because he chuckled.

"Last night, he told us if you ask questions about the prisoners or the cells, we're not to tell you anything."

"I see."

"What do you think of that, Josie?"

"I...I don't really know."

Hammer's order left me feeling a little hollow. If he could confide in me about his memory loss and the scars on his back, why not the prison cells? Who was kept there? And why?

"Seems to me he doesn't trust you," Brant said.

It seemed that way to me too.

"Wonder why, since you helped save Lady Miranda's life." He sniffed and wiped his nose on his sleeve. "I guess he has his reasons, and one thing I've learned about Hammer is he always knows what he's doing. He doesn't do anything without a reason. You know the other thing I learned?" He glanced at the door. "You don't cross him. Not ever. I've seen him almost kill someone from a beating. You best remember that, Josie. I don't want you getting hurt." He clamped his hand down on mine.

I sprang up and darted away. "Don't." I didn't know if I'd meant to say don't touch me or don't say such things about Hammer. Perhaps both. It didn't matter. My nerves were frayed and all I could think about was getting away from the sergeant.

I rushed to the door just as it opened. Hammer filled the space.

"What did he do?" he asked.

"Nothing. He gave me a drink." It was the truth. Brant hadn't done anything. Touching my hand didn't count; it was hardly a threatening gesture.

Yet I couldn't dislodge the cold lump of dread in the pit of my stomach.

"Why do you always assume the worst of me, Captain?" Brant asked. "You forget, we're the same, you and me."

Hammer's fists closed at his sides but he didn't disagree with Brant. Why didn't he tell him they were nothing alike?

"We need each other," Brant went on. "We need to trust each other. You've told us a dozen times, we can *only* trust each other."

And not outsiders like me, his unspoken words said.

"Josie, come with me," Hammer said.

I slipped past him and we strode together along the corridors. I had to walk quickly to keep up with him. "Captain, you *can* trust me."

"I know."

"Then why aren't you telling me some things?"

He stopped suddenly and rounded on me. "Because *you* shouldn't trust *me*."

CHAPTER 13

"What do you mean?" I asked on a rush of breath. "Why can't I trust you?"

"I don't know." He started walking again.

"Captain—"

"Don't, Josie. Just…don't."

He pushed open a door and I realized we'd reached Balthazar's office. It seemed to be the only place we could have a private conversation. I was glad Balthazar wasn't there, however. Hammer was difficult enough to manage at the moment, I didn't want to face the cantankerous master of the palace too.

"I'm sorry," he said, closing the door behind us. "None of this is your fault. I shouldn't take it out on you." He dragged his hand through his hair and down his face. He looked exhausted.

"Sit down, Captain." I poured him a cup of wine at the sideboard. "Drink. Midwife's orders."

He gave me a tired smile and accepted the cup.

"I have something to help you sleep tonight," I said, opening my bag.

He shook his head. "I need to stay alert. There's too much going on with the festivities tomorrow night."

"I noticed more comings and goings on my way here." I glanced over the desk, covered with sketches and notes. The disorder reminded me of my father's desk when he was buried under work.

"We can't stay long," Hammer said. "Balthazar is at the sunken garden but he'll return soon. I'd rather be gone by then."

"In that case, I'd better give you my report." I dug through my bag and pulled out five vials. "I've made an antidote for the poison."

"Finally, some good news." He accepted the vials and pocketed them. "Thank you. This is a relief."

"I also learned that a hooded man entered my house after my father returned on the day of his death. Unfortunately I can't tell you anything more."

"How did you learn that?"

"A neighbor told me after I came back from questioning my father's patients."

He lowered the cup. "You questioned your father's patients? Josie, you need to be careful. Someone killed your father because he knew their identity or the poisoner thinks he knew. If they hear you're making enquiries, they might come after you too."

"Asking my father's patients a few questions is hardly going to worry the poisoner, particularly when I learned nothing."

"Even so—"

"He was my father. I want to find out what happened to him, and I cannot sit idly by while I could be doing something." My anger dissolved as quickly as it flared, and was replaced with hot, burning tears.

His jaw softened and he lowered his head. "Promise me you'll be careful. If you learn anything, send for me."

"I may sometimes say things that get me into trouble, but I rarely do anything foolish. You have my word, Captain."

My promise seemed to satisfy him. "I have some more work for you." He set the cup on the desk and removed a small blue ceramic bottle from his pocket. "After what you told me about the duke of Gladstow holding a grudge against the Claypools, I searched his rooms."

I gasped. "You're allowed to do that?"

"I am the captain of the guards."

"Yes, but he's a duke. He outranks everyone except the royal family, of which the king is the sole member at the moment."

"And I have the king's authority to search rooms in times of danger. Or I would if I told him what I was doing." He handed me the bottle. "I found this hidden behind a panel in a drawer."

"You want to know if it contains poison." I removed the stopper and smelled the contents. It was pleasantly musky.

"I also questioned the Gladstow servants, but learned nothing of use. It does seem that this is the first time the duke has seen either Lord or Lady Claypool in over twenty years. Only His Grace's valet remembered what the feud was about. He confirmed that the duke had once been unofficially betrothed to Lady Claypool but she ended it to marry Lord Claypool. His Grace was livid at the time and took many years to accept her decision. Apparently he expected her to leave Lord Claypool and return to him, tail between her legs. He finally gave up only a few years ago and decided to marry."

"You learned all that from a long-time servant? He's not very loyal."

"I can be persuasive."

Watching him stand, his powerful frame towering over me, his broad shoulders and chest filling his uniform, I could well understand it. He held out his hand to me but retracted it when the door opened.

Balthazar sighed upon seeing us. "Again, Hammer?"

"Find me an office of my own and I won't need to come in here and drink your wine," Hammer said.

"You have a bedchamber."

"You want me to take Josie to my bedchamber?"

Balthazar looked as if he was about to say something, but Hammer's quelling glare stopped him. He limped past me instead. "I hope you haven't been peeking at my plans, Josie," Balthazar said as he slid a paper on the desk beneath another. "The entertainments are supposed to be a secret."

"I wish I could see them," I said. "It sounds like it will be glamorous."

"It's going to be a triumph. The most dazzling thing those spoiled brats have seen." His eyes shone and I couldn't help smiling at his enthusiasm. "They won't believe their—" He suddenly leaned heavily on the desk and dropped his walking stick.

Hammer caught him and guided him to the chair. "You're over-doing it," he said gently. "You need to rest."

"After tomorrow. If I rest now, the festivities will become the most pathetic thing the nobles have ever seen." He shoved Hammer away. "Leave me be. I have work to do."

"Will you let me take a look at you?" I asked. "I can prescribe something to calm you."

"I don't want to be calm, and you shouldn't be prescribing anything. I'm not pregnant."

His words stung, but he was right. I shouldn't have offered. If he told anyone, I could be in trouble.

Hammer led the way out and shut the door, but not before I saw Balthazar lean both elbows on the desk and lower his head into his hands.

* * *

THE CERAMIC BOTTLE contained nothing more harmful than fragrant oils. It was intended for a man, if I weren't mistaken. I was about to send word to Hammer when I spotted a boy watching my house from across the street. He looked familiar, but it wasn't until he came closer when I beckoned that I recognized the sick child from The Row whose mother, Dora, helped me escape.

"You look much better," I told him.

"Ma says I nearly died, but you saved me." He blinked up at me through strands of dirty blond hair, his eyes wary. Illness lingered in the shadowy hollows of his cheeks and the thin limbs poking out of too-small clothes. He was nothing but angles and edges covered by pale skin.

"What's your name?" I asked.

"Remy."

"How old are you, Remy? Five? Six?"

He looked at me like I was stupid. "Eight." He was far too small for eight.

"Come with me. I have a task for you."

He followed me into the house only to pause just inside the door and take in his surroundings. I'd not thought it possible, but his eyes grew even wider. It was easy to forget that I lived like a queen to some people.

I wrote a message for Hammer then handed it and two coins to Remy. "Get a ride on a cart heading to the palace. Pay the driver one ell. Save the other for the journey home. Don't pay him until he delivers you safely. Give one of the guards on duty at the gate this message and tell him it's for Captain Hammer from me. Can you remember that?"

He rolled his eyes. "Course I can."

"Good. Now, something for you for your trouble." I plucked a carrot from the bowl in the larder and gave it to him along with another ell. I really needed to go to the market.

Remy bit down on the carrot, mumbled something unintelligible then left.

He returned an hour later full of wonder. "It's made of gold, Miss Cully!"

"The palace? There's some gold on it, yes."

"And it's gi-normous. The whole Row could fit in it."

"Remy, the whole of Mull could fit in it. Did you deliver my message?"

He nodded. "Captain Hammer came out to see me and all. He gave me this." He opened his palm to reveal another coin. "Me and Ma are going to eat like them lords and ladies tonight."

"Did Captain Hammer give me a message in return?"

He nodded. "He says thanks."

"Is that all?"

"What did you want him to say?"

That was a good question.

* * *

THE FOLLOWING MORNING I searched again for the savings my father had hidden but found only dust and a dead mouse. I couldn't think where else in the house it might be. Luckily Hammer paid me for my work testing the dog's discharge or I'd have nothing to purchase what I needed at the market. The problem was, what I needed was food as well as supplies to replenish those I'd used in testing the poison and creating the antidote. There wouldn't be much left over.

The stall holders who'd lived in Mull for years all passed on their sympathies, and I had a hard time keeping my tears at bay. I finally shed some when Sara Cotter passed her baby boy to me. He was the last baby I'd delivered before Father's death.

"We named him Tristan, after your father," she said.

"Truly?" I said, trying to dash away tears on my shoulder without waking the baby.

Sara nodded. "You have friends here, Josie. Never forget that. If there's anything you need, call on me."

"Thank you."

"Speaking of your father, my mother says she heard from her neighbor's cousin that you've been asking if anyone saw him the day he died."

"It seems silly, but I'd like to know how he spent his last hours."

"My husband says he saw him here that day."

"At the market?"

She nodded. "Apparently he looked a little strange, that's why my Tolly noticed."

"Strange how? Ill?"

"Determined, like he didn't notice anyone or anything around him except Tam's stall. He went straight there, spoke to Tam's son, then left the market without buying anything."

I looked toward Tam's stall, partially hidden from view by a group of gossiping women. "Thank you, Sara." I attempted a smile as I handed back the little sleeping bundle. "He's beautiful."

I took my time buying what I needed, and could afford, all the while remaining close to Tam's stall. Tam didn't appear to be working today, but his son served customers with a cheerful smile. I had to wait until the morning's shoppers dispersed and the stall keepers began to roll down the shutters on their carts. Tam's stall, like many of them, was a permanent fixture at the market, but other stall holders wheeled their carts off-site, bringing them back in the morning and setting up all over again.

When I saw that Mika Tao was alone, I approached. He greeted me with a friendly smile, only to quickly look past me. I spun around, but saw only other stall holders going about their business.

"What is it, Mika?" I asked.

He shook his head. If his father had done that, the bells threaded through his long black hair would have tinkled musically. Mika may have the Zemayan coloring of his father, but he was more Glancian, having lived here his entire life. He wore his hair short without a bell in sight.

"Thought someone was about to come here until they saw you. Maybe you scared him off, Josie." He winked. "Don't know why. You're the least scary person I know."

"You're too sweet for your own good." I smiled, all the while trying not to let my imagination run away with me.

"You just caught me." He lifted the lid on a box of spice and was about to open a jar when I told him I wasn't there to purchase anything.

"I want to ask you something," I said.

He replaced the lid and continued to put jars and boxes away. "If you've come to ask me to a drink at The Anchor, the answer's yes."

I chewed my lip.

He laughed. "It was a joke, Josie. Go on, ask your question."

"Did my father speak to you here the day he died?"

He nodded. "I was sorry to hear of his death. Real sorry."

"Thank you. I'm trying to piece together his final movements that day for my own peace of mind."

He picked up a stick with a hook on the end and pulled down one of the stall's shutters. "I must have been one of the last people to see him alive. I can't believe it. He seemed fine. A little agitated, maybe. I heard he died of heart failure."

"Do you remember what you spoke about?"

"Sure do, because it was a strange conversation. He asked me about traitor's ease."

I held my breath. "And?"

He glanced past me then took his time lowering the two remaining shutters. He emerged from the stall and lowered the final shutter. "No one's supposed to know that we sell it," he whispered. "It can be used in poisons, and my father doesn't want the law coming here. Turns out he was right to be cautious, with that lady at the palace getting poisoned. It was nothing to do with us, you realize. My father only sells it in small quantities to people he knows and trusts. Like your father."

"Did my father say why he wanted it?"

He narrowed his gaze. "To kill rats, of course."

"Right. We have a rat problem."

"So he said."

"Was that the first time he'd bought traitor's ease from you?"

"Must be, because he wasn't sure we sold it. He was just asking that day. I told him he had to speak to my father. He keeps it at the house, not here."

"Did he go and see your father afterward?"

He shook his head. "I mentioned it when I got home, and he said the doctor didn't call on him." He shrugged. "He mustn't have felt well. Sounds like he died shortly after that. Such a shame," he added with a shake of his head. "What's the village going to do now? He was our only doctor. And what about you, Josie? What are you going to do now?"

"I...I'm not sure."

"Why not come home with me? My father would like to see you, and my mother won't mind. She doesn't like going out, but she's happy to have guests." He was so friendly that I was positive he had nothing to do with my father's death.

Tam, however, was in the thick of it. I was sure now that he'd lied to me, not only about selling traitor's ease but also about the other Zemayan he'd seen receiving the parcel at the pier. *Tam* was that Zemayan. *He'd* sold the poison to the poisoner.

And he may have killed my father.

I think I thanked Mika but later, I couldn't recall. Nor could I recall hailing a cart on the road to the palace, but I did remember sitting alongside the driver who talked of nothing else but his theory on how the palace might have been built without anyone seeing the builders.

Quentin was on duty at the gate and smiled upon seeing me. "Josie! You look—" He peered into my face. "You look terrible. What's wrong?"

"I need to see the captain urgently. Please find him and bring him here *now*."

"What's—"

"Go!"

He hurried off. A few moments later, he returned with Hammer, whose longer strides easily outpaced Quentin. "What is it, Josie?" he asked.

"It's Tam Tao," I whispered. I couldn't say it louder. It was far too shocking. "He sold the poisons to the poisoner. I'm sure of it."

"Go on."

"My father asked Mika, Tam's son, if they sold traitor's ease. I think my father specifically asked Mika, not Tam, knowing Mika would trust him. Mika confirmed they did, then told his father about the conversation. That afternoon, my father died."

"Didn't Tao tell you he didn't sell it?" Quentin asked.

I nodded. "That's the point. He lied."

Hammer ordered Quentin to take a message to the stables to prepare six horses and a carriage. "Josie, wait here," he said, already striding off toward the commons.

* * *

HAMMER RODE hard to the village flanked by five guards. I rode in the slower carriage. The driver had orders to take me directly home. Hammer shouldn't have bothered; I would have gone straight home anyway. I had no intention of following them to Tam's. I didn't want to be in the same room as the man responsible for my father's death.

But I'd hardly stepped out of the carriage when Max arrived on horseback and ordered me to follow him. "Bring your medical bag," he said.

"What's wrong?"

"Tao's been stabbed."

I thanked Hailia that the guards weren't hurt, then I prayed to the goddess that Tam would live; not because I cared but because I wanted him to give us answers.

At the house, four children huddled together outside a room

guarded by two of Hammer's men. A mournful wail came from inside the room and the children burst into tears.

I pushed past the guards and knelt by Tam's body. I hadn't seen Mistress Tao in years, but I recognized the woman with long gray hair kneeling on Tam's other side. She was much older than I remembered and her face swollen from crying. The wailing came from deep within her.

Someone had torn open Tam's shirt and tried to stem the flow of blood with a cloth. I removed the soaked cloth and inspected the wound. It looked deep and had been made with a narrow, sharp blade.

"Can you do anything, Josie?" Mika asked in a trembling voice. I hadn't seen him standing there in the corner.

I checked for a pulse at Tam's throat and shook my head. "He's gone."

The woman let out another wail. Mika crouched beside her and folded her into his arms. He stared at me over the top of her head, his eyes brimming with tears.

"I'm sorry," I said, pathetically. I felt awful for not caring more. Whatever he'd done, Tam had been a much loved father and husband.

The guards at the door stepped aside and Hammer entered with Max. He raised his brows at me and I shook my head. A muscle in his jaw bunched.

"Mika?" he asked. "Is that your name?"

Mika nodded.

"Come with us to the kitchen. We have to ask you some questions."

"Now?" I asked. "Captain, he's just lost his father."

His cool gaze connected with mine. "We haven't got time to waste."

Mika let his mother go and followed Hammer out of the room. Mistress Tao stared down at her husband and continued rocking back and forth. I wasn't entirely sure if she was aware of anything other than the lifeless body and her own grief.

"The festivities are tonight," Max told me quietly. "It'll be harder to keep an eye on things, and the captain won't rest until the poisoner is caught."

"Poison," Mistress Tao murmured. "He should never have sold it. Should never have supplied it."

"Mistress Tao?" I prompted. "Did Tam talk to you about traitor's ease?"

She nodded.

Max ordered one of the other guards to fetch Hammer.

"He hated himself for what he'd done," she went on. "He hated that he told the poisoner about your father. He didn't—" She closed her mouth when Hammer strode in.

"What do you know about the poison?" Hammer asked.

She sidled away from him toward me. I took her hand in mine. This was a woman who rarely left the house. Like my reclusive neighbor, she must find men like Hammer intimidating.

Hammer pressed his lips together and appealed to me.

"Mistress Tao," I said gently, "can you help us find who did this?"

"I don't know," she whispered. "I'll try."

"You said Tam regretted his actions. What precisely were those actions?"

"Wait," Mika said. "Don't say anything, Mother. You could go to prison."

"We want information to stop the killer," Hammer said. "If she can help us, she must. There'll be no repercussions for her."

Mika took his mother's other hand. "Go on then. What did Father do?"

"He sold a large dose of traitor's ease to someone."

"Who?" Hammer asked.

"I don't know. I never saw a face when they came here to transact business. He or she was tall and always wore a long cloak with a hood. It could have been man or woman."

"The other Zemayan he claims he saw at the pier," I said. "That was all a lie, wasn't it?"

She nodded. "He wanted to throw you off the scent. He didn't know your father knew so much about poisons, you see. He shouldn't have. He wasn't Zemayan."

"He traveled to Zemaya years ago," I told her. "He learned a lot about poisons there."

"Tam was worried about losing your business," she said. "Your father was his best customer. But he knew he had to lie. He knew your father would never understand why he did it. He had all these mouths to feed, Josie, and his father in Zemaya is sick. He wanted to visit him one last time, but sea voyages are costly. We needed the money."

"I understand," I said. "But Tam put himself at risk." I indicated the body. "He put my father at risk too."

She turned away and closed her eyes.

"That's my fault, isn't it?" Mika asked. "I told Father that Doctor Cully asked me about traitor's ease. Father told the poisoner, didn't he?"

"Tam panicked," she said. "He knew Doctor Cully would tell the palace guards that he supplied traitor's ease. He was worried and went to the poisoner to extract a promise that they wouldn't give his name. He got his promise," she said, her face crumpling. "Doctor Cully was killed to ensure his silence."

I pressed my fingers to my trembling lips and swallowed my tears. Two families destroyed because of Tam's desperate need for money.

"How did this happen?" Hammer asked, indicating Tam. "Did anyone see his attacker?"

"No," Mistress Tao said. "He was wounded when he came home."

"It was just after I arrived home from working at the market," Mika said. "He stumbled in here, all covered in blood. There was so much of it, and he was so white. I raced to your house, Josie, but you weren't there." He looked at the guards but said nothing.

"I couldn't have saved him even if I came straight away," I told him. "The wound is very deep."

"Why now?" he asked. "I don't understand why the poisoner would do this to the man supplying him?"

"Tam refused to give him more," Mistress Tao said.

"Why did Father refuse? Didn't he know his life depended on his usefulness?"

"The poisoner was probably watching your stall," Hammer said.

Mika gasped. "I thought I saw someone when I spoke with Josie, but I assumed it was a customer."

"He saw me and guessed that I'd learned my father's last act was to speak with you, Mika," I said. "He knew I'd tell the captain."

"Tao was the only one who could identify him," Hammer said.

Mika reached for his mother's hand. She began to cry again.

"Did you see the person watching the stall?" Hammer asked.

Mika shook his head. "He or she wore a long cloak."

One of the guards entered and handed a paper to Hammer. He whispered in Hammer's ear then stepped back. Hammer read the message.

"The supply of traitor's ease has been uncovered," he said. "I'm confiscating it." Hammer handed the paper to Mika. "Do you recognize this handwriting?"

He nodded. "It's my father's. 'Midday,'" he read. "'2 packets D.' What's D?"

"D for Deerhorn perhaps," I said.

Mistress Tao took the note. "A woman picked up supplies from your father at midday today. It must be referring to that appointment."

"What did she look like?" Hammer asked.

"I didn't see her face. She was tall and slim and had a noble-woman's accent."

The description fit all of the noblewomen at the palace. I looked to Hammer but he was once again giving orders to his men. They filed out and he thanked Mistress Tao and Mika for the information.

"Josie, Max will escort you home," he finished.

"I'll stay here a little longer," I said. "I'll help Mistress Tao prepare the body for burial."

He leveled his gaze with mine, and I could see he was consid-ering what to say next. Should he order me or ask nicely?

"Neither will work," I told him.

If he understood, he didn't let on. He didn't divulge any of his thoughts to me or to anyone else, not even through a twitch of an eyebrow. He simply stood there and waited for me to go with him. There was no sign of anger that I didn't obey, no sign of worry, simply a stoic presence that was more commanding than mere words could ever be.

Sergeant Brant's entrance broke the standoff. He had not been one of the original five guards with Hammer so must have just arrived from the palace. He spoke quietly to Hammer then they both looked at me.

"You're needed at the palace," Hammer said, indicating I should leave the room ahead of him.

I said quick goodbyes to the Tao family and grabbed my bag. "What is it?" I asked as Hammer held the carriage door open for me. "Is Lady Miranda all right?"

"It's the king. He's been poisoned."

CHAPTER 14

*T*he king sat propped against pillows on a vast bed, a sheet covering his legs to the waist. Several serious looking gentlemen stood on one side of the bed while Theodore hovered on the other. Yet another man held up a bottle of amber liquid to the bedside lamp, inspecting it. He must be Doctor Clegg. With the thick curtains pulled closed against the afternoon sunshine, the lamp's flickering flame and the dozens of candles spaced around the chamber provided the only light.

"Miss Cully!" the king cried upon seeing me. "Thank Hailia you're here." He flipped his hand at the man holding the bottle. "You're dismissed, Doctor."

Merdu.

The gentlemen exchanged glances. Doctor Clegg chuckled until he realized the king was serious. "But she's a—"

"A woman, yes. In my experience, women can be as capable as men, given the right training. Miss Cully learned about poisons from her father, a more knowledgeable doctor on the subject you won't find anywhere on The Fist."

"He was a village healer, sire," Doctor Clegg sneered. "What papers has he written? What classes has he taught?"

"If a doctor is spending time writing papers and teaching classes, he's not gaining experience. Now, please leave. All of you." The king shifted his weight and winced. His hand fluttered at his stomach. "Quickly, Miss Cully. The poison is working through me, I can feel it."

"You haven't been poisoned, Your Majesty," Doctor Clegg said in what sounded like a practiced monotone. "In my professional opinion—"

"I said get out! Go! If you don't leave immediately, my guards will throw you out of the palace."

The gentlemen couldn't leave fast enough. Doctor Clegg handed the bottle to Theodore, picked up his bag, and backed through the door, bowing as he did so. He lifted his gaze in the moment before Hammer closed the door on him. It was ice-cold and full of hate, and it was directed at me.

"Miss Cully," the king said on a groan. "Do you have an antidote in your bag?"

"I have to do some tests first to see what poisons were used." I looked around for the bedpan but saw none. "Have you vomited?"

"No."

"Purged your bowels?"

"Not lately."

I asked him to sit on the side of the bed then checked his vitals. His heart was regular and his eyes seemed clear. "Theodore, please open the curtains and put out the candles. Open a window too."

Hammer helped Theodore as I checked the king's temperature. He was a little hot but not dangerously so.

"Describe your symptoms," I said.

The king indicated his stomach and winced again. "It aches here."

I lifted his shirt. "When did the pain start?"

He sucked air between his teeth as I pressed into the soft flesh. "Just after lunch."

"Describe the pain to me."

He pointed to the exact location and I felt there. "It's not sharp but not dull either."

"Does your stomach feel as though it's churning?"

"No."

"Do you feel as though you want to throw up?"

"No." After a moment in which I continued to press into his stomach, he said, "It must have been in the duck. It tasted off."

"Did anyone else eat the duck?" Hammer asked.

"I don't know. I ate alone in my dining room." His breathing became deep, ragged, and I stopped inspecting his stomach. It seemed to be upsetting him.

"Take regular, slow breaths, sire," I said, gentling my voice.

"I can't!" He pushed to his feet and paced to the window and back. He pressed a hand to his stomach. "This is how I breathe, Miss Cully. I can't help it. I can't breathe normally. Merdu. You have to find an antidote, *please*."

"Sit down, Your Majesty," Hammer said. "She can't help you if you won't sit still."

The king sat and flopped back on the bed, his legs dangling over the edge. He groaned. "Why is everyone trying to kill me?"

"Not everyone," Hammer said.

The king pointed a finger at him. "You should have prevented this, Hammer. This is your fault!" He groaned again, drawing his knees up.

"It's not his fault," I said. "It's not—"

"Stop talking and find me a cure!"

"Don't speak to her that way," Hammer snapped. "She's trying to help you."

"She can help me by making an antidote. *You* can help me by finding the poisoner, Hammer. The festivities are tonight. Tonight! How can I enjoy it knowing someone is trying to kill me? It could be anyone. They all hate me. The ministers, my advisors." He stabbed a finger at the door through which the gentlemen had left. "All the nobles want me dead. They want my crown for them-selves. And those are my so-called subjects!" He groaned again and flung his arm over his eyes. "Something's going to happen at the festivities tonight. Something terrible. I know it."

Theodore signaled to Hammer and mouthed, "Shall I get Balthazar?"

Hammer shook his head. "We can call off the festivities, sire."

"No!" The king sat up again and pressed a hand against his stomach. "This is my opportunity to show them how powerful I am, how full my coffers. They'll be dazzled into submission, and will never doubt my right to sit on the throne, never doubt my ability to be a proper king. But Hammer, you *must* stay with me at all times. Station your men where you think necessary, but *you* must be with me every moment. Do not leave my side. Understand?"

Hammer gave a curt nod.

"You have mere hours, Miss Cully," the king said. "I want an antidote before then."

"It's not necessary," I told him. "Doctor Clegg was right. There's no evidence of poisoning."

Theodore slumped back against the window sill. "Thank God and Goddess."

"Not even a little?" Hammer asked. "Could it have been a mild dose?"

"Surely you're mistaken, Miss Cully," the king said. "I am in terrible pain."

"There's no discharge of any kind and no other symptoms," I said.

"Then what's causing this ache?"

If the king were an ordinary patient, I would tell him he was constipated without hesitation. But talking about bowel movements with the man who ruled the country, particularly when I wasn't qualified to do so, was not a task I wanted to undertake.

"Josie?" Theodore prompted.

"Miss Cully," the king began, "if you're not capable of a diagnosis, I'll have to call Doctor Clegg back."

"That's not necessary," I said. "I know what the problem is. You need to empty your bowels, sire."

He stared at me. Then he snorted. "You're wrong. I've been poisoned. It's obvious to anyone. Well, obvious to a *proper* doctor."

Sometimes, the only way to reason with petulant children was to call their bluff. "Perhaps we'll see what Doctor Clegg says after all. Since he's the finance minister's doctor, he'll need to report to his employer and the other ministers. They'll want to know what ails their king, after all." I nodded at Hammer, standing by the door. "Please fetch him."

"No!" The king scooted back up the bed and folded his arms over his stomach. "I can't trust him. He's on their side."

"There are no sides, sire," Hammer said with surprising gentleness. "Your ministers aren't trying to kill you."

"You don't know that."

Theodore cleared his throat. "Josie, do you have something that can make the king feel better?"

"Not in my bag, but the kitchen will have the ingredients I need. It'll work quickly and he'll…feel better in a few hours."

Theodore understood my meaning and thanked me. "I don't have to mention the need for confidentiality to you, do I?"

"You know you don't," Hammer said with a glare for the king's valet.

Theodore apologized. "I don't know what's got into me, Josie."

"It's all right," I told him. "I won't tell a soul. I'll tell the kitchen staff I'm making the king a tisane to improve his general health."

"Good," the king declared. "I just need a draft to counteract the poison. It must have been a mild dose, after all. Or perhaps the duck had spoiled."

None of us contradicted him. It seemed the best course of action to take to maintain the peace.

The king got up, winced, and headed for an adjoining room. "Theodore, help me choose an outfit for tonight."

"You've already chosen one, sire," Theodore said, trotting after him. "You preferred the silver and black."

"I'm having second thoughts." The king's voice sounded distant, as if he'd entered a long cave, not the next room.

I went to take my bag but Hammer had the same idea. Our hands touched. His fingers twitched, brushing mine. I didn't know if it was intentional or an innate reaction. He did not pull away, however, and neither did I. Our gazes met and everything seemed to stop. My breathing, my heart, time. The king's voice faded altogether. It felt like just Hammer and me in the palace, alone. His thumb stroked my wrist with aching tenderness and heat banked in his eyes.

Something behind me caught his attention and he let go. His gaze slipped away.

"Hammer!" The king's shout shattered the bubble I'd found myself in. Had he been shouting long? "Captain, get in here *now!*"

Hammer strode past me without a backward glance. I followed him into what appeared to be a dressing room. It was as big as the bedchamber with sofas, dressing tables, chairs, chests of drawers, trunks and more mirrors than one man needed. Theodore stood by a round table, studying a small wooden cabinet inlaid with gold in the shape of sunbeams radiating from one corner. The sleeves of the shirt he held brushed the floor, forgotten. He seemed worried.

The king looked more ill than when I'd entered his chambers. "It's been moved!" he cried, shaking a finger at the cabinet. "For Merdu's sake, I've told you both, *no one* is to touch it."

"It must have been a maid," Hammer said with a shrug. "Is it damaged?"

"No," Theodore said. "Just moved. It used to be over there." He pointed to another table. "Hammer's right, the maid must have shifted it. I think it looks well here." He tried to sound positive but I heard the uncertainty in his voice, saw the way his worried gaze flicked to Hammer.

It was at that moment I remembered Miranda's story about the lady who'd touched a cabinet in the king's rooms and been expelled from the palace for her impertinence. This must be the same piece. What could be so important about it that the king would be sent into a frenzy whenever someone touched it?

The king smacked Theodore's shoulder with his open palm. "I told you to tell the servants not to go near it! That includes the maids." Another smack. Theodore stepped back but did not attempt to deflect yet another strike. "Are you an idiot, Theodore? Do you think the maids are exempt from the rules?"

Theodore swallowed. "No, Your Majesty, of course not. Perhaps they forgot."

The king hit him again and drew his hand back to strike another blow.

Hammer clasped the king's shoulder. "The maids are only doing their job, sire. If you want to stop anyone touching it, it needs to be kept somewhere more private."

The king shoved Hammer's hand away. "I knew you'd be on their side."

"I'm on *your* side. We all are. Let me put it in a safe place where no one will find it. That way you can rest easily."

The king drew in several deep breaths. He looked down at his bare legs as if he just realized he was dressed only in his shirt. He blushed and looked sheepishly at me, the expression at odds with his tantrum. "My stomach still hurts. I need that draft, Miss Cully."

"Of course," I said. "I'll make it now. In the meantime, you should rest."

"Doctor's orders?" he offered with a wan smile.

I smiled back. "Doctor's orders."

"It contains personal things," he told me. "Private things. It's important to me."

I nodded.

"The maids have been informed not to touch it. If they broke it..." He thrust out his chin to Hammer. "Take it somewhere safe, Captain."

Hammer picked up the cabinet only to put it down again. He stared at it.

"What is it?" Theodore asked.

"It felt...strange."

"Just take it!" the king shouted.

Hammer continued to stare at the cabinet. Then he slowly picked it up again. He held it out from his body as if it smelled foul.

"Where will you put it?" the king asked, following Hammer out of the dressing room. "Wait, don't tell me now. Later." He tried so hard not to look at me that I suspected my presence was the reason for his reticence.

So be it. I couldn't expect him to trust me completely.

I picked up my bag and left with the captain. He acknowledged the guards at the door then walked quickly along the corridor to the hidden door. I opened it and we entered the labyrinthine service corridors.

"Where are you taking it?" I asked.

"To a safe room that hardly anyone will look in. The maids don't go in to clean it."

"Are we going there now?"

"I am. You're going to the kitchen."

"After I go with you to the safe room."

Hammer kept walking in silence. After a moment, he said, "I've never seen him so anxious. The poisoning is playing on his mind, and tonight's festivities are important to him."

"It's a pity he wouldn't consider delaying them."

Another silence then, "He's not always like this. The anxiety is making him do and say things he normally wouldn't." We stopped at a fork in the passages. "Can you find your way to the commons?"

"No." It was the truth. The hidden corridors were too complex for me. But I had to admit that I wanted to see where he took the cabinet.

"What's in it?" I asked, feeling bold.

"I don't know."

"You've never looked? Even though you know it's personal to him?"

"That's precisely why I haven't looked. There is such a thing as privacy. That goes doubly for kings."

"But considering he's probably lying about losing his memory—"

"Don't, Josie."

He quickened his steps. I had to trot to keep apace. My bag bumped against my hip and scraped along the wall. We passed two maids carrying trays. They stepped close to the wall, allowing us to pass single file. They both smiled at Hammer but I couldn't see his face to know if he smiled back.

"What if information about your pasts is in there?" I asked when we were alone again. "What if the reason for your memory loss can be explained by the contents of that cabinet?"

He suddenly stopped and rounded on me. I only just managed to halt before careening into him. "Enough, Josie. He's not hiding something like that. I trust him." He turned and walked off again. "I have to."

"Very well, perhaps he's not hiding anything. But something made you put that cabinet down after you picked it up the first time. You said it felt odd."

"I was mistaken," he tossed over his shoulder. "It feels normal."

So much for trusting me. I wasn't going to get answers now.

"This is where we part," he said when we reached an intersection. "You have to go that way." He nodded right. "Follow it as far as it goes then take the steps down one flight. You'll find yourself at the exit that leads out to the commons. When you've made up the draft, have one of the servants take you back to the king. On second thoughts, have them bring you to the garrison. I'll take you to him."

"Trying to keep an eye on me, Captain?"

"You require both eyes." He headed up the stairs, leaving me staring at his broad back and shoulders, wondering if he'd been flirting with me or threatening me.

I hoped for flirting. That touch in the king's bedchamber had been thrilling, and Hammer's gaze as intense as a firestorm. I was still feeling giddy from it.

So giddy that I couldn't recall if I was meant to go up or down the steps when I reached them. I stood there, hoping a servant would wander past, when I heard footsteps above me followed by a distant wail. It was the same sound I'd heard last time I'd been lost in the corridors yet this time I could tell that a person made that sound, not an animal. A woman, if I weren't mistaken.

That decided it. I headed up the steps and found myself in a corridor that looked the same as every other service corridor. Endless stone walls seemed to go on forever, broken only by lit torches. Their flames flickered in the drafts, creating ghostly shadows. The wail sounded again, this time stopping abruptly.

I shivered, although it wasn't cold, and forced myself to keep moving. I'd come this far. I rounded a corner and realized I was not far from the place Hammer had found me last time. The closed door with a thick padlock up ahead beckoned me. The lock was open and I could just make out a male voice coming from the other side. Hammer?

A moment later, the door opened. I raced back the way I'd come on tiptoes and didn't stop until I found the exit. I squinted in the bright afternoon sunshine. A footman eyed me curiously as he entered the palace, a vase of fresh flowers in his arms.

I walked quickly to the kitchen in the square commons block and informed the cook that I had to make up a draft for the king. He pressed his lips together as he wiped his hands on his apron.

"I'm supposed to be preparing food for tonight," he growled.

The kitchen did seem extra busy, with every bench and table surface covered with ingredients, pots, bowls, platters and utensils. Smoke swirled in the rafters high above us, its lingering smell mixing with a myriad of delicious ones, too numerous to identify. Staff stirred pots, chopped and measured ingredients, and kneaded dough, while yet others seemed to do little more than fetch and carry.

"Miss?" the cook prompted. "Did you hear me? I'm too busy to play tour guide to you."

"The king requires a healthful tisane," I said. "I won't get in your way, sir."

He grunted. "Oren will help you find what you need." He jerked his head at a young man. Oren put down the knife he'd been using to chop herbs and came running. "Stay out of the way. Don't distract any of my staff. Don't take more than you need. Don't sample the food. If you drop something on the floor, pick it up. We don't want mice."

He walked off, still wiping his hands on his apron, and barked orders at a terrified kitchen maid arranging flowers on a platter.

"Mice wouldn't dare come in here," I whispered to Oren.

He laughed only to suppress it when the cook suddenly turned and glared at us. He had excellent hearing.

Oren fetched what I needed and I brewed up the tisane, drawing the familiar, minty smell into my lungs. It was calming and allowed me time to think. But I could only think of one thing —Hammer had taken the cabinet to a room where a woman was kept prisoner.

I looked up from the bubbling pot. The kitchen staff went about their assigned tasks under the watchful eye of the cook. He stood like a general on a raised step, barking orders at his soldiers. Did he know about the cabinet? Did any of them?

I poured the tisane into a jug. I thanked Oren then left the kitchen and its heat and chaos behind.

It wasn't until I reached the service entrance at the palace that I realized I didn't know how to reach the garrison. There'd been two entrances to it—one from the maze of internal service corridors and another from outside. It was that entrance I decided to find since it would be more direct. I was about to ask a palace footman rushing toward the kitchen when I spotted a guard carrying a lidded pail by the handle.

He rounded the pavilion, crossed the large forecourt, and

passed the northern pavilion. He kept on walking, always far enough ahead that I couldn't shout out without attracting too much unwanted attention to myself. I already felt conspicuous with my medical bag under my arm and the jug in hand. The nobles must think it odd to see me in their midst.

The guard kept going, leaving the more populated part of the palace grounds behind. Sweat dampened me in uncomfortable places and my bag grew heavy. The tisane would have cooled by now, but it was probably nicer that way in this weather. The end of the palace was in sight. I could just make out the guards practicing their sword fighting through an arched gate to the north. I began to wonder if the guard I followed was going to the garrison at all when he suddenly pushed open a door.

Finally! I put my head down and rushed after him. The door was heavy and I had to put my shoulder into it to push it open. It took a moment for my eyes to adjust to the dim light and when they did, I realized I wasn't in the garrison. The room was small, a mere antechamber with an unoccupied chair by a door leading to another room. The door was open, a padlock swinging from it. It wasn't that which had my heart beating faster. It was the angry, sneering voice coming from beyond.

"Rancid slops again?" it said. "My fucking favorite."

"It's not rancid or slops," came another voice that I suspected belonged to the guard I'd followed.

I peeked around the corner and only just managed to suppress my gasp. It wasn't a room but a corridor with several barred cells on either side. This must be the prison Hammer didn't want me to know about.

Two guards stood in the middle of the corridor. One rested his hand on the hilt of his sword, strapped to his hip, while the other poured the contents of the pail into three bowls. He passed a bowl through the gap between one of the cell's bars then stepped quickly back as if he were afraid the prisoner on the other side would bite. He may well have. He looked like a wild animal, hunkered down on his haunches in the middle of the cell, his long gray hair a grizzled nest. He grinned, revealing blackened teeth.

"What are them up there eating tonight, eh?" asked the prisoner. He pushed the bowl away with dirty fingers. "Bet it ain't this muck."

"Shut it, Kai," said the guard who'd served him. "We eat the same as you, you filthy dog. Look at you. You're sitting in your own shit."

"Come closer and say that." After a moment, the prisoner named Kai chuckled. "You ain't got the balls."

"He ain't got no brains neither," came another voice from a neighboring cell. I couldn't see the occupant or any of the other cells further along.

"You're the one with no brains, Mal," the guard said, passing another bowl through a different set of bars. This time he didn't seem to fear the occupant. "If you were smart, you would know that you're lucky to be alive. Hammer could have killed you."

I bit down on my lip and backed away. My hands shook. My whole body shook. What had these men done to be kept in here like animals? The healer in me wanted to check on them, and make sure they ate good food and received some exercise and light. But the woman in me recoiled at the sight of the prisoner with the sneering grin and long hair. I didn't want to be anywhere near him.

An arm wrapped around me from behind and a hand closed over my mouth. It stank of cheese and something more rank. I tried not to gag as Sergeant Brant's sweaty cheek pressed against mine.

"Shhh," he whispered. "Don't say a word. You're coming with me."

CHAPTER 15

*B*rant dragged me backward through the door and outside. I lost my footing but his arm stopped me from falling. It tightened, squeezing me until I felt like I'd be cut in half.

"Let me go!" I said.

He did, and I scurried away from him, out of his reach. No one was near, but if I screamed, the guards inside would hear. Would they protect me or take Brant's side? I didn't dare test them.

"Wh—what do you want?" I asked.

He licked his lips and glanced past me to the door. "See enough in there? I know you heard enough."

I pushed past him, but he grabbed my arm. Some of the tisane spilled over the sides of the jug. "You afraid, Josie? Of the prisoners?" He leaned in, his face so close I could feel the heat of his breath on my forehead. "You afraid of Hammer now you see what he does to people he don't like?"

I jerked free and hurried off. He could have caught me, but when I glanced over my shoulder, he was nowhere in sight. I intercepted a maid and asked her to direct me to the garrison. It was a relief to see Hammer there, talking to half a dozen guards about the evening's security plans. He broke away from them upon seeing me and gathered his sword and belt from a hook. He opened the drawer of a nearby dresser and removed a set of keys, only to change his mind and drop them back in.

"You look like you ran from the kitchen," he said, as we headed into the service corridors. "Did you get lost again?"

I considered telling him the truth but quickly dismissed the idea. He didn't want me to know about the prisoners, and I didn't want him thinking I'd defied him to seek out the cells. "I wanted to get this to the king quickly," was all I said.

We delivered the jug to Theodore in the king's antechamber. In the bedchamber beyond, the king sat up in bed. "Finally!"

"Thank you, Josie," Theodore whispered. "He's been unbearable since you left."

"He should feel more comfortable after drinking this," I said. "Hopefully his mood will improve after it takes effect."

"Speaking of effects, what can I expect?"

"What do you think?" Hammer asked with a wry grin.

Theodore wrinkled his nose. "On days like this, I hate my job."

"Have a bedpan ready," I told him. "Or two."

He made a small sound of protest before squaring his shoulders and marching into the bedroom.

Hammer escorted me through the palace and outside to the forecourt. "I have to leave you here," he said. "Ask one of the guards on duty to have a carriage sent for you." He pulled a fat purse from inside his doublet and pressed it into my hand.

"This is too much," I said.

"King's orders. Apparently his life is worth it."

I doubted the king oversaw trivialities like payments but I didn't refuse it. The money would come in very handy.

"I have to go," he said, his gaze darting around the courtyard. Whenever he was outside, he always seemed on heightened alert, checking faces for unfamiliar ones, or looking out for potential trouble.

"Good luck tonight," I said. "I hope you catch the poisoner before then."

"I'm going to speak to Lady Deerhorn now."

"You think she is the D Tam was referring to in his notes?"

"It's possible. I don't expect her to admit it, but if she is the poisoner, she'll know I'm watching her closely and won't strike tonight."

"Or it might drive her to act sooner out of desperation."

Hammer's frown deepened. I wanted to smooth it away, perhaps even encourage a smile from him or a tender touch like the connection we'd shared in the king's bedchamber. But he looked far too serious and focused for tenderness.

"Be sure to stay indoors, particularly at night," he told me. "Don't trust anyone."

"Aye, aye, Captain."

"I'm serious, Josie."

"I don't know who the poisoner is, so my life is not in danger. But thank you for the warning," I said when he looked like he was about to argue with me. "I'll be careful."

He walked off and I headed to the gate, only to be intercepted by Miranda. She broke away from Lady Lucia, who watched on in dismay, her hands on her hips and a scowl on her face.

"Josie, how lovely to see you again," Miranda said. "You seem to spend more time at the palace than at home."

I smiled. "It's far more interesting here."

"Does that have something to do with the handsome captain of the guards?" Her gaze wandered in the direction in which Hammer had just left.

"More to do with the king's fear of being poisoned."

Her smile faded. "Is he all right? He sent word to me earlier that he couldn't join me for cards after lunch."

"He'll be fine. So, you're spending a lot of time with him since your recovery?"

She sighed. "He seems to prefer my company more than ever, even though I am the dullest of companions now."

I eyed Lady Lucia, who'd been joined by Lord Frederick. He whispered something in her ear that made her giggle behind her hand. "I find that hard to believe," I said.

"It's true. The other ladies have sharp wits and clever opinions, whereas I prefer to keep my own counsel, nowadays. Indeed, I hardly open my mouth at all."

"Afraid of consuming something poisonous?"

She tilted her head closer to mine. "Afraid of saying something that will propel me down a path I don't want to be on." She lowered her voice. "I've decided I'm not ready to marry. Unfortunately, everyone else thinks I am."

"Including the king?"

She sighed again.

I nodded at Lady Lucia. "She can help you with your predicament."

"Believe me, she's trying *very* hard to help. So hard, in fact, that I appear to have a new best friend. She and her brother are with me almost constantly. Between them and the king, I have to retire to my rooms to get any peace."

The Whippler siblings approached with matching smiles of dazzlingly white teeth. "Miranda, dear," Lady Lucia said, "come along. It's time to prepare for tonight."

"It's still early," Miranda said.

"It's never too early to prepare oneself for the king." She made it sound like she was serving herself to him on a platter. "Come with me if you don't want to dress yet. You can watch me."

Lord Frederick winked at Miranda. "What a privilege. Most would kill to be in your shoes."

His sister swatted his arm playfully.

"What will you wear tonight, Miranda?" Lord Frederick asked. "Or is that a secret?"

"Not at all," she said. "I have a pale blue and silver gown with a high neckline and elbow length sleeves."

"High?" Lady Lucia echoed. "That sounds very—er...safe."

"Demure," Lord Frederick countered. "I've been trying to tell you, Lucia, the king prefers sweet, demure women. If one wanted to attract his attention, an elegant but sensible gown is the perfect choice."

"No man prefers demure or sensible, Freddie. They only *say* they do. I'm going to wear something cut low to show off my best features."

Lord Frederick's lips flattened. "The king is not like other men."

"Of course he is. All men are the same." She waggled her fingers in a wave at Miranda then swanned off, her hips swaying.

He watched her go then turned a bright smile onto us. His eyes danced with mischief. "She's a menace. She always does the opposite of what I say." He bowed to us and followed her.

"I do believe he just manipulated her into wearing precisely what he wanted her to wear," Miranda said, watching them.

I hadn't thought of it that way, but she might be right. Lord Frederick didn't want the king to be attracted to his sister, and his keener observations had led him to believe what Miranda believed —the king liked a sweet natured, quieter woman who dressed sensibly. Lady Lucia wouldn't be attracting the king's eye tonight with a low-cut gown, and her jealous brother couldn't be more pleased.

"Perhaps I should start getting ready after all," Miranda said. "I think I need to choose a different dress. Something more daring than the silver and blue is in order."

I smiled and she grinned back.

"Come and help me, Josie.

* * *

MIRANDA WAS RIGHT. The blue and silver gown was lovely. It showed off her slim waist and the flare of her breasts and hips, but it showed no flesh from the neck down. While I agreed with Lady Lucia's opinion that men, on the whole, preferred to see bare skin, it would seem Miranda and Lord Frederick held a different view of the king. He wanted his future wife to be a modest, elegant noble-woman. Miranda, in the blue and silver dress, was a perfect match.

Miranda in the pink one was far more *obvious*, once we set about lowering the neckline. It didn't take long to cut away the excess fabric at her décolletage and finish it off with a row of beads to draw the eye.

"What about jewelry?" she asked, holding the dress against her body and checking it in the mirror.

"What would you usually wear?"

"I have some diamond earrings that would look sweet once my hair is up."

"Sweet is too…sweet. Wear something bigger. And a necklace, too."

Her reflection smiled at me. "How about two necklaces?"

"The more the better. Paint your lips a bright color too."

"That may be more difficult. Perhaps I can borrow Lady Lucia's."

Hilda the maid arrived with a light supper on a tray. The guard with her informed Miranda that the taster had tested it first. She thanked them and set the tray down but didn't eat.

"Are you nervous?" I asked.

"About the poisoner? A little." She lay the dress on the bed and eyed the food. She picked a nut off the plate. "I'm more nervous about the king's reaction. What if we've misjudged him, Josie? What if Lucia's right and he secretly likes this sort of dress? It might make him more interested, not less." She sighed and flopped back on the pillows. "I wish I could go home. Everything's so much simpler there. Here there are more intrigues than people, and friendships are formed according to political alignments. Ever since the king showed interest in me, I've felt as though the eyes of the entire court follow my every move." She patted the space beside her on the bed and I sat too. "You're lucky you get to go home."

"There are certain benefits to living in a palace that I can see." I indicated the platter. "Someone cooks you delicious food and serves it to you."

"I do like that part."

"There are lovely grounds to walk around at your leisure."

"The problem is, I have too much leisure time. There's nothing to do except walk and gossip. Some like to gamble."

"You attend parties dressed in beautiful gowns," I said.

"They're just trimmings, Josie. Don't envy me because of those." She hooked her arm through mine. "And anyway, you have a lot that I envy. Chief among them is your freedom. You can choose whomever you want to marry."

"I can now," I murmured.

She hugged my arm. "I'm sorry. That was insensitive of me."

I gave her a smile, determined not to let thoughts of the loss of my father dampen my spirits. I'd enjoyed helping Miranda with the dress and plotting ways to diminish the king's interest in her.

Hilda returned with a pot of Lady Lucia's lip color. She helped Miranda dress in the pink gown and fixed her hair. Miranda insisted on wearing it in a loose, slightly messy arrangement with flowers threaded through it. I didn't think the style suited her, which was perhaps why she chose it.

"The torches in the gardens are being lit," I said from my position by the window. "It'll look so pretty once it's completely dark."

Miranda joined me and pointed out the path the torches made. "We've not been informed what will take place, or where, but I think we'll be led off that way through the garden. It'll smell lovely at this time of the evening."

"It seems to lead to that bank of trees to the right of the big lake."

"That's Lake Grand, and those trees hide a sunken garden. It's been off limits for days. I imagine there'll be some kind of performance there."

I sighed. "It sounds wonderful. I wish I could see it."

She smiled a slow, devilish smile. "You can." She grabbed my hand and dragged me to the bed where the blue dress still lay. She picked it up and held it against me.

"No. Oh no, no, no. I can't," I said.

"You can. We're the same size."

"I'm not a noblewoman."

"Nobody will notice. There are so many here at the palace, and we don't all know one another. Just keep your head down if you pass someone who might recognize you."

It was a very bad idea. But sometimes, bad ideas are the most exciting and refuse to be dismissed. The dress certainly was beautiful, and the thought of seeing the festivities up close would be a sight I'd never experience again.

"Say yes," Miranda said, pushing the dress into my arms. "I know you want to."

I held the dress against myself and checked my reflection. It was simple yet elegant, with silver threads embroidered into the hem and down the central panel in a wave pattern. The bodice was a plain ice-blue all the way to the neck.

"I do want to," I said, "but that doesn't mean I should. What if I'm found out?"

"Who will find out? Everyone will be too busy watching the king and the entertainments he has planned for us."

"But I should go home."

She rifled through a box on the dressing table. "Don't take this the wrong way, Josie, but why should you go home?"

She was right. It wasn't as if I needed to be home for anything or anyone. None of the expectant mothers were due soon.

"Change in my dressing room. Hilda, where is that brooch? The crystal one shaped like a sun?"

I changed into the dress but Miranda wouldn't let me look in the mirror until everything was complete. Hilda spent more time doing my hair than her mistress's, positioning a crystal comb at the back to complete the arrangement. Miranda pinned a matching brooch to the gown at my throat then stood back.

"There," she said on a breath. "Lovely. You wear it better than I ever did."

"I doubt that."

Miranda turned me to face the mirror and I gasped. The woman in the ball gown wasn't me. It couldn't be me. I was a simple village girl who barely remembered to brush her hair in the mornings. The woman in the reflection was elegant and pretty.

"A little color on your lips and cheeks," Miranda said. "Not as dark as the one I'll wear."

Hilda handed me a pot of the palest coral, and Miranda positioned me in front of the mirror again. I watched her apply a vibrant shade to her own lips and copied her technique with the coral. We finished by smoothing the lightest amount on our cheeks.

A trumpeter blasted a tune from the garden. Several others joined from positions throughout the palace, like a call to arms. The palace filled with their brassy chorus.

"It's time, my lady," Hilda said. "If Miss Cully is to go unnoticed, she should stay here while you take the guard with you. Then she can join the others assembling downstairs."

"Good plan." Miranda gave me another thorough inspection before announcing I was ready. "Remember, head down, and don't engage anyone you know in conversation. Avoid the guards." She gave me a brief hug. "Most of all, enjoy yourself. I'll meet you back here afterward."

I bit my lip and nodded.

"Don't do that to your lip," she scolded.

I nodded again. Just as she was about to leave, I remembered I had advice for her too. "Please be careful tonight, Miranda."

"I'll be perfectly fine. The captain is assigning two guards to me at all times. I'm not sure it's necessary, but I am grateful."

"If the captain thinks it's necessary then it is. Don't eat or drink a thing."

"I won't." She raced out of the room, and I followed a few minutes later.

The guards had left with Miranda, and the corridor was empty. I descended the grand staircase behind a group of nobles. They complimented one another on their outfits and speculated on the type of festivities the king had in store for them. They were as giddy and giggly as children presented with a shop full of sweetmeats. Perhaps they were already drunk.

There were so many ladies and gentlemen milling at the twin ponds outside that it was easy to blend in, dressed in Miranda's ball gown. Nobody paid me any mind. Even so, I quickly scanned the faces of those nearest me. I recognized none. I drew in a deep breath, but the air was filled with a cloying mix of perfumes that caught in my throat. I coughed uncontrollably, earning me a glare from those nearest.

A footman passed with a tray of drinks and I plucked off a crystal glass. The cool wine washed away the irritant and steadied my nerves a little. They returned when I spotted Lady Violette Morgrave talking to a gentleman. I dipped my head but kept her in my line of sight. Fortunately, she did not look my way.

The ebb and flow of conversations suddenly stopped, and a wave of whispers flowed through the crowd. "The king."

All eyes turned to the palace, where the king stood at the top of the steps, flanked by Hammer and Max. Lady Lucia dropped into a graceful curtsy and only rose when the king bade her to. Beside her, her brother bowed, but the king only had eyes for Lady Lucia. Other ladies curtseyed too, but it was too late. Lady Lucia already occupied the king's left arm. His right remained free. He searched the faces, but not finding the one he wanted, he headed down the steps. Lady Lucia's smile widened.

The crowd parted for them. Gentlemen bowed and the ladies curtseyed in a sea of rustling silks. The king strode slowly among them, looking comfortable and benevolent. My tisane must have worked.

"Follow me!" the king announced. "Follow me into a magical world filled with wondrous sights. Prepare to be dazzled."

The crowd made suitably amazed sounds and fell into step behind him. We formed a long line that snaked slowly through the partitioned gardens. Torches lit the gravel path, and thanks to the overcast sky, the darkness beyond the torches was absolute. Behind, however, the palace was brightly illuminated. Every window was ablaze with light as if it were on fire. That sight in itself amazed me.

Our promenade continued through the vast formal gardens that I'd only ever seen from palace windows and Lookout Hill. Paths divided the garden into sections, with each section featuring a different color grouping of flowers laid out in patterns—stars, circles, diamonds. Many featured a fountain in the middle, others statues, all lit up by lanterns and torches. Footmen stood to one side with trays of more wine so that no one went without.

But it was the dancers everyone clamored to see. Men and women dressed in fitted costumes with wings at their backs performed to music that seemed to come from all around us. They flitted through the shallow water of the fountains as lightly as butterflies, splashing themselves and each other, and occasionally sprinkling one of the guests. Each fountain featured a different set of dancers, dancing to a different style of music, dressed in a different color. One set wore gold, one silver, another red. I'd never seen such graceful moves, such daring outfits that sparkled in the light, and was one of the last to leave each performance.

The procession snaked its way further from the palace, drawing ever closer to the sunken garden. We passed ponds, rockeries and more gardens, drenched in light by lanterns that directed their glow to a featured statue of prancing nymphs, or the god and goddess kissing, or a golden orb on a pedestal, or yet another fountain. The crowd had grown quieter with each new sight. They spoke in hushed, expectant whispers at the turn of each corner.

Finally we reached Lake Grand, where we paused for refreshments. Two long tables were set up on the lawn, each decorated with tall white vases overflowing with pristine white flowers. Platters were piled high with pink marzipan, and others held crystalized plums, oranges and peaches. What appeared to be yellow flowers turned out to be nuts covered in borrodi spice. The bed of green leaves in which they nestled was an edible confection that melted on my tongue and left it tingling.

Small cakes formed pyramids at intervals along the table cloth, each one iced with a delicate touch so that it appeared to be covered in lace. Beads in pink, blue and green topped each cake. When the nobles flocked to the cakes like gulls to the fishing boats, I realized they weren't beads but gemstones. The cakes were all gone before I had the chance to take one. When the procession set off again, there was nothing left of the towers, and crumbs littered the lawn.

With the formal gardens behind us, we traversed a path lined with shrubs and trees a little taller than me. Instead of torches to light our way, lanterns hung from boughs. Floral garlands draped between them, their sweet scent lingering in the warm, still air.

The path opened up to a grove surrounded by trees, also lit with lanterns. The grove itself was the sunken garden Miranda had mentioned. There were no flowers in this garden, only an empty expanse of lawn. It could hardly be called a garden either, it was more like a circular theater. The tiered seating around the perimeter were covered in lawn, as was the raised dais down below. A throne of gold decorated with pink and white flowers on vines stood in the middle of the dais. It looked as if it had grown out of the lawn. A canopy of crimson velvet protected the dais. If it rained, the king and his guards would be the only dry ones.

He flipped out the long tail of his gold brocade coat and sat. He crossed his feet at the ankles, showing off his gem-studded shoes, and spread out his hands, welcoming his guests to the grove. Hammer and Max stood on either side of him, slightly set back in the shadows. I couldn't see Hammer's eyes but I knew his gaze would be darting around the crowd. I had expected to see more guards. Perhaps they were hidden, like the musicians.

Footmen ushered guests to the tiers to sit and it wasn't until one drew near me that I realized the guards had been disguised as footmen. I refused his assistance and quickly turned away, hoping he hadn't recognized me.

With everyone settled, the king stood. He raised his arms to the sky, puffed out his chest, and bellowed, "Let the entertainments begin!"

A trapdoor I hadn't noticed opened near the dais and four women and two men emerged. The women wore bands over their breasts and skirts no bigger than a handkerchief, and the men wore nothing but loincloths. Their oiled skin gleamed. They danced and tumbled, performing acrobatics, sometimes with fire. When they finished, another act followed then another and another. Some acts incorporated magic tricks. The final performance with six horses that the acrobats leaped over while the horses trotted around the arena had the crowd gasping in awe and me on the edge of my seat.

Afterward, we were directed back to the banks of Lake Grand where the tables had been set with more food. All remnants of the earlier refreshments had been replaced. Even the crumbs had been swept away. Footmen wove through the crowd and I plucked another glass of wine from one of their trays.

I caught sight of Lady Deerhorn standing in the shadows at the edge of the clearing. She appeared to be waiting for someone. A moment later, her daughter joined her. Lady Violette Morgrave glanced around and sidled closer to her mother. Their hands touched, and Lady Morgrave opened the purse dangling from her wrist and slipped something inside. Without a word to one another, the two ladies separated.

I tried to see where Lady Morgrave went but I lost her among the crowd. It was easier to find the king, however. He was the center of attention, regaling several ladies and gentlemen with a commentary of the performances that had them listening intently. Hammer stood a few steps away, looking serious and impossibly handsome in his black uniform with the gold braids, sword strapped to his hip, and piercing gaze that saw everything. Including me.

I knew the moment he realized I was there when his eyes briefly widened then tightened at the edges. I suspected I was not a welcome sight. Even with the possibility of a scolding, however, I had to warn him.

He moved away from the king and positioned himself where

he could speak with me and see the king at the same time. His gaze darted back and forth, and didn't settle on me again.

"You didn't go home," he said simply.

"I wanted to see the entertainments." It was hardly a good defense but considering I didn't have one, it was all I could offer. "Miranda loaned me a dress."

"I didn't think you'd brought it in your medical bag."

"There's no need for sarcasm, Captain."

His gaze met mine. "Would you prefer I tell you how angry I am?" He looked away again.

"Sarcasm is fine."

"Now that the revelries are over, you can leave. The sooner the better. Make sure no one sees you. I'll have one of my men—"

"For goodness' sake," I hissed. "There's no need to assign anyone to me. You can't spare any men, and I am perfectly capable of asking for a carriage to take me home."

He regarded me with severely arched brows as if questioning *my* right to be angry with *him*. It was unnerving. "I know I don't belong here," I said hotly. "I know this dress doesn't hide the commoner I am underneath."

His jaw softened and he shifted his stance. "If the king sees you here, he'll be furious. He won't allow you back to the palace, not even for a medical emergency. That's not what I want. Do you?"

Well, when he put it like that, it was almost flirtatious.

"I'll go," I muttered. "But first I need to tell you that I saw Lady Deerhorn surreptitiously pass something to Lady Morgrave just a few moments ago. It was small enough to be concealed in her hand."

"Thank you."

"Did you speak to her about buying poisons off Tam?"

"She denied it," he said. "She denied going to his house at all but she was lying."

"How do you know?"

"I can usually tell when someone is lying."

"Good to know." I smiled.

He scowled.

"I'm going, I'm going."

I took a circuitous route back to the palace, avoiding the king and the people near him. Lady Lucia was still glued to his side, but he often glanced around, looking for Miranda, perhaps. I spotted her near one of the tables, surrounded by gentlemen who couldn't keep their gazes off her. Two guards dressed as footmen stood nearby, holding trays. I hoped Hammer could see her from his vantage point. I glanced back at him, only to find Lady Deerhorn right behind me.

We both gasped, but she recovered from the surprise quicker. She grabbed my wrist. "You're the doctor's daughter."

I tried to pull away but her grip tightened, cutting off my circulation.

"What are you doing here?" she snapped.

I jerked free, picked up my skirts and rushed away. This time I did not look back. I followed the path into the formal gardens, only to stop again when I heard a distressed woman's voice coming from behind a hedge.

"Stop this, Lucien," she said. It sounded like Lady Claypool.

"Stop what?" The man's voice was familiar, but I couldn't quite place it. "Stop loving you? I can't. I've tried and I can't."

"I'm a married woman, and happily so." It was definitely Lady Claypool.

"Happy? Living in the middle of nowhere with that arrogant prick? You don't have to pretend with me, Minette."

"I'm not pretending. Now let me go." She gasped. "Lucien! Enough!"

"Merdu, but you're a cold-hearted bitch."

"Stop it! Stop this at once. Let me go or I'll scream."

"Go ahead. No one can hear you."

"Don't!" The crack of a hand slapping skin seemed far closer than the voices.

"You bitch!"

Her response was muffled. I picked up my skirts and raced around the side of the hedge. Then I did what any woman from the village would do if a friend was being attacked by a man—I jumped on his back, forcing him to let her go.

She fell backward into the hedge and stared up at me, riding on the duke of Gladstow's back. He grunted and growled like a wild beast, swatting at me with his big paws, turning around and around in an attempt to dislodge me.

When Lady Claypool was well clear of him, I jumped off him, grabbed her hand, and ran.

Once back on the path, I gave her a little shove in the direction of the revelers. "Go that way. I have to return to the palace."

"Thank you, Miss Cully," she said, her voice shaking. She gave me a wobbly smile then hurried off in the direction of the chattering voices.

I ran toward the palace, honing in on it like a moth to a beacon. When I reached the twin ponds, I slowed to a walk. No one had followed me, and I was quite sure the duke hadn't seen my face. I hoped he left Lady Claypool alone, not just tonight but every night. Perhaps I should inform Hammer.

I sat on the edge of the fountain and dipped my fingers into the cool water. It was blessedly quiet here. I couldn't even hear the music. Lake Grand seemed miles away, as far off as Mull. The two worlds were as disparate as the sun and moon. Life's mundane moments took place in Mull. In the village, people lived and died and went about the business of survival in between. The revelries, however, were all about glamor and amusement and enjoying *this* moment.

The description didn't really do the village the justice it deserved. There was joy to be had in the friendships, the daily routines of going to market, of seeing patients. Not to mention the perpetuity of the village itself. Mull had existed long before I was born, and it would exist long after my passing. Each year, new life was added while others were taken away, and each life wove another thread through the village's fabric. In comparison, the palace felt like a shell. Without their memories, the staff would never fill it with chatter and laughter. It would never feel like a home for them.

I couldn't help wondering about Hammer and the others— where they'd come from and what made them lose their memories. The lack of answers frustrated me. It frustrated me even more that the king seemed to be withholding information from them. The more I thought about it, the more convinced I became. Hammer's insistence that he trusted the king no longer rang true either, but I couldn't explain why. The problem was, he was too loyal to admit it to me, and perhaps even to himself.

I was not so loyal.

I strode into the entrance hall and emerged on the palace's eastern side beneath the pink colonnaded portico. It was darker here, although a few torches had been lit to keep the shadows at bay.

Now that I knew where it was, I easily found the external entrance to the garrison. I was surprised to find the door unlocked, however, despite all the guards being on duty at the revels. I found the set of keys in the drawer then grabbed a lit torch from the wall sconce.

The right room wasn't as easy to find. I traversed passages, climbed stairs and descended them again. I backtracked twice and almost bumped into a maid carrying a bedpan. She looked as surprised as I felt.

"Are you lost, my lady?" she asked, bobbing a curtsy. She must think me a noblewoman.

I was about to give her an excuse then thought the truth might be better, but not all of it. "Actually, I'm Miss Cully, the doctor's daughter. Captain Hammer asked me to check on the woman."

"Woman, miss?"

"The one kept in the room. The one who cries out." I held my breath, hoping it was a good enough description yet vague enough too, and hoping she even knew the answer. I showed her the keys.

It seemed to convince her. She pointed along the corridor. "Next right will take you there."

I thanked her and didn't wait to see if she found my request odd. I recognized the corridor and the padlocked door. It was my third time there, so I ought. The fourth key on the iron ring slipped easily into the lock. The clank of it opening echoed all around me and seemed to follow me as I entered.

I thrust the torch out front like a weapon but remained in the doorway, prepared to back out and slam the door shut if someone attacked. But nothing moved, and no wailing greeted me.

I took a step inside, two, and held the torch high. The room was more comfortable than the prison cells. Indeed, it was cozier than my own room, with a big bed, dressing table, table and chairs. Blue velvet cushions softened the wooden chairs, and a thick rug covered the stone floor. The pile of blankets on the bed looked warm, inviting.

They moved.

I held my breath as fingers curled over the blankets and pushed them down, revealing a mass of dark hair framing a pale, oval face. Small eyes blinked against the light. I recognized her. It was the maid who'd run into the village months ago, before I'd ever been to the palace. The guards had retrieved her. It would seem they'd locked her away in here with no light, no fresh air, and no company.

Merdu, why?

"Who're you?" she said, voice cracking. "Where's Hammer?"

"My name is Josie. Hammer is...he sent me." I approached slowly, carefully, not sure whether my caution was for her reassurance or mine.

She shifted away, taking the blankets with her, revealing the space beneath the bed and the box stored there. No, not a box; a wooden cabinet.

The king's cabinet.

I was caught between my desire to see what was in it and to find out more about the woman. My hesitation cost me.

My only warning came in the widening of the woman's eyes as her gaze shifted to the doorway behind me.

Then pain tore through my skull and I couldn't stop myself falling.

CHAPTER 16

*M*y head felt like it had been split in two, but somehow, by some miracle, I didn't black out. I fell forward, landing heavily on my hands and knees.

The woman in the bed screamed, the piercing sound shattering my nerves as thoroughly as the blow had. It roused me into action, and I managed to look over my shoulder at my attacker.

Lord Frederick stood over me, raising a bloodstained club above his head. His lips parted with his gasp and his grip slackened. "You're not Miranda."

The moment's hesitation was all I needed. I kicked as hard as I could, smashing my foot into his knee. He fell, roaring in pain, and dropped the club.

I scrambled backward until I hit the bed. The woman still screamed.

Lord Frederick lurched to his feet and limped toward me, his face twisted with pain and distress. He began to cry, the tears streaming down his cheeks. He looked like a man standing on a cliff, about to reluctantly throw himself off it.

"I'm sorry," he said through his tears. "I thought you were her. But you're not, and I can't let you live now. I'm so sorry."

A maid appeared in the doorway only to disappear again. Lord Frederick hadn't seen her, thank the goddess.

He kept advancing toward me, his limping gait slowing his progress. "Hailia, forgive me."

"Please, don't," I begged. "Killing me won't help your sister with the king."

"It will when I remove Miranda."

Merdu.

I felt behind me but my fingers met only floor and bed. "Why do you want Lady Lucia to be with the king? I thought you loved her."

"That's precisely why I'm doing it. She wants to be queen, and I want to please her. Once she delivers him a prince or two, she'll be mine again. I simply have to bide my time and give her the thing she desires the most. Then she'll love me again."

I shifted to the side, my fingers dancing behind me, searching. Finally I touched wood. "They'll know it's you," I said.

"They'll think the madwoman did it. I've kept enough poison for her that it'll look like she took her own life after taking yours. I'm sorry, Miss Cully, but you shouldn't have dressed as Miranda." His mouth twisted and his sobs made him difficult to understand. "You shouldn't have become involved in this. Nor should your father. I didn't want to kill him or Tao, but I had to. Your father's prying left me no choice. And now you leave me no choice." He bent to pick up the club.

Terror and desperation must have propelled me because in the barest blink of an eye, I'd dragged the cabinet out from beneath the bed and jumped to my feet. I lifted it above my throbbing head and brought it down on Frederick's.

He collapsed onto the floor, face first, unconscious.

The woman did not stop screaming, but I had no capacity to comfort her. My heart felt like it would smash through my ribs and my head was on fire. I could do nothing more than sit on the floor and lean back against the foot of the bed.

Running footsteps echoed along the corridor and Erik appeared. He took in the scene and swore in his native tongue. He nudged Lord Frederick with the point of his sword. Frederick groaned but did not get up.

"Are you hurt, Josie?" Erik asked.

I touched the back of my head. The hair was sticky and my

fingers came away bloodied, but it seemed like the bleeding had stopped. "Not too badly."

He helped me to my feet then leaned over the bed. "Hush, Laylana. It is over. You are safe."

Her scream changed to a wail, the same one I'd heard before. She looked terrified. Erik sighed and moved away. He nudged Lord Frederick with the toe of his boot.

"Why did he want to hurt you?" he asked.

"He thought I was Lady Miranda," I said.

His gaze took in my dress. He nodded. "He is poisoner?"

More footsteps thudded along the corridor and Hammer stepped into the room. "Josie!"

Brant bumped him as he passed and Hammer had to put his hand on the doorframe to regain his balance. He leaned heavily on it for a moment then pushed off with effort.

"What in the god's name is going on here?" he snapped. I opened my mouth to speak but he put up a finger to stop me. "Erik?"

"A maid tell me there is trouble here," Erik said. "I come and see Lord Frederick like this." He shrugged. "He is not dead."

Brant kicked the body. Lord Frederick groaned.

"Josie?" Hammer prompted.

"He came up behind me and hit me on the head." I touched the spot again, pressing gently to test for fractures. Merdu, it felt like I'd been hit all over again. I'd tested for fractures on others dozens of times under my father's guidance but never realized how much pain that alone caused the patient until now. "When I turned around, he saw that it was me and hesitated," I went on. "He thought I was Miranda. I was able to take advantage of his hesitation and hit back."

All three men looked at Lord Frederick as he groaned again. He managed to roll over and open his eyes. He closed them again upon seeing the guards and whimpered.

"You are strong woman." Erik clapped my shoulder. "Good."

Brant's gaze scanned my length and heat flared in his eyes. "Well, well. She can heal *and* kill. Impressive."

"He's not dead," I shot back.

"He could be." His fingers tightened around his sword hilt as he arched his brows at Hammer.

Hammer gave his head the slightest shake. Brant sighed and released his sword.

"He is poisoner," Erik announced.

"How could he mistake me for Miranda?" I folded my arms and rubbed, but a chill sank into my bones anyway. "We look nothing alike."

"From the back you do," Brant said with a lift of his top lip that was part sneer, part accusation. "And in that dress. What's she going to say when she finds out you stole it?"

"I didn't steal it. She loaned it to me so I could blend in at the festivities. As to looking alike, everyone in Glancia is tall and blonde. Half the women at court look like this. Why would he—? Oh." I touched my temple and looked down at my clothing. "I remember now. She told him she was wearing a blue dress with a high neckline then she changed her mind and wore something else."

"It was foolish to borrow her dress," Hammer growled. "It was foolish to join the others at the sunken garden and to come here."

I bristled. "I disagree. The first two should have been a little harmless fun. There hasn't been a lot of fun in my life lately, and I wanted to forget my troubles. As to your third point, not even you could have foreseen this, Hammer, so do *not* lecture me."

His back stiffened and his jaw hardened. He would not back down and apologize, and I wouldn't allow him to make me feel guilty. Everything between us would change now, and that I did regret. There'd be no more easy conversations, no more flirting, if that's what it was. There would only be his words hanging like a weight between us. I liked him, but not enough to allow to him speak to me in such a manner.

He finally looked away and drew in a deep breath. "Erik, escort Josie to the garrison."

"Not Mull?" he asked.

"Not yet."

Was I a prisoner too, or merely temporarily restrained? It would have been a more palatable order if he'd directed it at me and not his guard.

"Brant, take his lordship to the cells," Hammer went on.

Brant smirked down at Lord Frederick. "My pleasure."

Lord Frederick gulped.

"And you, Captain?" Erik asked as he stood by the door, waiting for me.

Hammer looked to Laylana, mewling like a sick cat, the blankets drawn up to her chin. "I'll wait here until Laylana settles."

Brant grabbed Lord Frederick by his doublet only to let him go again. He frowned at the cabinet, noticing it for the first time. "What's that doing here?" He reached out but suddenly recoiled. His fingers curled into a loose fist. "What was that? Did anyone else feel it?"

Hammer picked up the cabinet and tucked it under his arm. "Sergeant," he barked. "The prisoner."

Brant swallowed and tore his gaze away. He pulled Lord Frederick up without a care for his injuries, and forced him from the room.

"You're hurting me," Lord Frederick whined.

Brant merely grinned.

Erik and I followed them part of the way, but Brant stopped when the corridor intersected another.

"Why were you in there?" he asked me.

"I wanted to check on Laylana," I said, using a similar excuse as I'd given the maid. While the cabinet had been my main reason for entering the chamber, I had also wanted to see the woman kept in a locked room. For now, I thought it best not to mention that to this man.

"Without Hammer asking you to?" He snorted. "You really are a fool. I hope I get to see how the captain deals with you later. It could be more entertaining than the party." He forced Lord Frederick down the corridor to the left while Erik and I headed right.

"Do not listen," Erik said. "The captain will not hurt you."

"There are ways to hurt someone that aren't physical," I murmured.

The garrison was empty, and I suspected the guards were still on duty as the revels continued in the gardens. Erik told me he'd been the lone guard stationed at the palace. He must have stepped out of the garrison when I entered and stole the keys.

"The captain will be angry with me," he said from the sideboard where he poured ale into a tankard.

"I'm sorry. I'll tell him I tricked you."

He thanked me, but we both knew it wouldn't save him from a scolding.

"Did you hear Laylana screaming?" I asked. "Is that why you came?"

He nodded. "I see maid too and tell her to get the captain. I would say you are lucky I come but you do not need me."

He handed me the cup and I drank, only to splutter at the strong, bitter taste. It wasn't ale.

"Drink," Erik said. "It helps the heart." He tapped his chest.

I was skeptical about its health benefits but it did slow my racing heartbeat a little.

That is, until Hammer returned. "Erik, take Brant and return to the king's side. Stay with him until I return."

"But there is no danger now," Erik said. I thought him brave for speaking at all. A glare from Hammer sent him on his way, however.

Hammer waited for the door to close before perching on the edge of the table. He crossed his arms and watched me. He didn't speak and the only movement came from the steady rise and fall of his chest. His gaze held neither heat nor ice, but it stretched my nerves to breaking point. I needed more of that drink.

I refilled the tankard only to have it plucked out of my hand before I could sip. I hadn't heard Hammer move. He stood close, trapping me against the sideboard. My heart raced, my breath quickened. Every piece of me became very aware of every piece of him. The way the light cast deep shadows across his eyes, beneath his cheeks, the way his hair was tousled, and the way he was so much taller and broader than me. Very much that.

"Josie," he began, then did not continue.

Part of me wanted to prompt him to go on, but part of me didn't want to hear his admonishment. There were only so many times a woman could bear hearing that she was a fool, particularly from a man she found so compelling.

Because despite his physical presence and strength, despite his anger, I was still attracted to him. My attraction galled me as much as being told I was a fool. I wished I felt otherwise. In time, I would, if I could stay away from the palace and him. But for now, I *was* a fool.

"There's blood in your hair." He lifted a hand and I instinctively leaned away. He dropped it back to his side. "You're afraid of me."

I swallowed and tried to think of an answer, but my tongue failed me.

As if he realized he was too close, he stepped back. He tucked his hands behind him and lowered his head. After a moment, he said, "Come with me." He strode to the door leading to the service corridors, not the one leading outside. So he wasn't about to throw me into the prison cells for unlawfully entering a private chamber, nor was he sending me home.

"Where are we going?" I asked, following him.

"To ask Laylana some questions."

"Which questions?"

"Whichever ones you want."

Laylana was still skittish but at least she wasn't screaming or wailing. Hammer had managed to calm her. I suspected a herbal tisane of some description, but there was no evidence of anything stronger than water in the cup on the bedside table.

"Laylana, this is Josie," Hammer said. "She's a doctor."

I didn't correct him. I smiled at her but did not approach the bed. After the incident with Lord Frederick, I was skittish too.

She lowered the blanket she'd drawn up to her chin upon our entry. "Will you cure me?" she asked.

I looked to Hammer but he offered me no guidance. "What ails you?" I asked.

"I...I don't know." Her voice was thin, reedy, and seemed to come from far away.

"Do you have any aches or pains in your body?"

She shook her head. "It's my mind. I can't remember."

"None of us can," Hammer said. "We've spoken about this, Laylana."

"Why, doctor? Why can't we remember?"

I was about to tell her I couldn't give her any answers, but she looked at me with hope and trust, and I couldn't destroy that. "I'm looking for a cure," I told her.

She smiled tentatively. "Until then, I'll stay in here."

I tilted my head to the side. "Why?"

"It's safer."

I glanced at Hammer but his face was a blank mask. "With the door locked?"

"To keep me in," Laylana said. "I've run off before when I... when I had a turn. I don't want to do that again. I want to wake up here afterward." She smoothed her palm over the blanket. "Sometimes, I think I remember this room."

"What do you mean by a turn?" I asked.

"You tell her, Captain. I don't remember them."

"Laylana has episodes where her memory is wiped clean," he said.

I gasped. "All of it?"

He nodded. "Her name, her recent experiences. It's worse than our memory loss. We at least remember everything that has happened to us from the moment the palace was completed. Laylana loses her memory again and again. Sometimes it happens two or three times a week, sometimes she can go a few weeks without an episode."

"That's awful. So she can't remember any of you? She doesn't remember the palace, or your problem with memory loss?"

He shook his head.

"How frightening," I said. No wonder she screamed in terror and wailed mournfully. Imagine knowing nothing about yourself and those around you. Imagine waking up surrounded by strangers. "Do any of your memories ever return, Laylana?"

"No. I do have a vague sense of belonging in this room, though." She clutched the blankets to her, as if those were the only constant in her ever-changing world.

"Captain, why didn't you tell me?" I asked.

Finally, his mask slipped. He lowered his head, shrugged. "I don't know."

"You don't trust me," I murmured.

His head snapped up. "I trust you." He swallowed. "I trust you, Josie." Was he trying to convince himself or me?

I rubbed my temples. Hailia, my head hurt. I needed some

hollyroot. A lot of hollyroot. "Even after I went behind your back to look for this cabinet?" I said. "I doubt it, Hammer."

He winced, and it took me a moment to realize it was because I used his name, not his rank.

"You have every right to distrust my actions." I was digging my own grave, but it seemed fair and right to admit guilt where I was guilty. He couldn't be blamed for everything, although I was still reeling about being called a fool. "But I went behind your back for a reason. I want to help you find answers." I nodded at the cabinet, now sitting on the dressing table. "If I have to go behind your back again in my search for the truth, I will."

Hammer eyed the cabinet. His fists curled at his sides and the knuckles went white. He wanted to open it, yet he didn't either. It was the first sign of a crack in his iron-willed resolve. I could widen that crack, if I was careful.

"What are you afraid of?" I asked.

He said nothing, just stared at the cabinet.

A different tactic was required. "I understand why you trust him. I understand why you *want* to trust him. But he's lying to you. You know he is, Captain."

He rubbed his thumb over his fisted knuckles. "I do."

"So why don't you open it and find out what he's hiding?"

"I will." But he didn't move toward it. He just continued to stare. "I've been biding my time, gathering information, looking elsewhere for answers and cures."

"But you've found none, have you?" I kept my voice calm, gentle, the way my father spoke with distraught villagers after they'd lost a loved one. For all his briskness toward patients, he could be the most caring man when he tried. "The answers may be in there," I went on. "They may not be bad answers, either; they might be good ones. But you won't know until you open it."

"He'll have my own men throw me in the cells if he finds out."

"I know that's not worrying you. I know you're more afraid of losing a friend's trust than going to prison."

He looked sharply at me. The sudden movement startled Laylana. She shrank back behind the blankets. If she knew what we talked about, and who, she gave no indication. Hammer seemed to trust her enough to have this conversation in front of her, although he did not mention the king by name.

"He's not your friend, Captain. He's keeping secrets and lying to you. He doesn't deserve your loyalty."

He turned back to the cabinet and with a deep intake of breath, strode toward it. He withdrew a flick-knife from his pocket and forced the doors open, only to fall back as if an invisible hand had pushed him.

I stepped closer but his outstretched arm blocked me. "Don't touch it," he said.

I had no intention of touching it. I simply stared. Sitting at the bottom of the cabinet was an egg-shaped gem, the color of freshly spilled blood. If I held it in my palm, I would just be able to close my hand around it completely. Its facets swallowed the light, causing the gem to glow from the inside. The glow grew brighter the longer we stared.

"What is it?" I whispered.

"A stone," Hammer said.

"A cure?" Laylana asked.

"It's just a stone."

Hammer removed the gem, studied it then went to put it back. Only he didn't return it. He slipped it into his sleeve then dipped his hand into his pocket. He closed the cabinet doors. His sleight of hand must have been to trick Laylana because I'd seen everything.

"May I borrow this blanket?" he asked Laylana.

She nodded and he wrapped the blanket around the cabinet. He tucked it under his arm and bade Laylana goodnight.

"I'll see you in the morning with breakfast," he said with a smile that didn't reach his eyes.

"Flat cakes?" she asked.

"With syrup."

She smiled.

"Goodnight, Laylana," I said. "I hope I can visit you again, if that's all right."

She nodded but looked uncertain. Perhaps she wondered what I'd think if I returned and she'd forgotten me.

Hammer locked the door and together we headed up to Lady Miranda's rooms and fetched my bag and clothes before exiting the palace altogether on the forecourts side. The revelers must still be in the gardens, enjoying the music and wine in the warm night air. If I listened very hard, I could hear laughter on the breeze.

The two guards on the gate stood to attention and greeted their captain. As we drew close, a faint glow shone through his pocket, only to recede the further away we got from the gate. No, not the gate, the *men*.

"Captain, the gem," I said when we were out of earshot. "It responded to those guards."

He opened the flap of his pocket and looked inside. "How?"

"It glowed."

"It's still glowing."

I looked into his pocket. "Yes, but not much. When you opened the cabinet doors, it began to glow. The color brightened when you touched it. I think it becomes more active when it's around people."

He checked the vicinity. We were half way between the palace gates and the stables and coach house. No one was near. This side of the palace was empty, silent. He pulled out the gem. Its glow strengthened.

"Hold it," he told me.

I put out my hand and he dropped the gem onto my palm. The glow diminished but didn't extinguish.

"Do you feel anything?" he asked.

I caressed it with my thumb. The facets were smooth, their edges sharp. It was cool but not cold. "No."

"No pull? Like it's...?" He shrugged, as if he couldn't think of the words. "Like it's drawing on your vitality?"

"No. It feels like a stone." I handed it back to him and it instantly flared to life.

He dropped it in his pocket. "It's responding only to those of us who've lost our memories." He started walking again. This part of the avenue wasn't well lit and, with the moon hidden behind clouds, I couldn't make out his features. His strides, however, were long and I had to walk quickly to keep up.

"It's not just a stone though, is it?" I asked.

"No."

"What do you think it is?"

"I can't begin to answer that."

I could, but I didn't say it out loud. Not because I didn't want him to hear, but because hearing it spoken might make it seem more real. I didn't want it to be real. I didn't want it to be the answer for their memory loss, for the existence of the palace, for the very existence of all these people. It would mean they shouldn't even *be* here. It might mean they'd disappear one day without warning, never to return.

Magic.

"Will you confront the king about it?" I asked.

"I don't know."

I wanted to press him further but kept my mouth shut. I'd said enough for one night. He'd *done* enough for one night. Now he needed to think about what that gemstone meant.

"If you need to discuss it with someone, you can talk to me," I said. "You know where to find me."

"I do." It was impossible to gauge his intention from those two words. It was entirely possible he never intended to speak to me again. Part of me wouldn't blame him. I'd caused him a few problems and undermined his loyalty to the king.

But all of me would be very disappointed.

We reached the coach house and he sent a sleepy groom to prepare a carriage to take me home. We stood on the avenue outside the building to wait. Neither of us spoke for some time, and I felt the blanket of awkwardness keenly. I couldn't think of a safe topic to ease it, however.

"Will you be all right?" Hammer eventually asked. "Your wound…"

"It'll be fine. There are no fractures, just a headache the size of the palace. A tisane of hollyroot and a good night's rest will get rid of it."

"Send word to me if it doesn't disappear by morning. I'll bring Doctor Clegg out myself."

I smirked. "He'd love that. Tending the midwife who thinks she's a doctor will give him a laugh."

"If he laughs, he might find himself relegated to an attic room."

"I thought Balthazar decides who is assigned to which room."

"Balthazar likes me."

I wasn't quite sure of that but said nothing. It was enough that he'd been disloyal to the king tonight; I couldn't ask him to question Balthazar's motivations too.

Silence fell again. Hammer leaned against one of the columns holding up the stable portico and shifted the cabinet to his other hip. "Josie," he said softly. "Well done tonight. You single-handedly captured the poisoner."

His earnest praise caught me off-guard and set my heart hammering again, so much so that I blurted out the first thing that entered my head. "You called me a fool. Three times, as I recall." *Ugh. Why did I have to bring that up?*

He shifted his weight again. "I'm sorry. I have a temper. It tends to make me say the first thing that enters my head, and sometimes that's the wrong thing."

I laughed. "Believe it or not, I do that too. But only when I'm nervous, not angry. I'm sorry I made you angry."

"It wasn't you, it was..." He sighed. "Very well, it was you. You're so..." He shook his head. "Never mind."

"It's all right. I've heard it all before. Stubborn. Headstrong. Selfish."

Thanks to the flickering light from a nearby torch, his crooked smile looked wicked. It quickly vanished, however. "When I walked into Laylana's room, you looked pale. You were shaking. And there was nothing I could do because you'd already done it. I felt useless."

"You're not useless, Captain. You've got a thousand-strong household to worry about, plus all the visiting nobles with their jealousies, not to mention a king with a bowel problem."

He smiled again. "It's never dull here, that's certain."

"Perhaps it will be now that Lord Frederick has been caught. What will you do with him?"

"He'll face Glancian justice. Whatever that is," he added in a mutter.

I wondered why he faced justice when the other prisoners did not. "Keep an eye on the duke of Gladstow," I said. "I caught him arguing with Lady Claypool tonight. He tried to restrain her."

"Did he?" He nodded thanks. "You have had a busy evening."

I rubbed my head. "I'm looking forward to peace and quiet."

A carriage rolled out of the coach house gates and stopped beside us. Hammer pushed off from the column. He kissed my forehead then opened the door.

I climbed in, too stunned to think of a response. Too stunned even to say goodnight. I ended up turning around and waving at him through the rear window as the carriage drove off in the direction of the village. But he was already walking away, back to the palace.

* * *

THE WORST THING about the patients staying away was that it made the days feel longer. There was only so much cleaning to do. I couldn't even visit Meg because her brother thought I was there to visit him. She did come to me when she could spare the time, and we went for long walks, often up to Lookout Hill where we could gaze upon the palace. It looked like a shiny pearl in an oyster from up there, a precious gem in otherwise bland surroundings. We were too far away to see figures moving about, but I wondered what my new friends were doing. Had Miranda managed to avoid the king? Had Laylana's memory been wiped again? Had Hammer spoken to the king about the gem yet?

News of Lord Frederick's arrest had traveled quickly through the village, and Tam's part in the crime shocked many. I'd mentioned the Tao family's innocence to everyone I knew, but they must have been feeling the weight of the villagers' censure. Mika in particular seemed to withdraw into himself. He still manned the family spice stall, but he wasn't the same friendly youth anymore, and business appeared to be suffering. Many customers frequented the other spice seller in the market, and without my father's business, the stall must be struggling. I must continue to purchase my supplies for medicines from him, but not yet. It was too soon. Seeing him reminded me of his father's hand in my father's death.

At least I was allowed to continue with the apothecary work and midwifery, but I wouldn't grow rich from either. It would barely cover my living expenses.

The worst part about being bored was it allowed me time to think. Not just about the palace and its inhabitants, but about my parents and how much I missed them. I visited their graves every day, usually sitting with my back against one of the headstones until it became too hot.

On the fourth day after the palace's revels, I strolled to the graveyard just outside the village in the afternoon, but found I wasn't the only visitor. Hammer knelt behind the headstone marking my father's grave. He appeared to be digging, but it wasn't until I looked over the headstone that I saw he'd just finished planting a seedling. The sight was so unexpected that I giggled, only to smother it when he looked sharply at me.

"Gardening is one of your many skills, I see," I said.

"I don't think so." He pushed his sword out of the way and sat back to admire his work. "I had to get instructions on what to do from the palace's head gardener. This is a riverwart plant."

"I know. Why are you planting a riverwart plant behind my father's headstone?" I couldn't keep the amusement out of my voice. It was so absurd to see the captain gardening in a graveyard that I couldn't summon the solemnity the site required. My parents wouldn't have minded.

"Once it grows, you can harvest the leaves, dry them, grind them, and use the powder in poison antidotes. I thought it a fitting tribute for your father."

"Very useful. He'd like that. Thank you."

He thrust the trowel into the soil and dusted off his hands as he stood. "Why is it called riverwart when it doesn't grow on riverbanks?"

"I don't know. It's one of life's many mysteries."

"The gardener told me it'll require watering every day while it's young."

"I'll bring a jar of water with me when I come here."

"He also said you should talk to it." He looked at the plant. "I don't think it's much of a conversationalist."

I laughed. "So you do have a sense of humor."

"That depends on who you speak to."

"Don't flatter yourself. I don't speak about you to anyone."

He smiled and, for once, it reached his eyes. They sparkled. "How is your head?"

"Fine, thank you."

"Will you sit with me under that tree?" He walked with me between headstones to the shady spot.

"I'm glad you're here," I said, settling between two thick tree roots at the base of the trunk. He adjusted his sword and sat beside me. "I've been dying to know if you spoke to the king about the gem."

"Not yet. I haven't told anyone, not even Theodore." He shook his head. "The king is, well, the king. He can throw me in jail, if he wants. He can have me executed. If he knows that I know he's lying, he might be prepared to do whatever it takes to stop me learning more. I'm going to proceed cautiously. But I am going to proceed."

I didn't know how but I didn't question him. It was his decision to make, not mine.

"And how is everyone at the palace after Lord Frederick's arrest?"

"Shocked. Relieved that the poisoner has been caught. Saddened, too. He was liked by most."

"What will happen to him?"

"His trial is tomorrow. If he's found guilty, he'll be executed."

"Is there enough evidence for him to be found guilty?"

He nodded.

I wasn't quite sure how I felt about that. I'd liked Lord Frederick. Then again, he'd hidden his true nature from everyone except his sister. "And his family? How is Lady Lucia coping?"

"They were expelled from the palace the day after the revels. They've gone home."

"They're not staying for the trial?"

He shook his head. "They know there's no hope for him. They have to redeem themselves now. Going home and keeping low for a while is the best way to start, but it'll be a long time before the king trusts them again, even though there's no proof that Lord Frederick acted on the family's behalf."

"And what of Lady Deerhorn and Lady Morgrave? Do you think they were involved in the poisoning too?"

"I searched their rooms but found only a sleeping draught in Lady Morgrave's bedchamber. When pressed, she confessed that her mother bought it from Tamworth Tao. Lady Morgrave planned on giving it to her husband in the evenings to send him to sleep."

"Did he confirm it?"

"He didn't know about it and still doesn't. She begged me not to tell him." He stretched out his long legs. "She was going to use it on him that night and sneak out for a rendezvous."

"With whom?"

"She refused to tell me but I suspect with the king."

I blinked at him. "I thought he wasn't with anyone in that way."

"He hasn't been. But if she'd succeeded, that would have changed the night of the revels."

"Oh. I see." It was, perhaps, a good way to secure the king's favor, particularly if she got herself pregnant. He might not be able to marry her, but he could keep her as his mistress and shower her with gifts. For some women, that would be enough.

"Speaking of Lady Deerhorn," I said, "I ought to tell you that she saw me the night of the revels wearing Miranda's dress. She might inform the king." I bit my lip and steeled myself for his reaction.

After a moment he said, "We'll worry about that when and if it happens. Thank you for telling me."

I wound a blade of grass around my finger then unwound it. "I thought I should. You'll probably find out sooner or later, and I don't want to give you any more reasons to mistrust me."

He drew up a knee only to stretch his leg again. He blew out a measured breath. "I want to tell you that you're wrong, Josie, that I have always trusted you, but you'll know it's a lie."

I hazarded a glance at him only to see him watching me closely, carefully, as if he were trying to gauge my thoughts. He should be able to read them easily enough. I was an open book, so everyone told me. It was for that reason I stared down at the grass again. Sometimes, a girl doesn't want to be too obvious.

"I didn't trust you because you weren't from the palace," he said. "You might have helped save Lady Miranda's life, but you were still an outsider. It's difficult for me to trust anyone from the outside. I don't know why. I'm sorry. I should have told you about Laylana."

"You *should* trust your instincts."

"What if my instincts are terrible? They very well could be. I used to trust the king and look how that turned out."

"I think your instincts told you he was lying long before you could admit it. Your instincts *are* good, Captain. I believe so, anyway."

"Call me Dane," he said on a rush of breath.

"Pardon?"

"My name is Dane."

I turned to see him properly and fell into his sea-blue eyes. He stared back at me and seemed to be waiting for me to say something. "Dane Hammer?" I asked.

"Just Dane. I don't think Hammer is a family name. The other servants aren't known by anything other than their first name so why would I be any different?"

I shook my head. "I don't understand. Why do they call you Hammer if it's not your name?"

"On that first day, when our memories began, we knew three things—our position on the palace staff, our own name, and the name we knew the other staff and the king by. They all called me Hammer. I didn't correct them. They just seemed to assume I was called Hammer, just like I assumed Max was Max, Theodore was Theodore, and so on. At first, everyone thought it odd that they all had ordinary sounding names and I didn't, but that was soon forgotten. Not by me, though. The thing is, I knew my name was Dane." He tapped his temple. "In here, I knew Hammer was wrong, that the name wasn't mine."

"So who *is* Hammer?"

"I believe it's a nickname they gave me for some reason. No one else knows my real name is Dane except me."

"Why not correct them?"

He looked off into the distance. "What if there's a reason I never told them? If I had a good reason for keeping it a secret before, I'm going to keep it a secret now, at least until I know more."

He spoke as if he had a life before the day his memories began. I hoped so. It meant these people weren't a figment of a magic trick, that they were real and had lives but had simply forgotten them. I liked that explanation better than the idea that they never existed before that first moment of consciousness.

And then something else hit me. Hammer—Dane—was telling me something he'd not told anyone else. He didn't trust them with the knowledge, but he trusted me. It was humbling. I was grateful and immeasurably relieved. It meant we hadn't ruined all the good things between us. It meant we could start again.

"Thank you, Dane." I lay my hand over his on the ground between us. "I appreciate you telling me."

"It sounds odd hearing you say it. Odd but good."

"I'll keep your secret."

"I know." He turned his hand palm up and twined his fingers with mine. He held tightly, as if anchoring himself to me. Perhaps that's what he needed, a safe port to harbor, somewhere outside the palace, somewhere immune to its influence. I was happy to be that port. I needed the connection now too.

"I wish I had something important to tell you too," I said. "Something that shows you I trust you, but all I have is a story about how I stole a handful of sugared almonds from Old Man Olly's stall when he wasn't looking. I was six and they tasted delicious but I was sick the next day." I smiled at him but he was still staring into the distance. My story hadn't amused him in the slightest. I wasn't sure if he'd even been listening.

He untangled his fingers from mine and stood. "You shouldn't trust me, Josie," he said, striding past the headstones.

My heart dove. Why did he have to ruin a perfectly pleasant moment? "I am aware of your temper, Dane," I said, following him. "But I know you won't hurt me or anyone who doesn't deserve it. If Brant has tried convincing you otherwise, he's wrong."

"That's not it." He pulled the trowel out of the soil where he'd plunged it near the seedling. "Since you mentioned Brant, you should know he's the reason you can't trust me."

I frowned. "That doesn't make sense."

"We both have similar scars on our backs. We were both whipped. That links us, links our pasts. I don't trust Brant."

"Nor do I, but—"

"Then you shouldn't trust me either. Not until we find out why we both have those scars."

I folded my arms and glared at him. "That's absurd."

"I can't trust myself, Josie. Not until I know for sure what happened, who I am, and what I've done in the past. I can't expect anyone else to trust me either. I don't *want* anyone else to trust me. Especially you."

I'd been about to argue with him again, but his final words stole my breath. I could only stare at him. Why *especially* me?

He looked away. "Stay vigilant around me—around anyone from the palace. It's wise to be wary." He thrust the trowel through his belt as if it were a knife. "I have to go."

He strode off. I stared at his back, too stunned to move, until he reached his horse, tied to a tree on the far side of the graveyard. I picked up my skirts and raced after him, but he rode off without a glance back. Perhaps it was just as well that I hadn't had the opportunity to ask if I could visit him at the palace. He might have forbidden it. This way, I didn't have to defy him. I could just show up in the garrison without guilt. I would need to be armed with a good excuse, however. One where he couldn't send me on my way as soon as I arrived.

The problem was, I had no ideas. No ideas, yet a keen sense that I was needed, not just by Hammer—Dane—but by everyone in the palace. I was determined to help them regain their lost memories, whatever the cost.

Pre-order now:

THE ECHO OF BROKEN DREAMS
The 2nd After The Rift novel by C.J. Archer.
When a palace maid is attacked, Josie and the captain investigate. Meanwhile, a visit from an expert on magic brings both hope and danger.

A MESSAGE FROM THE AUTHOR

I hope you enjoyed reading THE PALACE OF LOST MEMORIES as much as I enjoyed writing it. As an independent author, getting the word out about my book is vital to its success, so if you liked this book please consider telling your friends and writing a review at the store where you purchased it. If you would like to be contacted when I release a new book, subscribe to my newsletter at http://cjarcher.com/contact-cj/newsletter/.

ALSO BY C.J. ARCHER

SERIES WITH 2 OR MORE BOOKS

After The Rift

Glass and Steele

The Ministry of Curiosities Series

The Emily Chambers Spirit Medium Trilogy

The 1st Freak House Trilogy

The 2nd Freak House Trilogy

The 3rd Freak House Trilogy

The Assassins Guild Series

Lord Hawkesbury's Players Series

The Witchblade Chronicles

SINGLE TITLES NOT IN A SERIES

Courting His Countess

Surrender

Redemption

The Mercenary's Price

ABOUT THE AUTHOR

C.J. Archer has loved history and books for as long as she can remember and feels fortunate that she found a way to combine the two. She spent her early childhood in the dramatic beauty of outback Queensland, Australia, but now lives in suburban Melbourne with her husband, two children and a mischievous black & white cat named Coco.

Subscribe to C.J.'s newsletter through her website to be notified when she releases a new book, as well as get access to exclusive content and subscriber-only giveaways. Her website also contains up to date details on all her books: http://cjarcher.com She loves to hear from readers. You can contact her through email cj@cjarcher.com or follow her on social media to get the latest updates on her books:

CPSIA information can be obtained
at www.ICGtesting.com
Printed in the USA
BVHW07s1606300918
528866BV00001B/1/P